**Praise for the bestselling
NASCAR Library Collection titles**

TO THE LIMIT
"An edge-of-the-chair, heart-racing, can't-put-down read."
—Wendy Keel, *Romance Reader Connection*

"A fun, lighthearted NASCAR romance."
—Harriet Klausner, *The Best Reviews*

ON THE EDGE
"This story provides a fascinating look at
NASCAR racing, with all of the excitement
and tension, along with an interesting look at the
behind-the-scenes preparations."
—*Romantic Times BOOKreviews*

"*On the Edge* introduces us to racing in a spectacular
way...hurry out, not race, and buy *On the Edge.*"
—Carolyn Crisher, *Romance Reviews Today*

IN THE GROOVE
"Start your engines...Britton delivers big-time on the
atmosphere and details about the racing circuit, and the
drivers and the lives they lead."
—Ginger Curwen, *Barnes and Noble*

"*In the Groove* is a fun, light-hearted, love story with
racing as the backdrop and a feel-good ending."
—*Racing Milestones*

PAMELA
BRITTON

total **control**

HQN™

ISBN-13: 978-0-373-77242-1
ISBN-10: 0-373-77242-4

TOTAL CONTROL

This page is for Codi, my lovely little girl, who's sitting next to me as I write this. I get teary eyed just knowing you're old enough to read this now. Isn't it cool to see your name in print? I know, I know…you want me to write a story about unicorns. I will one day. I promise (pinky promise!). In the meantime, know that I love you and that I often think of you while I'm working. But you need to share this page with Daddy because he's gotten used to seeing his name here. (Spoiled man! But, shhh, don't tell him.)

Michael, I love you more and more each day. You truly make me understand the meaning of the words soul mate. When the days are long, and your subcontractors are driving you nuts, put on Rascal Flatts's "*Bless the Broken Road.*" It says it all.

Hugs and kisses to you both,
Mama Bear

total control

RED FLAG

Love 'Em or Leave 'Em

By Rick Stevenson, Sports Editor

It's no secret that there are some drivers in the NASCAR series whom everybody loves. Lance Cooper comes to mind. And lately, Adam Drake.

Then there's the opposite: Those drivers everyone loves to hate. Okay, one driver in particular.

Todd Peters.

Rarely do I see so many people boo as when Todd Peters is introduced. But then they cheer him, too—when he suffers some bad luck. At Dover this year when Todd wrecked on lap fifty-three, I honestly thought a favored driver had taken the lead until one of my journalist friends pointed out that it was actually the crowd shouting in delight that Todd Peters's day was over.

And all because he's accidentally "bumped" someone off the same track *last year.* Of course, he ended up sending that driver to the Infield Care

Center. And many a NASCAR aficionado will argue that the driver he punted ended up not making the Chase for the NASCAR NEXTEL Cup because of Todd's little stunt, although with the revisions to the Chase system this year, maybe not.

But, you know, all that aside, I have to wonder what all the fuss is about. In the past, drivers like Todd were revered for "bumping" and "nudging." If someone was sent into the wall, so be it. Nine times out of ten the crowd cheered. They *loved* it. That's racing, they used to say. What happened to those days?

And I have to wonder: does Todd care? He certainly hasn't done anything to change that unfavorable image. Should he?

Do *other* "bad boys" worry about their public image? Does it matter to them that they might end up losing a sponsor because of their tarnished image?

Todd Peters is poised to make the Chase. With one race left to go—Richmond—he might just find himself in the thick of things.

How will fans react to that?

I suppose time will tell.

CHAPTER ONE

"YOU ARE THE BIGGEST jerk that ever walked the earth."

Todd Peters froze, sunlight refracting off the water and momentarily blinding him.

"It's all I can do right now not to push you off the pier."

He squinted and turned, but it was hard to see with his eyes momentarily blinded by the sun. A woman. That much was clear. Blond haired. Skinny. And really, really angry.

"With any luck you'd land in a pool of piranhas. Hopefully a whole school of them. Maybe they'd eat your pestilent flesh, nibble out your eyes, then snack on your pea-sized brain for dessert."

Todd pushed himself up. "Can I help you?" he asked.

Out behind him a Jet Ski roared by. The *wha-wha-wha* of the engine popping in and out of the water made Todd long for the smooth surface of Lake Norman, too.

"Yeah, you could help me. You could help me by showing up when you're supposed to. By not blowing off my clients. By being kind and thoughtful and considerate instead of selfish and pigheaded and a self-centered ass."

Okay. That was harsh. "Do I know you?" he asked.

"No, you don't know me, but I know of *you,*" she said. "And what I know, I don't particularly like."

She'd started to come into focus. The hair went from mouse-blond to platinum with reds and browns mixed in, the strands loose and well past her shoulders. The oval face suddenly had the cheekbones of a ferocious feline. The brown eyes weren't just brown, they were a brilliant, nearly green-hazel— and they were furious.

"How'd you get down here?" he asked, glancing back toward his house and at the French doors at the rear of his multileveled home. They were closed. He leaned forward, hoping to see past the lush foliage that surrounded his backyard. The side gate appeared closed. And locked.

"I climbed over the fence," she admitted.

"You climbed over?" he asked, wondering if he needed to call the police.

"I wanted to see you. And since neither you nor your assistant, Jennifer Scott, seem willing to call me back, a padlock gate wasn't going to stand in my way."

Jennifer. She knew his PR rep. Maybe not a crazy woman after all. "I see," he said. "What'd you need to see me about?" he asked.

"I work for *Miracles,*" she pronounced, an expectant expression coming to her face at the mention of the charity group.

"Who?"

"Miracles," she said again. "You know. Formerly known as the *Wishing Tree* Foundation."

Okay. *That* rang a bell.

"I see. And what does *Miracles* want with me?" he asked, although he already knew. It wouldn't be the first time the wish-fulfilling organization had asked him to grant a wish, although this was the first time one of their volunteers had ever accosted him in his home.

"You mean you can't guess?"

"Why don't you just fill me in instead."

She looked incredulous. Behind him, water splashed against the front of his boat. He braced himself for the inevitable rocking of the dock beneath his feet.

"You're unreal, you know that?" she said. "You show absolutely no remorse."

"Remorse? For what?" he asked.

"Blowing off two meetings."

"I did?"

"Are you denying it?"

"I don't manage my schedule," he said, going back to his task of untying his boat. "So if I did blow you off, chances are I didn't know it was you."

"How can that be?" she asked, following him from cleat to cleat.

"I'm told where to go, and if I can't make a meeting, I tell my reps to cancel it." He untied another line. The Scarab was thirty-five feet long, sleek and heavy. It'd been a gift from one of his sponsors, its red, yellow and orange paint scheme seemingly luminescent. The minute he untied a line, the fiberglass hull started to drift away. He moved quickly to the next cleat.

"You blew off *two* meetings with us. One last month and one this month."

"That's unusual," he said. "I don't usually cancel meetings with charity organizations," he added.

That wasn't exactly true. Over the past few months he'd canceled a lot of meetings—thanks to his relentless pursuit of Kristen, a woman who he'd hoped to have a future with, but who'd ditched him in favor of another man.

"Yes, but what makes your behavior all the more deplorable about canceling *this* meeting is that *these*

weren't with us. They were with one of our clients—
a terminally ill child named Benjamin Koch, who,
for some misguided and totally incomprehensible
reason, wants to meet you—his favorite race car
driver—before he gets sicker than he already is, only
you…" Red blotches of color stood out on her
cheeks, the splash of crimson spreading all the way
to her neck. "*You* stood him up."

He straightened, nylon rope forgotten. "I did?"

"You did, and to be perfectly honest, I was hoping
that after the second time he'd start rooting for, you
know, Adam Drake. Alas, he's still enamored of
you—goodness knows why—and so this time I'm
leaving nothing to chance. I want to set up another
time for you to meet Benjamin, only this time I need
to warn you that if you stand him up again, I'll hire
a hit man, have you boiled in tar, hung out on a rack,
tortured and then dragged behind one of those race
cars you drive, preferably one piloted by one of your
arch enemies."

HE DIDN'T SEEM AMUSED. Or threatened. He didn't
look anything, Indi thought.

"Wow," he drawled, his accent making him sound
like a Southern gentleman. But she knew for a fact
he was *no* gentleman. "That's harsh."

"*That's* only the first part."

She thought he might have smiled, saw the very edges of his lips tip up, but then he frowned. "Like I said, sometimes I cancel meetings without even knowing who they're with."

"Well, maybe you should take the time to unearth that little tidbit of information."

"Maybe I should," he said, going back to work.

"Will you meet with him then?"

"Of course," he said, peering up when he knelt down by another line.

"When?"

"I'm not certain." He tossed the rope into the boat. "Like I said before, I don't handle my own schedule."

"Well, if you don't mind, I'd like to call whoever *does* manage your schedule and arrange for a meeting now."

"Sure," he said. "But is it going to make a difference if we do it right this minute? Or in a couple hours?"

"Well...I—"

"'Cause if you don't mind, I'd like to enjoy what's left of the day."

Spoiled race car driver. They were all alike. "It'll only take you two minutes to do it."

"Actually, it might take longer than that, depending on if I can get a hold of Jen or not."

"Please try."

He patted his pockets. "Don't have my cell phone."

"Use mine," she said.

He glanced from the boat to the lake to the boat again, his body language telling her that he wasn't happy to have to deal with this now. But to give him credit, he held out his hand.

"I'll be right back," she said. "I have to go get it."

He stiffened. "What?"

"The battery was low. The phone's charging in my rental car."

"Fine," he said, dismissing her with a wave of his fingers. "And go though my house," he called out after her. "That's all I need for you to do—break your neck on my fence."

Blah-blah-blah-blah, she silently mimicked. He could just sit there. It was the least the jerk could do. Whenever she thought of the way poor Benjamin's face crumpled the second time Mr. Fancy Pants Race Car Driver had stood him up, well, it infuriated her all the more. She'd take her time, and Todd Peters would learn to like it, she thought, inhaling the sweet scent of lilies someone had planted along a winding pathway. The air was heavy with the exhalation of foliage: ferns, ivy and some kind of tree with thick, glossy leaves.

"Whoa," she said, the minute she pulled open a French door that, like about a half a dozen others, lined the rear of the house.

The inside was *huge.* But of course she'd known it would be the moment she'd pulled up in front of the split-level mansion. She was in some sort of game room. There was a pool table, plasma TV and a pinball machine in the corner that she'd passed as she walked across a hardwood floor and toward the front of the house only to discover there was no exit, just stairs. She climbed those next. At the top she found a mammoth-size kitchen—complete with its own hearth—and one very large family room off the side of it. Windows stretched up ten feet high, allowing her a view of the dock. The egomaniac stood there, glanced at his watch, then at his boat that was still tethered by a single line to his private dock.

You can just wait, she thought again.

She didn't deliberately take her time. All right. Maybe she did. But it was hard not to gawk at the main foyer that rose up three stories tall. Single-paned windows allowed light to filter onto the off-white marble floor. There was a fixture hanging from the middle of the ceiling some thirty feet above her head, one with bulbs that were made of blown glass and that were elongated and twisted in such a way that the fixture resembled a giant sun. She would bet with the lights on that's exactly what it was supposed to look like. Unbelievable.

She let herself out before she was tempted into doing something stupid, like turn on the switch. Her car was parked atop a brick driveway, one whose color complemented the rose-colored stucco of his home. The outside was landscaped just as beautifully as the back, lush crepe myrtles splashing color amongst a green lawn backdrop.

"I'm back," she called a few minutes later, almost out of breath. "My name's Indi Wilcox, by the way."

"Indi?" he asked, black brows hiked up over impatient eyes.

"I was born early while my mom and dad were driving through Indiana," she said, weary of the explanation that inevitably followed her name.

"Well, all right, Ms. Indi Wilcox," he said. "Hop on in."

"Excuse me?" she asked, watching as he untied the last line, then climbed aboard the shiny ski... boat...thing. Strangest shaped boat she'd ever seen with its long, pelican-nose front end and bright color scheme.

"If you want to schedule something," Todd said. "You'll have to come aboard. I'm heading out."

"Oh, I don't think so."

"Okay, then," he said, moving to the rear of the boat and pulling on a rope with a rubber thing on the end that she assumed kept the fiberglass hull from rubbing against the dock. "Call Jen at my office. Tell her that we met, and what happened. I'm sure she'll make things right."

"I already *have* called Jennifer," she said, following alongside the boat when he moved to the front, the dock beneath her feet hot. She could feel warmth ebbing through the rubber soles of her white tennis shoes. And she had to cover a lot of ground. The boat was at least thirty feet long. "That was the point of tracking you down. Jen isn't calling me back."

"Really?" he said, pulling a canvas cover off the driver area, which was more to the rear of the vessel, the snaps giving a *pop-pop-pop*. "Tell her I told you to call."

"What if she doesn't believe me?" she asked, having to lift a hand to shield her eyes against the glare of the sun. Did it ever cool off in North Carolina? "What if she doesn't call me back again?"

She heard a *chu-chu-chu* and stepped back quickly. He was trying to start the damn boat.

"That's the risk you take, Ms. Indi Wilcox," he said, the engines flaring to life with a roar that made her lean back. Holy cripes. What did he have under there? A 747?

"You either come with me now," he called, slipping on a pair Ray-Ban sunglasses, "and I'll give Jennifer a call while we're out on the lake, or you go home and take your chances."

Hotel. Not home. She'd flown all the way out here on her own dime. And she wasn't going to leave without getting him to set up a meeting.

"Why can't you call her now?" Indi asked, her irritation mounting. "I'll dial her number for you."

"Go ahead," he said. "Try. But she won't answer. It's after five."

Damn it.

"Look, I only have two hours of freedom left," he said, bending. He pulled out a dark blue baseball cap from somewhere, tucked it on his head. "After today it's back to the grind. Press conferences, photo shoots, PR appearances. I want to enjoy what's left of the day, and if I can't get a hold of Jennifer right away, it might take me some time to track her down."

"Can't you just leave her a message?"

"Not if you want to resolve this thing tonight. I'll have to call her house, her boyfriend, maybe her private line at the office. I'll do it out there," he said, nodding toward the water.

"But—"

"See ya," he yelled, the engines changing pitch.

"Wait," she cried.

He cut off the motor so abruptly she knew he'd been waiting for her to do exactly that. She felt her insides burn, and not in a *good* way, either. Drat the man. "Fine," she said, walking to the back of the boat. "How do I get on this thing?"

"Just step onto the back. I'll help pull you aboard."

"No, thanks," she said. "I can manage on my own."

She couldn't believe he was forcing her to do this. She could dial his assistant's number *for* him. She'd called the woman enough times. It'd take her two seconds to hand him the phone, and if the woman didn't answer, he could leave her a message. Instead, she was waving carbon monoxide fumes away from her face.

Maybe, just maybe, he'd choke on them.

She put her foot on the chrome ledge that jutted out from the back of the boat, suddenly afraid to lift her other foot because what if the boat drifted off when she moved? Or if the boat tipped? Or she slipped or something?

And then the boat *did* start to drift away, its colorful stern bobbing on the water…ever farther away.

She lunged.

Her worst fear came true.

Her foot slid off the slick metal. She gasped, flinging her arms over the back end. Todd grabbed her and heaved.

He landed beneath her, Indi sprawled atop his surprisingly muscular chest. She drew back, her palms digging into the scratchy indoor/outdoor carpeting that lined the bottom of the boat.

Now it was Todd Peters's turn to seem unhappy. "Well, now," he drawled, the expression on his face belying the sexy drawl of his words. "If I'd known you wanted to do that, I'd have asked you aboard sooner."

CHAPTER TWO

SHE WANTED TO DIE.

Todd could see the desire plainly in her eyes.

Either that or she wanted *him* to die. Maybe both. Either way, she wasn't happy.

He shifted beneath her, setting her aside. He had no idea why he'd just made such a suggestive comment. Guess old habits died hard. But he felt immediately disloyal to Kristen, even though he had no reason to feel that way. She'd made her choice of boyfriends— scratch that, it was *fiancé* now—plain enough.

"In the future you might want to move a little faster when climbing aboard," he said, pushing himself to his feet.

"I'll remember that," she muttered. "If I'm ever blackmailed into getting on board one of these things again."

Blackmailed. Yeah, he supposed he'd done that. But it served her right for making him wait while she got her damn cell phone.

"Can you try calling Jennifer now?" she asked.

"Nope. I'll call her when we're out on the lake."

"What if you don't get service out there?"

"We do," he said, starting the engines again. The speed limit was twenty-five miles per hour in the tiny cove where his house and three others sat.

Todd *never* did the speed limit.

"Where do you want me—"

He gunned it.

"Yipers," he thought he heard her say, glancing back. She'd fallen onto the ice chest he'd put behind the passenger seat.

"Sit here," he warned, pointing to the spot next to him.

She heaved herself forward, sprawling onto the white chair. "Slow down," she yelled.

Nope, he thought, a tight smile coming to his face. His neighbors knew what to expect. He left his dock in a blaze of glory, rooster tail drenching the wooden slats. Sometimes the spray would reach the edge of his lawn.

"Hang on," he warned, then turned right.

"Hey—"

He brought the engines up to full speed; the long prow rose higher, and even higher. He loved this part. Loved blowing by the houses that lined the shore. Loved scandalizing the uptight old biddies who lived nearby. They were always lodging complaints. He ignored them.

Out onto the lake they zoomed, a small smile coming to Todd's face. This. *This* was what he lived for. The feel of the wind. The mossy smell of the water. The roar of two big block engines.

"Do you mind slowing down?" she called, her words torn back.

"Yes," he called, tilting the wheel just a bit. They shot to the right and out onto the main portion of the lake. This time of day there were others out, too. The Jet Ski that had passed by earlier was far, far ahead of him, the water still rippling from his wake. A sailboat cut through the water on his left. He smirked and turned his Scarab in the boat's direction.

They roared by. A couple seconds later he glanced back. The sailboat rocked like a hammock in the wind, a gray-haired man standing near the middle of the ship, left fist clenched, right hand raised, middle finger—

That wasn't nice.

He chuckled, faced forward again. It was the first time he'd laughed in weeks.

"If you were trying to sink that boat, you failed," she yelled.

His amusement faded as quickly as it'd come. Yeah. He really should cool it, and call Jennifer. He felt bad about standing that kid up, although to be honest he hadn't exactly been in his right mind recently. And in his own defense he really didn't know where he was going from one minute to the next. Sometimes he glanced at his itinerary, sometimes not. More often not. Ultimately, though, it was his choice to follow his schedule and lately, he'd been blowing off a lot of people, much to his PR person's dismay.

"If I'd wanted to sink him, believe me, I could have," he said, easing off the throttle.

"How heroic of you," she called.

He drew back even more. The front of the boat dipped into the water like a goose coming in for a landing. The lake stretched out before him, the gray-blue water seeming to mesh with the sky like a two-toned paint scheme. On the left and right a tree-studded shore concealed multilevel homes from his view, some hugely ostentatious—like his—some far more plain. The older homes had been around a while, the lake having been developed some thirty odd years ago, long before it became trendy to build on the shores of Lake Norman.

He cut the motors.

"What's the matter?" she asked. "Can't find any new targets to drench?"

She clutched the edge of her seat as if she

expected to be ejected. Her hair looked as if it had suffered through a lightning storm. And her eyes. Well, her eyes called him every dirty name in the book.

He swiveled sideways on his captain's chair, the boat drifting along the water. "You really don't like me, do you?"

"Oh, no," she said, faking innocence. "You're my favorite driver in the whole wide world."

"You can cut the sarcasm. You're right. I should be boiled in oil for standing up one of your kids. That was inexcusable, and I'm sorry. Now, hand me your phone so we can set things right."

Her mouth had dropped open. He held out his hand. She stared at him a second longer, her eyes sweeping over his face like a timing light. He thought he heard her let out a little "humph" before fishing into her pocket and handing him her cell phone.

If he'd been thinking clearly earlier he'd have grabbed his own cell phone off the kitchen counter. He could have used Direct Connect to page Jen. Now he was stuck dialing numbers, none of which she answered. But he left messages, used the pound key to have her paged at one point, Todd having to ask Indi what her cell phone number was.

"Now we wait," he said a few minutes later.

"Out here?"

"Sure. Why not?"

The wild-haired thing worked for her, he noticed. It made her seem like a model, one who posed for a shampoo ad, albeit one where the picture had been freeze-framed right as a giant fan had been pointed in her direction.

"I'd rather go back, if you don't mind."

"And I'd rather you tell me about Benjamin."

"Benjamin?" she asked in surprise, smoothing her hair back from her face almost as if she could sense he'd been looking at her hair.

"Yeah," he said, glancing up as a ski boat motored by.

"Go number twenty-six," the skier yelled, Todd rolling his eyes at the mention of a competitor's number. Figured he'd be recognized, and that he'd run into someone who felt the need to rub his nose in it. Then again, his boat had been profiled in enough NASCAR magazines that the boat's paint scheme and specs were no secret. Most fans knew he had a super crankin' stereo system on board (as one magazine put it), as well as a surprisingly spacious bunk below.

"Tell me about him," Todd ordered again.

"What's there to tell?" Indi said, her gaze moving back to his. She'd been studying the ski boat, too.

"He's your typical little boy. Loves football, hockey, but mostly anything to do with NASCAR."

"What's he sick with?"

She lifted her chin. "Chronic myelogenous leukemia."

Todd felt his stomach burn. "Poor kid."

She turned her head, her profile every bit as—all right, he'd admit it—*beautiful* as the rest of her. She was one of those women that he would bet other women loved to hate. Perfect skin. Slim figure.

A breeze caught a strand of hair, sunlight turning that skin pale ivory. The anger seemed to have drained out of her, he noticed, replaced instead by sadness. "He's only ten years old," she said, lifting her chin. "*Ten* and he's fighting for his life. Every time I see him he's weaker and weaker and yet still, still…" she said, her jaw jutting out as if she either fought the urge to cry or to hold back her anger once more. "All he wants to talk about is racing, or more specifically, you. But you…you stood him up. Twice."

She wanted to kill him, she really did. Todd could see that.

"I'm sorry," he said.

"You should be."

"It won't happen again."

"I hope not," she said, inhaling so loudly he could hear it over the sound of water slapping the side of the boat. She turned away from him, Todd was certain, so she could collect herself.

Indi. He liked her name. It suited her in a weird way.

"Benjamin's lucky to have you," he said.

She squared her shoulders and faced him again. "Yeah, well, for every Benjamin out there there's a dozen others just like him."

A couple of months ago she'd have been just his type, but that would have been before Kristen, the woman who'd tossed him over for another man.

Kristen was now with Matt.

"Have you worked for *Miracles* long?"

"A few years," she said.

"It must be tough. All those sick kids…"

"Are you kidding? It's the most rewarding job I've ever had." And suddenly she seemed ferocious again. "Just last month we sent one of our kids to Montana, to an archeological dig. He loved dinosaurs, could name just about every one of them. Helping out on that dig was the highlight of his life. For weeks afterward he glowed, until…"

She shook her head and stared out at the water again. "It's not easy watching kids fight for their lives, but at least *Miracles* brings a little joy to their lives. I quit my job as a broadcaster to do this and I've never regretted it, not even for a minute."

"You worked for a network?"

"Just a local affiliate, nothing big. What I do now is much more important."

She reminded him of Kristen, Todd thought. There was so much passion in her voice, such a light in her eyes....

"I'm sorry," he said again. "I had no idea—"

Her cell phone rang. She jumped. They both glanced down at it. Indi pressed the green button and handed it up to him.

"Todd Peters," he answered.

"Hey, Todd. I wondered who was calling me," Jen said. "What's up?"

"Hey. Sorry to bug you after hours, but I'm standing here with Indi Wilcox."

"Indi Wilcox," Jen murmured, as if repeating the name in an effort to jog her memory.

"She works for *Miracles*."

"Oh, yeah. Right. They used to be called *Wishing Tree.* How strange. I called her today, but they said she was out of town."

"She's here, with me."

"What a coincidence."

"Not really," Todd said wryly, deciding to forego an explanation. "She told me about Benjamin."

"Yeah, poor kid."

"Do me a favor. Next time, don't let me cancel appointments with sick children."

"I tried to tell you—"

"I'm sure you did," Todd said, shaking his head. "In the future just slap me upside the head if I'm not listening."

"Will do," Jen said, and he could hear the smile in her voice.

"I think I owe Benjamin an apology," he said, glancing at Indi.

"I would say so," Jen agreed.

"Why don't we fly him to the race this next weekend?"

"Great idea," Jen said. "I'll start working on it right away."

"He can hang out with me." He met Indi's gaze. "If it's okay with his doctors, of course."

Indi nodded encouragingly.

"Sounds great," Jen said. "I'll let you know what I come up with by tomorrow."

"Oh. And one other thing." He smiled back at Indi. "Make sure Ms. Wilcox gets passes to the race, too."

CHAPTER THREE

"I DON'T WANT TO GO," Indi said the moment she walked into their shoebox-shaped office.

Maggie Taylor looked away from the computer screen she'd been studying and met Indi's gaze. "I know," she said, glancing back at the monitor, tapping some keys, then pushing her keyboard back under her desk and giving Indi her undivided attention. They had desks that faced each other. Because the two of them had combed garage sales for office decorations, the walls were adorned with an eclectic selection of art and the room was filled with used office furniture. But they didn't care—their clients rarely visited the space.

"You *have* to go," Maggie said when Indi remained mutinously silent.

Maggie Taylor was not just her boss. She was Indi's best friend. They'd met five years ago when Indi had chucked her broadcasting career to go to work for *Miracles*. Indi hadn't known what to think of the soft-eyed, perpetually kinky-haired brunette. She was a single mother whose perky attitude and energized personality always astounded Indi. Coming from the über cutthroat world of broadcasting, Indi had been taken off guard by Maggie's crinkled, sometimes coffee-stained clothes. But Indi had soon learned that Maggie didn't care what she looked like, just that her "kids" were taken care of.

"Are you sure there isn't any way I can get out of this?" Indi asked, shifting on her leather chair. The things were about as comfortable as amusement park rides.

"Not if you don't want to disappoint Benjamin."

Indi sighed. Benjamin. He deserved this trip. But Indi's joy at having secured the elusive Todd Peters was overshadowed by Benjamin's latest test results. According to Linda, Benjamin's mom, the chemo they'd flooded his bloodstream with wasn't working. Soon they'd try something new, and if that didn't work...

Indi refused to think about it.

"I just wish someone else could go."

Someone like *you*. At least Maggie knew something about NASCAR. She even had a crush on one of the drivers—Mike Morgan. But apparently she hadn't wanted to get close to the object of her infatuation because she'd passed this NASCAR task to her.

But she didn't point that out to her friend because it was completely unfair to expect Maggie to go, especially when her reasons for not wanting to attend the race centered solely around one egotistical, misogynistic race car driver.

Maggie pushed her chair sideways so that it was more centered to her desk, and if she'd been wearing glasses, Indi was pretty certain she'd have peered over the top of them.

"Indi, I know you hate racing—"

"I'd rather go get a pap smear," Indi muttered.

"—but you need to think about Benjamin."

Indi held up her hand. "You don't need to say it," she said. "I'm going."

She just wished the trip came *without* Todd Peters. The man bothered her, and not just in an I'm-a-famous-race-car-driver-and-I-do-as-I-please way. No. There was more to it than that; she just didn't know *what* yet.

She looked out the window to the left of Maggie's desk. They'd taken space in a single-level office complex, one whose rent the property owner donated as a write-off. Donated space meant that they were at the farthest end of the flat-faced building. The only view the space offered was out the front, and it was of a wall that was supposed to shield them from one of the Bay Area's busiest freeways. However,

Maggie was convinced the wall *amplified* sound rather than kept it away from them. Recently someone had spray painted graffiti all over it and, Indi had to admit, the colorful display was a definite improvement.

"How is Benjamin, by the way?"

The *woosh-woosh-woosh* of cars roaring by was nonstop, the sound worse on rainy days like today when tires sloshing through the rain added a whole new decibel level. "What's that?"

"Benjamin," Maggie said, getting up and resting her back end against the front of her desk. She always smelled like cinnamon, and today was no different. Indi knew the smell came from her addiction to Hot Tamales. "How is he?"

Indi had to look away. She focused on a raindrop that dashed down the window only to stop abruptly. Sometimes her life felt that way, especially on days like today when she couldn't get Benjamin off her mind. She knew why, too. He reminded her of her nephew. Even their diseases were the same. They looked alike, too.

"Sick. In pain. Tired of all the needles."

She looked back at Maggie just in time to see her friend's gaze lose focus for a second. "Sometimes I wonder why we do this for a living."

Indi sighed. She knew why she did it. What she

hadn't told Todd was that she did this just as much for herself as the kids she helped. "And then you remember the look on their faces when a wish is finally granted," Indi said. "And you know why you do it."

"For a day at least, they feel well."

"Like any normal kid," Indi added.

It was a conversation they'd had many times before, and it always ended the same way.

"It's the best job in the world, and the worst job in the world," Maggie said, true to form.

Indi nodded, recalling the glee in Benjamin's eyes when she'd told him not only would he be flying to Virginia that next weekend—doctors permitting— but he'd be Todd Peters's special guest for both days. His whole face had lit up like birthday candles, the exhaustion and misery that had filled it only seconds before momentarily banished.

That's why she did it; *that's* why she'd fly to Richmond next weekend, darn it all. She owed it to kids like Benjamin to help them out.

Because she hadn't been able to help her nephew.

BUT KNOWING HOW EXCITED Benjamin was didn't make it any easier to pack the next week. Nor did it make the drive over to Stanford Children's Hospital any easier to bear. Dealing with sick children stank.

Every time Indi entered the children's wing, she felt her insides turn over, especially when she spotted any of the hospital's many patients, their pale faces and anxious eyes never failing to tug on Indi's heart. It reminded her of Kyle.

"Hey there, Indi," the pink-clothed receptionist said, her winsome smile always making Indi grin in return.

"Hi, Sam," Indi said right back.

"Today's the big day, huh?" Sam said, spinning the visitor sheet toward her.

"Yes, it is," Indi said, signing her name with a flourish.

"You know," Sam said, her frizzy brown hair bouncing along her shoulders as she abruptly stood, the bright blue countertop she sat behind nearly the same shade as her eyes. "My boyfriend's a huge NASCAR fan. He would die, just *die* to meet Todd Peters."

Indi's smile dissolved like rained-on sugar. "Tell your boyfriend he's not missing much."

Sam's smile fizzled, too. "Really?"

"Really," Indi said.

"Wow," Sam said, sinking like a spent balloon. "He seems so nice on TV."

Indi leaned toward Sam. "That's just it," she said. "Every celebrity seems nice, at least until you spend some time with them. Then they become self-centered, egotistical brats…at least in my experience." Like her ex-boyfriend. But she didn't need to go down *that* road today.

"Huh," Sam said, her eyes going dim, as if she were erasing her memory banks of every secret feminine fantasy she'd ever had about Todd. "Don't forget your badge," she murmured distractedly.

"Thanks," Indi said, clipping the thing on before heading toward Benjamin's room. If she felt a little twinge of guilt over Todd losing one of his fans, then she pushed it aside.

Sunlight illuminated the tips of her black tennis shoes as she walked through the facility. The rain had finally stopped, leaving behind a crystalline blue sky that she could glimpse through tall windows to her right. Outside, oak trees pointed dark green leaves heavenward. Indi thought that nowhere on earth could there be a more beautiful place than Palo Alto, California.

Certainly *not* Richmond.

She sighed, her grimace fading when she spotted a little girl being wheeled toward her, the red, white and blue scarf on her head a bright contrast to her pale face.

"Indi," the little girl cried, a smile breaking out on her face, her dull blue eyes seeming to light from within when it finally registered who was smiling down at her.

"Erin," Indi said with a big smile of her own, one that included the nurse who pushed Erin's wheelchair. "Has he asked to marry you yet?"

"Not yet." The thirteen-year-old's smile grew, if possible, even bigger. The nurse slowly rolled to a stop as, above Erin's head, the IV bag swung on the end of its hanger. "But he calls me once a week."

And just like that, Indi's overactive tear ducts switched on. She had to work hard to keep Erin from seeing the sudden moisture in her eyes. *Miracles* had recently arranged a "date" with one of Erin's favorite pop stars. Maggie had been the one to orchestrate the whole thing, but Indi had been the one to accompany Erin on her big night out. Much to Erin's surprise, the object of Erin's affection turned out to be a "hip-hog"—a high-profile person with a heart of gold—as Maggie and Indi liked to call them.

"I'm not surprised," Indi said. "He'd be a fool not to fall head over heels for you."

Erin's laughter was as carefree and high-spirited as any other child's, and Indi felt her heart lurch all over again. This was why she did what she did. Erin's joy was so palatable, Indi could feel her own spirits lift in return.

"I wish," Erin said, the nurse pushing her forward again.

"I don't know," Indi teased in singsong voice, walking backward a few steps and nearly crashing into a potted palm in the process. That made Erin laugh all over again. "I think I hear wedding bells in the air."

Erin giggled some more and waved, her hospital gown dropping down and exposing the plastic ID bracelet around her wrist.

Indi's smile faded, but she'd turned away before Erin could see it. Another case of non-Hodgkin's lymphoma. The hospital was full of them. One-in-five chance of survival. Before her wish had been granted, hospital scuttlebutt was that Erin wouldn't make it. Her health had deteriorated, her body had grown frail, her blood work didn't look good. It had just about taken an act of Congress to get her down to Los Angeles, but they'd done it and the results had been…magical. She was rallying. Indi hoped Erin would continue to improve, and she had high hopes she would—what with weekly calls from her hip-hog.

Indi paused outside Benjamin's hospital room, one cluttered with stuffed animals and get-well cards from his fifth-grade class, all the while hoping Benjamin's trip to Richmond would garner the same results as Erin's trip.

The boy sat in a stickered-out wheelchair, his back to her while he talked to his mom. On the wall above him, the one opposite his rumpled bed, a TV played—what else—a rebroadcast of last week's race.

"You ready there, buddy?" Indi said.

With an expertise that bespoke months of experience, Benjamin spun his chair around, just about doing a wheelie in the process.

"Indi!" he cried, his dark green eyes as bright as the sunshine that filtered into the windows behind him.

"Today's the big day," she said after washing her hands and then bending down to give the little guy a hug, his shoulders feeling even more frail than usual, she thought. Or maybe not. She couldn't be sure. She straightened, noticing then the bright red number 82 scrawled across the front of his T-shirt…and the face that went with it.

Todd Peters.

"Hey there," she said to Benjamin's mom, but Indi checked the rest of her words when she spotted Linda's swollen and red-rimmed eyes.

"What's wrong?" Indi whispered, giving her a hug.

Linda shook her head, her blond hair brushing Indi's cheek. "Later," she whispered back.

Indi struggled to hide her concern, her attention falling on Benjamin again and searching the boy for telltale signs that something might be more seriously wrong—as if having lymphoma wasn't serious enough. But he looked the same as always—bright green eyes that belied the bruised flesh beneath them, a complexion that paled against his wide smile. He'd lost his hair, although not as thoroughly as Erin. Benjamin covered what was left of the strands with a red and gold ski cap. Number 82 was on the side.

"How are you feeling, kiddo?" she asked. "You ready for your trip?"

"Are you kidding?" Benjamin asked with all the excitement a sick ten-year-old could muster. "I was ready at five this morning."

"You were up at five?" Indi asked, her focus settling on Linda.

He got sick, she mouthed.

"Couldn't sleep," the boy said, missing the exchange. His hands clenched in his lap, his jaw sticking out as if daring his mom to contradict him.

She didn't.

"I know how that is," Indi said, giving the boy a smile that she hoped shielded the concern she felt budding in her chest. "So. Are we ready to go?"

Benjamin's mom pushed a piece of hair off her

face, but not before Indi spotted the way her hands shook. And the uncertainty in her eyes as she stared at her son.

"As ready as we'll ever be," she murmured, her voice cracking a bit.

What had happened?

Indi knew it couldn't be good if brave, always optimistic Linda reacted this way. The woman was a rock, both she and her husband constantly at Benjamin's side. Indi had often marveled at how the three of them had pulled together. So often a terminally ill child put an unbearable strain on a marriage. Indi had lost track of the times she'd watched a formerly strong union crumble. Not so with Linda and Art Koch.

. "Anything you need me to grab?" Indi asked, biding her time. She'd uncover all later.

"Nope," Benjamin said. "My mom's got my bag all packed."

"Then let's go. We have a little under three hours before our plane departs."

Benjamin smiled excitedly, his tiny shoulders hunching as he struggled to push himself forward. Indi almost helped him, but Linda stayed her with a hand. "Let him do it," she said. "He needs that."

Indi nodded. "What's the matter?" she asked when Benjamin rolled through the door.

"They're going to stop giving him the Phelbu-teral."

"The chemo? Why?"

Linda's eyes welled up, and Indi knew she was trying to stop the tears from falling. Indi had had to do the same many times herself, but Linda's eyes couldn't hold back the tears brought on by this latest setback, whatever it was.

"It's too hard on his system. His latest blood work came back." Linda shook her head. "It was pretty bad. They almost didn't let him go."

Indi took the news like a physical blow. "Oh, no."

"*I* would have canceled except I knew how badly Benjamin wants this, *needs* this. I've spent the last twenty-four hours praying that nothing bad will happen while we're gone."

Indi almost stopped, almost put her arms around Linda's shoulders, except she knew if she did that, the woman would crumble. And if Linda crumbled, then Indi would break down. Damn it.

"What does Art think?"

Linda looked away, all the troubles of the world seeming to reflect from her eyes. "That we should stay home. But he knows, just as *I* do, that if we put this off again…"

Benjamin might not make the trip. Ever.

Frustration boiled up deep inside Indi, the same

frustration she always felt against the unfairness of Benjamin's disease. It showed no prejudice. No sympathy. No desire to ever let up. Yes, it was a disease, technically not sentient, but sometimes Indi swore it knew when it was under attack.

Damn that Todd Peters.

If he hadn't canceled the first two meetings....

"We'll get through this, Linda—" she squeezed the woman's hand, Linda's cold fingers clutching hers back "—I promise, with Benjamin none the worse for it. In fact, nine times out of ten a trip like this will do more good than harm."

"Do you really think so?" Linda asked, her eyes filling with grudging hope.

"I *know* it," Indi said, because this battle was never over until it was over. She would make certain the weekend was every bit as special as Benjamin hoped. And if Todd Peters made the mistake of brushing Benjamin off again, well, the driver would be the next person to end up in the hospital.

CHAPTER FOUR

"I'M LATE," Todd said, jumping into the rented SUV.

"Yes, you are," Jen said, sliding onto the seat behind him. Someone called his name—probably a fan who'd spotted him from the grandstands across the track.

"You suck!" the man yelled.

"Yeah, yeah, yeah," Todd said before slamming the door. "And you paid a couple hundred bucks to watch me drive," he muttered under his breath.

"Are we in a hurry?" his chauffeur, Ron, asked, peeking at Todd above dark sunglasses.

"Yes," Todd said with a jerk of his chin. "We're in a hell of a hurry."

"Better buckle up then," Ron said.

Todd cursed inwardly. He hadn't meant to leave the media center so late. But he'd been screwed since the beginning of the day, having arrived ten minutes late to a radio station. They'd zoomed him back to the track for a driver appearance, but he'd been fifteen minutes late for *that,* then afterward he was off to practice, which he'd had to cut short to make up time. He'd thought he was in the clear then, but Dan, his crew chief, requested a meeting. That had made him late for his media center interviews, which in turn had made him late now.

"You should have gotten me out of there sooner," Todd grumbled, his body tipping sideways as Ron barreled around a corner. Richmond's infield was tiny—network trailers, vehicles and what seemed like a million golf carts—but Ron didn't let that bother him. He shot toward the exit tunnel like a bullet down a barrel. Thank God the directional light was green.

"I tried," Jen said plaintively. Todd caught a glimpse of her in his visor's mirror. "The network refused to give you up. Said you were late and so it wasn't their fault."

That was probably that producer, Barney whatever-his-name-was. The goofy-looking guy with the big eyes and thin lips rubbed Todd the wrong way.

"Son of a—" Todd said when they slowed just outside the infield tunnel.

"I'm trying, I'm trying," Ron said, his horn blaring at the golf cart in front of them. They'd just passed the security station that guarded the infield entrance. That meant they now blended in with a stream of NASCAR fans. The narrow road they traveled upon was lined with pedestrians. They couldn't get around the damn golf cart. The driver obviously thought he was on the seventh hole judging by the rate he toddled along.

"Is the strobe light on?" Todd asked, leaning forward and peering up at the front of the rearview mirror.

"Yup," Ron answered right as Todd spotted the flickering blue-and-white light. "But it doesn't do any good if the guy isn't paying attention," Ron said with another beep of his horn.

The golf-cart driver gave them the bird.

"Why that little piece of sh—"

"Todd, calm down," Jen said as they crossed by a chain-link fenced parking area to their left, which was filled with trailers belonging to television media. "I've already called Ms. Wilcox and explained the situation."

Terrific. Indi would be in a fine frame of mind by the time they arrived. "Why couldn't they come to the track?"

"Something about the boy being sick."

"Of course he's sick. He's got cancer."

Jen shook her head. "It's something else. A cold, I think."

"Great," Todd muttered as they turned down another road. Unfortunately, the golf cart went the same way. With the way his day was going, he'd probably end up catching whatever the kid had. And then he'd be sick while driving on Sunday.

Todd.

His inner conscience—yes, he did have one—reminded him that at least he'd get over the cold, whereas little Benjamin was sick for life. Maybe. What was the survival rate for the type of leukemia he had, anyway?

"What the heck is it?" Todd asked, splaying his hands toward the front windows and the infamous golf cart which, instead of pulling over when the road cleared, kept on driving at five miles an hour. "Is he a Lance Cooper fan or something?"

"Just a sec," Ron said.

The road split into a Y. Ron yanked the wheel right, giving the golf cart a honk. He, in turn, gave them the finger. Again.

"Whatever," Ron grumbled, stepping on the gas.

"Finally," Todd said, their sudden burst of speed startling a state trooper who directed traffic coming off the main road. He yelled something at them as they raced by.

"Go ahead. Write us a ticket," Ron told him.

"After this, you've got that thing with the

sponsor," Jen, ever the efficient PR rep, said as they were waved through a special exit used for race teams and the media. In a few seconds they were out on one of the thoroughfares, Ron flicking off the strobe lights.

"What time?"

"Six o'clock."

"Damn. I wanted to watch the Busch race to-night," Todd said, clutching the dash as Ron made a sudden left onto a side road—the main road was clogged with traffic—but he nearly ran over a gaggle of race fans in the process.

"You can TiVo the race," Jen answered, flipping through some pages. "It's a cocktail party hosted by one of the associate sponsors. And wait until you see what they want you to drive to the event."

"What do you mean?"

"They have a MINI Cooper for you to drive—and don't worry, I already cleared your driving a foreign car with your manufacturer. They understand it's a sponsor thing."

"A MINI Cooper, eh? I've always wanted to try one of those."

"Even one that's decked out with the Snappy Lube mascot on the roof?"

"Huh?"

"Roadrunner is on the roof."

It took a moment for the words to sink in. "You're kidding?"

"Nope. And it's painted the Snappy Lube colors. Orange, yellow and white."

The chuckle emerged before he could haul it back. "Great," he said.

"But you don't have to drive the car to the event. Not if you don't want to. I can have someone meet you at the track with the car."

He thought about it for a moment. "Actually, I think I kind of want to drive the thing." A little self-humiliation was never a bad thing, at least according to his mom.

"Terrific," Jen said with a blinding smile. "I'll arrange for it to be delivered to your hotel."

"I can hardly wait," he said.

The engine whined as they flew down the road. Barely any traffic. Todd felt himself relax a bit. "What's on for tomorrow?"

"You have an appointment at that fitness club at seven. Someone named Andy will be your trainer for the day. Your first interview is at nine. Local affiliate. After that, there's a lot of corporate stuff—a whole day of it, actually. You have a team meeting at four, then another souvenir rig signing after that. From there you'll go to the media center. Everyone wants to talk to you since you just might make the

Chase. Immediately following that is another interview, then driver intros at seven—"

"Do I have time to breathe?" he asked, refusing to think about the word *might*. He would make the damn Chase.

"I've arranged for a stop at an oxygen bar in between the hospitality tents and the team meeting."

Todd glanced back at her. Jen gave him a blinding grin.

"Cute," Todd said, trying, but failing, to hide his grin.

"I might be able to get you some nitrous instead."

"Go for it," Todd said. Because he refused to wear a seat belt, he nearly slid off his seat when Ron slammed on the brakes at a red light.

"And don't forget you offered to let the boy shadow you tomorrow."

"Yeah, but he's sick."

"Something tells me he'll be all better by tomorrow."

"You think?"

"Todd," Jen said. "He's meeting his hero—"

"A *late* hero."

"Doesn't matter. The adrenaline rush he'll get from meeting you will fuel him for hours."

"Twenty-four of them?"

"Maybe," Jen said.

"Maybe we should check with his caregiver and see if it'll be all right."

"His mom. That's who's with him. And Ms. Wilcox. And I'm certain they'll let you know if he's too sick to go."

"Hang on," Ron said, gunning it through a light about to turn red.

"Damn," Todd said. "If you ever want a career racing dragsters, I'm sure they'd take you."

"You said we're in a hurry," Ron said, his big shoulders shrugging.

Todd shook his head and settled back in his seat. It was a twenty-minute drive to the hotel. Ron might make it in five. Okay. Ten.

It took fifteen minutes, as it turned out. The tires screeched on the concrete beneath the porte cochere that extended out from the front of the hotel, the sound echoing on the high-beamed ceiling above. Someone leaving the building jumped back when Todd opened the SUV's door and flung himself out.

"Hey," Todd said to the pedestrian when the guy's eyes widened.

"You're Todd Peters," the man said.

"In the flesh," Todd said as he rushed past the guy, only to stop just on the other side of the sliding glass doors. "Jen, what room number?"

"I was wondering when you'd ask that," Jen said,

coming up behind him. "We've got them in a suite. Number ten-thirteen."

"Got it," Todd said.

"You want me to go up with you?" Jen asked.

"Nah," Todd answered, dashing toward the elevator.

He drew up short when he saw who stood nearby.

Indi Wilcox, her arms crossed and lips pursed together as if she were a cop and he'd been caught drunk in public.

"Well, well, well…if it isn't Todd Peters." She made a point of glancing at her watch. "And he's only twenty minutes late."

"At least I made it," he grumbled as they both got in.

"There is that," she said with a grin as fake as the painted-on headlights on his car.

"Were you going somewhere?" he asked, wondering what she'd been doing down in the lobby.

The smile grew even more false, if such a thing was possible. "Nope. I was just on my way to hire a big rig. I was going to send him out to the track and have him run you down, but there's no need for that now that you're here," she said, pushing the elevator button for the correct floor. "I'll wait until *after* you meet with Benjamin."

The doors started to close. Todd glanced through

the slit in them just in time to catch the "who is that?" look Jen shot him just before she was cut off from view.

Who *was* this?

The thorn in his side. The bane of his existence. The acid in his stomach.

"I told you I'd be here," he said, remembering how pretty she was only when she stood next to him. She had a tiny chin set in jawline that looked almost delicate, or at least it *would* have looked delicate if it hadn't been jutted out in disgust. Cheekbones that were almost feline in appearance shot up below a pair of emerald-gold eyes that reminded him of a tabby cat he used to own as a kid.

Striking.

That's the word he'd use to describe her. Too bad the perennial scowl detracted from her pretty face.

"Oh. That's right. And I had no reason to doubt that."

He pressed the stop button. He had no idea why he did it, except something about the woman rubbed him the wrong way. And, really, another couple of seconds wouldn't hurt little Benjamin.

"I know you don't like me," he said, over the sound of an ear-piercing buzzer.

"Whether I like you or not is immaterial," she said, plugging her ears before she obviously lost patience. She reached around him to pull the button out to start the elevator again.

He blocked her with his body so that her hand poked his abs. Her gaze snapped to his.

"Firm, isn't it?" he asked, leaning toward her.

"I've stepped in cow patties that were firmer." She had to yell to be heard over the stop button's shriek.

"You're just saying that to cover your surprise."

"And that smelled better, too," she said, her eyes mocking him.

"And now you're trying to get on my nerves because you don't want me to know how much you want me."

He was just razzing her, Lord knows why, but he was unprepared for her sudden burst of her laughter. Her whole body shook, her satin-smooth cheeks filling with color. "Are you kidding me?"

Well, yeah, but now that she'd laughed in his face, he was starting to feel the buzz of a challenge burn through him.

"I want you about as much as I want diphtheria. Scratch that. Come to think of it, I'd take diphtheria over you any day of the week." She stepped around him, pushed the stop button in and then crossed her arms.

He couldn't take his eyes off her. He'd never, in

all his years of being Todd Peters, famous race car driver, been as thoroughly peeved at a woman as he was at Indi Wilcox right at that moment. In her tan slacks and a satiny white shirt that matched the highlights in her hair, she looked as cool as the ice that lingered in her eyes.

"You don't really mean that," he said.

"Trust me. I mean it." She took another step away from him, tossed her long hair over the back of her shoulders and said, "But you've reminded me. You'll need to wash your hands before touching Benjamin."

"Why's that?"

"We don't want him catching anything."

"I thought *he* was the one with the cold."

"Yeah, and the last thing he needs is a case of scabies on top of that."

"Scabies—"

"You know when you start itching your skin like that it's a sign that it's spreading."

He looked at the top of his hand, realizing only in that moment that he'd been scratching it. He must be nervous about making the Chase this weekend. "I don't have scabies," he said, staring at the slightly reddened skin. He needed lotion.

"Might want to get that looked at," she said as the elevator door opened with a stomach-dropping stop and a happy little *bing*.

"I don't have scabies."

They stepped out. "We're right here," she said, guiding him down a corridor off the main one.

Todd watched her stop in front of the suite. The wall next to the doorjamb had a gouge in it, as if someone had kicked it or hit it with a suitcase.

"Now." She turned back to him and crossed her arms. "Benjamin will be excited to meet you… finally," she muttered. "Don't confuse his excitement with energy. He's had a rough go these past few weeks so he's not as energized as he might look. Don't offer to give him a ride in your car, or to take him out to dinner, or anything else that might get him all excited and that we'll have to put the kibosh on two seconds after you say it."

"What about tomorrow?" he asked, glancing toward the door, surprised to feel a tinge of trepidation. Maybe that's why his hand itched. Same kind of apprehension he felt before a race.

Scabies.

Ha.

"Tomorrow is up in the air. I know you offered to take Benjamin out to the track, and that was very kind of you, but I just don't know if that's in the cards."

"Then we'll have to do it some other time."

She cocked a brow at him, her look seeming to mock him somehow. "Really?"

"Really," he reiterated.

"Well, let's not mention that to Benjamin just yet."

Wouldn't want to get his hopes up.

She didn't say the words aloud, but she didn't need to. He could read her face as easily as he could his sister's. Odd how he could do that. He opened his mouth to tell her to bring the boy to the race next weekend, only she didn't give him time. With a squaring of her shoulders she faced the door, using a white key card to open it.

And when he caught sight of the pallid-faced child on the other side, he forgot all about what he was going to say.

CHAPTER FIVE

"MR. PETERS," Benjamin cried, Indi wincing at the high-pitched squeal of delight. With a show of strength that took Indi by surprise, given the boy's weakened state, he thrust his wheelchair toward the driver.

"Hey, there, buddy," Todd said, holding out his hand.

"Uh-uh-uh," Indi quickly interjected, stepping around and in front of Todd. "Wash your hands."

"Oh, yeah, right," he said, winking at Benjamin. "I'll be right back."

"Aw, man," Benjamin said with a sniff of disappointment, one that tugged at Indi's heart because it was obvious by his red nose and pallid complexion that Benjamin didn't feel well. She could hear how stuffed up he'd become. And yet he still all but bounced in his chair.

"It'll just be a second," Indi said over the sound of running water. She glanced up and caught Linda's eye. Benjamin's mother had the strangest look on her face, one Indi didn't immediately recognize, probably because she was so used to Linda looking tired or worn-out or depressed that the momentary twinkle that glittered from her eyes didn't immediately register.

He's cute, Linda mouthed.

Who? Benjamin? Indi wondered, glancing back at the boy. The water shut off.

Indi stiffened.

Oh, brother. Todd.

"All right," Todd said, wringing his hands together. "I'm all washed up. Give me a high five."

When Benjamin lifted an arm that bore bruises from all the blood tests and IVs he'd received in recent weeks, Indi's disgruntlement at Linda's suggestive eyebrow wiggle immediately faded. This was about Benjamin, not Todd Peters. It would *never* be about Todd Peters. There was a better chance that she'd find the backside of a steer more attractive than the NASCAR driver, especially after her last disastrous relationship with a professional athlete.

"Ouch," Todd said after Benjamin slapped his hand. "That stung."

Benjamin laughed. Indi pursed her lips as she watched the exchange. For some reason she'd expected Todd to be aloof. Sometimes celebrities were uncomfortable around sick children, but Todd didn't appear to be so. She watched as he squatted down by Benjamin's chair, one of his hands resting on Benjamin's knee.

"How's it going?" he asked.

"Awesome," Benjamin cried. "I can't believe I'm getting to finally meet you."

Indi rolled her eyes, the snort of derision she bit back turning into a sigh of long-suffering resignation. Linda must have heard it, because she looked in her direction. Todd must have caught it, too. He glanced up.

Indi colored.

"Hi," Linda said, covering for Indi. "I'm Linda, Benjamin's mom."

"Hey," Todd said, holding out his hand again.

"Thanks for coming," Linda said, her attention settling on Benjamin. Indi spied the instant flicker of emotion in her eyes, one that seemed to turn her brown eyes gray. "He's been looking forward to this for weeks."

"Yeah, I'm sorry about the wait," Todd said, his eyes moving back to Benjamin. "I've had a lot going on lately, but that's no excuse for blowing you off."

"Nah," Benjamin said with another wiggle. "I understand. You're a famous driver. Of course you're busy."

"No," Todd said with a shake of his head. "It was wrong, but I've taken steps to ensure it never happens again."

"I didn't mind. At least I got to go to the track."

"Yeah, Sonoma. I heard about that," Todd said. "Did you have fun?"

"Yeah, but it would have been better if you'd won."

Todd chuckled softly, and Indi found herself wondering what Linda saw in the man. Yeah, he was cute, if one liked dark-haired, dark-eyed men, which she didn't.

"It's always more fun when I win," Todd said.

She supposed he had nice shoulders, but that was it.

"You've been doing a lot of winning this year," Benjamin said enthusiastically.

"Yeah, it hasn't been a bad season," Todd said. "But I've had a lot of help from the shop."

And he had a lot of body hair. Okay, maybe he wasn't caveman-ish, but there were a lot of dark strands on his arms. And he had big hands. Ugh.

"You can't win races without a good driver, and you're one of the best," Benjamin said.

Okay, that did it. Indi couldn't stomach another minute. "Listen," she said. "I think I'll grab a bite to eat downstairs while you two chat."

"I thought you were going to wait until after to find that big rig?" Todd asked, his mouth tipping up on one side with what she assumed was a teasing grin.

"Changed my mind," Indi said, trying to tell him without words that the jury was still out where *he* was concerned.

"What big rig?" Benjamin asked.

"Oh, you know," Indi quickly improvised. "One of those big trailer things with souvenirs on it. I was going to get you some stuff."

"No need to do that," Todd said. "I'll have my PR rep send some stuff over. What do you want?"

"An autographed ball cap," Benjamin answered immediately.

Indi saw Todd's gaze slide up, and it was only because she'd been studying him closely that she saw the way his eyes dimmed for a moment as he took in Benjamin's hairless scalp.

"I think we might have a few of those lying around."

"Cool," Benjamin said with another jiggle.

"Linda," Indi asked over their heads. "Do you want me to grab you something?"

"I'll eat later," Linda said.

Indi nodded, though she knew the woman wouldn't. She'd watched Linda drop what must have been thirty pounds over the past few months. It was hard to eat when your child couldn't even keep his own food down.

Indi looked away before Linda could see the way her own eyes dimmed, but Indi's gaze became entangled in Todd's. She saw the driver's eyes flick over her face just before she turned away. Well, whatever. If the man reasoned out that her job depressed her from time to time, so be it. After today she'd never see him again. And that was good, because she didn't like the way she flinched inwardly when she'd spied the commiseration in his eyes.

"I don't think she likes me," Todd whispered to Benjamin when the door closed behind her.

Benjamin's attention shot to where Indi had just stood. "Indi?" the boy asked, sounding so stuffed up Todd all but winced. Poor kid.

"Nah," Benjamin added. "Indi likes everyone."

Except me.

"Have you known her long?" he asked, standing up a second later so he could claim one of the chairs that framed a coffee table. The room was spacious. It had two bedrooms and a sitting area. Benjamin wheeled himself closer as Todd took a seat.

"Indi's been with us from the beginning," Benjamin's mother said, pulling out a matching side chair. She handed her son a tissue so he could wipe his nose. "She's practically a staff member at Children's Hospital."

Todd nodded, noticing the same thing Indi must have spotted a moment before. The woman was exhausted. Dark smudges smeared the skin beneath her eyes. She looked gaunt, too, her shoulders seeming to carry the weight of the world.

"It must be a tough job," Todd found himself saying, but he wasn't necessarily referring to Indi. It must be tough on them all. Sure, he'd met terminally ill children before. What professional athlete hadn't? But those meetings were invariably conducted at the track, and they were usually quick. He'd arranged to spend some time with Benjamin because he felt bad about blowing him off. Only now that he was alone with the boy he found himself wondering why he hadn't done more for other children in Benjamin's condition. Even with a nasty head cold, Todd could practically feel his excitement.

It made his concern about making the Chase seem irrelevant and silly.

They chatted for a bit about racing, Todd feeling every minute slip by. He had less than an hour, thanks to his late start, and it sucked. And even though Indi had told him not to get Benjamin's hopes up, he couldn't help but think of things he could do for the kid in the future. Indi might think him a flake, but Todd knew better.

"Something tells me you won't be able to make it out to the track tomorrow," Todd said as he prepared to leave.

"I can make it," the boy said.

"No," Linda said. "You won't."

"But, Mo-om—"

"Don't 'but Mom' me, young man. You're too sick to go to the track."

Where he might pick up another virus. Or overexert himself. Or do any number of things that might jeopardize his health. Todd could see that now.

"But we came all this way," Benjamin said.

"Tell you what," Todd said. To hell with Indi's directive. He didn't want the kid thinking this was it. "If you can't make the race tomorrow, maybe you can come to a race next weekend."

Benjamin's head shot up. "You mean it?"

"I do," Todd said. "I'll talk to Indi about it when I see her."

"Mr. Peters," Linda said, leaning toward them. "It's really kind of you to offer that, but I'm not certain Benji's doctor will allow him to travel again."

Because the child was getting sicker by the moment. Todd didn't need to be a doctor to see that. "Well, maybe we can do a race closer to home."

"Yeah," Benjamin said. "Phoenix. That's pretty close to California."

But Phoenix was weeks away, and when Todd looked at the boy's mom, he could tell she was thinking the same thing he was.

Linda Koch stood, turned away, ostensibly to look out the window, but Todd knew better.

"Listen," he said. "I know you can't do anything this weekend, but I think there's a camp or something coming up, one that's for kids just like you." Todd remembered reading about it a few weeks back. He'd been invited to attend, but he'd turned it down. He always turned that kind of stuff down. Too depressing. Only now did he realize how selfish an attitude that was. "It'd be a perfect place for you to visit because there are doctors on staff. And I won't be the only driver there. You could meet Lance Cooper and Adam Drake and who knows who else."

"But, it's not a race," Benjamin said, sounding like every other ten-year-old who wasn't getting his way.

"And I don't know that his doctors will allow him to go anywhere," Linda said, facing them again.

Todd leaned toward Benjamin and said in a low voice, "I'll be right back."

The boy nodded, hope still shining from his eyes.

"I know this is short notice," Todd said. He could tell Linda had been doing her darnedest to hold back tears while she'd been studying Richmond's tree-studded skyline. Her red-rimmed eyes gave her away. "And I know that Benjamin has a really bad cold right now, but if he starts to get well, maybe he can make it."

"That's the problem, Mr. Peters—"

"Todd," he quickly corrected.

"Todd," she whispered back, her voice equally low. "He's *not* getting better. Chances are this cold will hang on, or turn into something worse. God forbid it should settle in his lungs. Damn it. We shouldn't have come."

But they had. And it was his fault they'd had to fly all the way out here. They were supposed to have met up in Sonoma, but he'd stood the kid up. And now they would have to fly back home.

"If he starts to get sicker, I will personally see to it that he has the best care."

"That's very kind of you, but it's not necessary. I already have the name of a local pediatric oncologist."

God forbid it should come to that. "Good. But I don't think we're going to need him. Or her. He'll get better with the right motivation," Todd said, echoing what Jen had said earlier. "And you won't have to fly on a commercial airline to get him home. I'll fly him home myself."

"Excuse me?" Linda said.

"I have a jet. We can fly him back when he gets better. I'll fly him to the camp, too."

"You don't have to do that."

Todd reached for her hand. "I *want* to do that."

He saw Linda's lip tremble. Saw her eyes flick away for a second. When she looked up at him there was a glut of pain in her eyes. And sorrow. And flagging hope. "I don't know."

"Talk to his doctors."

She thought about it for a moment, then said, "I will."

Todd released her hand. "Good."

They heard someone at the front door. Indi, no doubt. Todd was surprised when Linda took his hand and said quickly, "In the meantime I want you to do something for *me*."

"What's that?"

But before Linda could answer, Indi asked, "What did I miss?" She gave Benjamin and Linda a wide smile, but her eyes pointedly avoided him.

Linda dropped Todd's hand and turned away, Todd watching in puzzlement as she moved toward her son. What could she want?

"Todd wants me to go to another race," Benjamin announced.

"Really?" Indi said, glancing in his direction, her eyes rebuking him for ignoring her directive.

"And a kid's camp."

"Really?" Indi repeated.

"I know you didn't want me to say anything, but I really think this is doable. It's a camp geared toward kids just like Benjamin," Todd said. "It has doctors on staff."

"Oh, wow. Great," she said, shooting Todd another false smile.

"But we're not going to the track tomorrow," Linda said.

"No?" Indi said, looking at Benjamin and then Linda. "Well, that's a bummer."

"But Todd offered to show you around tonight," Linda said.

Todd's attention shot to Linda. The woman smiled sweetly. This, he realized, was what he could "do" for her.

"Yeah," Linda said. "Just because we can't go anywhere doesn't mean you have to stay behind. What's on your schedule tonight, Mr. Peters?"

"Oh, but Linda," Indi said. "I'm tired, and I was hoping to catch up on some paperwork—"

"I have a cocktail party to go to. It's a sponsor thing—"

"You should go," Benjamin interrupted. "You can tell me all about it."

"But I don't think—"

"You're going," Linda said. "*Don't* think you're not. You never have any fun, Indi. I've been telling you that for months. Todd's offer is a generous one. Go. Have fun with him."

But he hadn't offered, Todd almost said. Only, as he watched the way color filled Indi's face, he couldn't stop himself from feeling a surge of self-satisfaction.

"It's a cocktail party," he said. "Snappy Lube is sponsoring it. There'll be a few other drivers there, maybe even some celebrities."

"I still don't think—"

"Please," Benjamin said. "Will you go? If I can't make it, at least one of us can."

And that, Todd realized, was a plea Indi couldn't refuse. Her eyes narrowed just before she said, "All right."

But I don't have to like it, she seemed to silently add.

Todd would just have to see about that, he thought, feeling anticipation run through him. That and something else.

Interest, he realized. Indi challenged him.

And he never could resist a challenge.

CHAPTER SIX

SHE WANTED to kill Todd Peters.

Indi paced the lobby of the hotel, the heels she'd been forced to don catching in the hotel's plush carpeting. It was a Friday night and so the lobby was packed, people coming and going, most of them wearing T-shirts bearing the car number of their favorite driver. She'd seen more than a few eighty-twos. In her formfitting red cocktail dress, Indi felt more than a little out of place.

"Mmm-mmm-mmm," cooed someone walking by. Indi glanced in the man's direction, her eyes narrowing when she spied the salacious grin on his face.

"Lookin' good," he drawled, nodding his head in approval as if she might have missed his meaning.

She turned on her heel, hissing under her breath, "This sucks."

For the past two hours she'd been forced to undergo a makeover at the hands of Linda and Benjamin Koch. Thanks to Linda's generosity, Indi now found herself the proud owner of an overpriced dress that Linda had found at a boutique located in the hotel lobby. Indi had tried to refuse Linda's generosity, but it had been impossible to say no to a woman who had the determination of a dog with a new chew toy. Benjamin had decided that Indi would be his emissary, and that nothing would do but that she look "hot" for his favorite driver. Indi hadn't had the heart to tell the boy that she'd rather dress herself in a paper bag and bunny slippers than the ankle-length dress and the slinky, rhinestone encrusted heels that Linda had picked out for her. But that she couldn't do and so here she was.

She paced in front of the mirrors that framed the hotel's lobby. She was just turning around when she caught sight of Todd in the mirrors, the man who'd been ogling her earlier just about colliding with him thanks to his head being turned as he checked out Indi's rear.

"Oh, excuse me," he said, and then straightened. "Hey," he all but yelped. "You're Todd Peters."

"Hi," Todd said, eyes scanning the lobby.

"Damn. Where's my camera?" the guy asked. "Shoot…up in my room. Are you going to be here long?"

"Nope. I'm meeting someone."

"How about an autograph then?"

Todd's expression grew more perplexed. His gaze caught on her for a second, or more appropriately, her rear end. Indi stiffened, waiting for recognition to dawn.

It didn't.

She began to turn, thinking that she couldn't look that different with her hair swept atop her head. Then again, she never wore her hair in tight curls. But Linda had curled it like a poodle's, all before stuffing it atop her head. Indi felt ready for a dog show.

"You're meeting that blonde, aren't you?" the guy asked.

Todd looked at the man in askance.

"She was just here," the man said.

Indi readied herself, surprised to realize she had to resist the urge to pat herself in place. She turned around.

"There she is," he said, pointing.

Todd followed the direction of the man's finger. She smirked, her lips pursing in derision as she waited for his reaction.

"Wow," was all he said.

"Todd," she said with an inclination of her head.

"Man, she's hot," the race fan said, as if Indi wasn't standing right there. Todd glanced back at the guy before heading toward her. "You think maybe I can get a picture with the both of you?" the guy asked when Todd stopped in front of Indi. "Really. It'll just take a second to go get my camera."

"Let's go," Todd said.

"What about my autograph?" the guy asked.

"Stop by the front desk tomorrow," Todd said, motioning toward the reception area where more than one hotel worker stared in their direction. "I'll have my PR rep leave a signed race card."

"Cool."

"Come on," Todd ordered again.

Indi followed, but only because she needed to speak to him alone.

"I'm not going with you," she said the moment the glass front doors slid closed.

"Excuse me?" he asked.

He stood on the red carpet that some industrious hotel manager had strategically placed to make a guest feel special.

"Let's just part company right here. I'll go hide out in the hotel bar or something. Linda and Benjamin will never know."

"*I* would know."

She felt her body tip back in surprise. "Don't tell me you're suddenly developing a conscience?"

He ran his hand through his hair, or he would have, if it hadn't been slicked back. Actually, he didn't look half-bad. The jacket he wore made him look fitter than she'd thought him to be. And the white shirt set off his tanned skin.

"Look," he said. "I told Linda I'd take you out. I'm taking you out."

"We're outside," she said, splaying her hands. It was a warm night. The clear sky had turned a molten pink thanks to a setting sun. A crescent moon could be seen in the sky—like a sideways smiley face.

Indi didn't feel much like smiling.

"Yeah, so?" Todd asked.

"Well, you can now officially claim we went out. No need to go anywhere."

She heard him expel an impatient breath. Saw him tip his head sideways and forward as if to chide her for something. But then he shook his head. "We're going to this event. Once we get there, you can do whatever you want. But I'm taking you there, for Linda and Benjamin's sake, and that's that."

Indi watched him walk away, envisioning Linda and Benjamin's disappointed expressions if they caught her returning to her own room. But maybe they wouldn't catch her. Maybe she could just pretend to have gone to the event.

"You coming?" Todd asked, pausing by the side of a car that...

Whoa! What *was* that thing?

A MINI Cooper, she recognized, but one painted

to look like a rolling billboard, complete with an orange roof, yellow sides and a white bottom. Across the doors and hood were the words *Snappy Lube*— a company famous for doing oil changes "in a snap"—the words done in a speedy-looking script. But what made her pause, and all right, bite back a smile, was the roadrunner on the roof. It wasn't like the one in the cartoons. No, no, no…this bird sat down, leaning over like a drunken sailor, long legs splayed out in front of him like Big Bird, wingtips down as if he were propping himself up, and the silliest, goofiest grin she'd ever seen on his long-beaked face.

Todd opened the passenger side door.

Realization dawned.

"Oh, no," she said before she could stop herself. "I'm not riding in that thing."

"Come on," he said. "Where's your spirit of adventure?"

He couldn't be serious. Could he?

"But I thought…"

"That we'd be riding in a limo?" he finished for her. He shook his head in mock commiseration. "'Fraid not."

"I was actually kind of expecting a rental car."

"This is *better* than a rental car," he said with a wide smile.

Indi glanced back at the hotel. The night just kept getting better and better.

"You coming?" he asked, and when she glanced back at him, his eyes were bright.

Todd Peters *laughed* at her. He also didn't expect her to ride with him.

"I refuse to wear an Elmer Fudd hat," she said, sauntering by.

"I don't blame you," he said.

And as she slid inside, she realized she had a choice. She could enjoy the night and all the surprises it might bring, or she could continue to be a party pooper. She watched Todd cross in front of the car, his hand lifting as he waved to yet another fan. But who was she trying to kid? The guy really *was* trying. He could have blown them off again. Heck, he could have completely ignored her. She'd met more than her fair share of celebrities who did exactly that. Todd hadn't done that at all. In fact, there might even be hints of a hip-hog in him.

"All right," he said, sliding into the driver's seat. "Let's see if we can get to this party in a snap."

He had a sense of humor, too. She'd always been a sucker for a man with a funny bone.

She stiffened because she couldn't actually be starting to *like* Todd.

Could she?

When he opened his mouth and did a perfect Roadrunner, "Beep, beep," she realized she was.

And that wouldn't do. That wouldn't do *at all.*

SHE LOOKED *HOT.*

It was all Todd could do to keep from staring at her as they drove to the event. Every time he glanced in her direction his eyes hooked on her legs, the sculpted length of them so tanned and toned and smooth—they looked like polished marble—he felt an inexplicable urge to reach out and run his hands up the sinewy cords of her calf. Man, he'd been without a woman for too long.

"Look, Todd. You really *don't* have to do this," she said when they stopped at a light, the driver of the car next to them doing a double-take when he caught sight of the bird atop the car. Todd hid his smile.

"You could just drop me off at a local restaurant," she added. "I'll have dinner there and then take a taxi back to the hotel. Linda and Benjamin would never know."

"*I* would know," he said again.

She frowned. Todd found his gaze settling on her legs again. "Besides," he admitted, "I want to spend time with you."

The sun might be sinking beneath the horizon, but

he could still see the surprise on her face. When her lashes widened, it turned the color of her eyes the same hue as freshly sprouted leaves. "Why?"

"Because your job fascinates me." And because he wanted to know what motivated a person to do something so remarkable as to work with terminally ill children.

"But I've been such a—" She bit the words off.

"Brat?" he finished for her.

"I was going to say something else," she admitted with—could it be? A wry grin.

"Yes, you have. And I've been a self-centered ass. So why don't we just bury the hatchet?"

She stared at the hand he held out. "All right," she said, clasping his fingers lightly.

Todd expected her to be cold, perhaps because of the ice that was usually in her eyes, but her grip was warm and surprisingly firm.

"Tell me about Linda," he said. The light turned green and he was grateful for the distraction of driving.

"Linda? She's great," Indi immediately answered. "She's devoted to Benjamin."

"He's a good kid."

"I know," Indi said.

"But he's pretty sick, isn't he?"

"He is," she admitted. "This cold is a sign of his weakened immune system."

"I'm sorry I put off meeting with him."

"So am I," she said, and Todd realized that with Indi, he'd always get the truth. She said exactly what was on her mind.

"Spending time with him today," he said, "it changed things. Helped me to realize that the little everyday stresses were nothing compared to battling for your life. I'll admit I was torqued that Linda arranged for me to take you out. And I'll admit that I planned to use tonight as a way of getting back at you."

She jerked toward him. He could see it out of the corner of his eye. "How?"

"I was going to flirt with you."

Then she laughed for the second time that day. Todd felt the strangest urge to stop the car, pull her to him, and kiss her...*really* kiss her. Make her moan and sigh and maybe touch him back...

Drive, Todd.

"I think you've bumped that head of yours one too many times."

Yeah. He'd been thinking the same thing, too. "It wasn't anything personal," he said, and yet, still, the aftereffects of his minifantasy tingled through him. "I just thought it might be fun to rile you."

"You'll find I'm impossible to rile."

Yeah, he sensed that about her.

"Why is Benjamin in a wheelchair?" he asked, trying to change the subject. They were on a freeway, trees and buildings speeding by, the darkened sky shrouding everything in gray.

"He's weak. The chemo's taken almost everything out of him. It's not uncommon for kids at his stage of CML to be in chairs. Sometimes they're almost too tired to hold their head up."

"What's CML?"

"Chronic myelogenous leukemia."

"I know that, but is it a bone cancer or something?" Todd asked.

"Yes. The kind that causes the rapid growth of blood-forming cells that can lead to tumors and bone marrow failure."

"I can't even begin to imagine how hard that must be on his parents."

"No," she said. "You probably can't."

They lapsed into silence again. Todd searched for something to say. But what *could* he say? He was blessed with a healthy family. His mom and dad still came to watch him race. His sisters routinely had babies. Until that moment, he didn't realize how blessed they were.

"What," she surprised him by asking, "does one do at a sponsor event, by the way?" and Todd was glad they seemed to be on even ground.

"Eat food. Shake a lot of hands. Imbibe alcohol."

"I see," she said with all the enthusiasm of some-one about to dig out an ingrown toenail.

"It won't be that bad. And, anyway, it'll be over in a couple of hours and you'll have lots of stuff to tell Benjamin. I'm sure he'll want to hear how you got to meet Lance Cooper and a few of the other drivers I'll be introducing you to."

"Who's Lance Cooper?"

And that, he admitted, summed up every reason why he shouldn't be thinking—yet again—how much he'd like to kiss the pique right off her face. Not only was he still sort of stinging from Kristen's rejection—and therefore in no frame of mind to pursue another woman—but even if he was, he and Indi were total opposites.

And yet as Todd drove toward their destination, he admitted Indi was a conundrum he wanted to try and decipher. Not because he was attracted to her.

His gaze caught on her legs.

Okay. So maybe that was a lie. But what red-blooded male wouldn't find her attractive? She was like one of those paintings where the artist draws a picture within a picture. At first all you saw was the initial drawing—a thing of beauty—but the more you looked, the more you saw other layers.

Those layers fascinated him.

CHAPTER SEVEN

SHE NEVER FELT so out of place in her life.

Indi sat at a table set up near the perimeter of the room all the while having one of those out-of-body experiences, the kind that made you wonder just where, exactly, you'd gone wrong. And just what, exactly, she'd done to put herself in this predicament.

She was here for Benjamin, she reminded herself. And so far it hadn't been all *that* bad. Todd was actually *nice*. When they'd arrived in the MINI Cooper, he'd asked her if she wanted to go inside while he did his thing with the media, who were waiting for him to arrive. He'd asked the press to wait a second while he escorted her inside. Indi would have to have been inhuman not to feel special when he'd done that.

"He's so totally *hot*," the woman to her left said, someone Indi had originally guessed to be at least twenty years younger based on her "totally" comment but who was, upon closer examination, closer to Indi's own age. Indi squinted her eyes, the low light making it hard to see ten feet beyond one's own circumference. She had to peer through the crowd to see which driver was "hot." It wasn't Todd, it was some blond-headed guy, but that wasn't to say that Indi hadn't heard more than her fair share of comments about how good-looking Todd was.

Deciding that the blond guy wasn't her idea of "totally hot" *at all,* she turned her attention to the people milling about. They weren't in a room. They were in a giant white tent sponsored by Snappy Lube. Yellow and orange appeared to be the color scheme for the night. Indi's arms rested on an orange tablecloth. The buffet table sported yellow fabric. Even the chairs had been outfitted with yellow slip covers. Indi felt as if she sat inside a giant candy corn.

Worse, the big top was set up near the front of the racetrack and, since a race was going on, she could hardly hear herself think, between the elevated conversation echoing off the canvas top, the pitiful music being played in the background, and the race cars out on the track, which were a constant hum.

"I heard Todd Peters works out at a local fitness club whenever he's in town."

Indi glanced right. It was the same woman who'd made the comment about the blond guy, a woman with big hair and a lot of makeup.

"I got the name from one of his fan club presidents," the woman said with a nod to her two dinner companions.

Indi had actually spotted the three women when she'd arrived. They hadn't seen her with Todd because they'd been hanging on to the coattails of another driver, but once he'd ditched them they'd been skirting the room ever since, looking for big game. She had no idea why they'd taken a seat next to her except she would bet it had something to do with their stiletto heels and the numerous laps they'd made around the room.

"Do you think we should go there in the morning?" the blonde asked.

"I think definitely," one of the other women said. Another blonde with hair so short and so full of gel it resembled Lady Liberty's torch—right down to the pointy tips.

"Not with me," a third woman said, a brunette with long, pretty hair and a surprisingly makeup-free face. "I'm sleeping in."

"You're such a party-pooper, Diane," flame-head said.

Diane shrugged. "And you and Amber are stalkers."

"Here, here," Indi muttered.

But the words came out during one of those weird

lulls in conversation, the kind when a previously noisy room turns absolutely quiet.

Three faces swiveled toward her.

Indi met each one unflinchingly. "I mean, um, I hear Todd's really nice."

"So have I," Amber said.

"Uh-huh," flame head said. "Todd Peters shirtless is something I'd pay money to see."

Indi just smiled. Todd Peters without his shirt on is something she'd pay money *not* to see.

She remembered his wide shoulders.

Or maybe not.

But the women weren't paying attention to her. Even Diane, the friendly one, looked past her, all three of the ladies blinking like beauty pageant contestants just before the winner was crowned. And Indi knew, she just *knew* who stood behind her.

"Oh my gosh, Todd Peters," Amber said.

"Hi, ladies," he said before coming around to her line of sight. "You want something to eat?" Todd asked. One of his arms rested on the back of her chair, the other on their table. And really, he had rather taut arms. Two sinewy cords of muscle ran up from the wrist. For a moment she found herself wondering if race car drivers had stronger forearms than normal men. Wrestling with that steering wheel had to take some effort....

"Uh…no," she said.

"Good," Todd said. "Then let's dance."

"Dance," Indi immediately countered.

"Yeah," Todd said, grabbing her hand and trying to tug her up. She resisted, but a surprisingly large hand that was amazingly strong pulled her up as if she weighed no more than paper.

The three women's eyes widened.

"Oh, hey," Barbara said. "If she doesn't want to dance with you, I will."

"That's okay," Todd said at the same time Indi said, "Great," which caused Todd to glance at her. "Don't you want to dance?"

"I do," someone said behind her.

"Todd, I—" Crud. She didn't know *what* she wanted.

"Hey. Can we get a picture?" Amber asked.

"After my dance, ladies," he said, beaming at the besotted women.

"Aw," Barbara pouted.

But Todd was already leading her away and Indi let him because, truth be told, there was a part of her that really wanted to be with him and that alarmed her. That alarmed her *a lot*.

"There's really no need to do this," Indi said when they were far enough away.

"You're right," he said. "But we are."

"Todd, I—"

He spun her onto the floor, if one wanted to call asphalt covered with some type of rubber a dance floor. And that was when Indi got her second surprise of the night.

Todd Peters knew how to dance.

The band played oldies. The tune Todd spun her around to had been recorded by some pop band that Indi was sure no longer recorded music. So as they dipped and swayed, Indi tried to hide her surprise. Todd would throw her out, then pull her back in with both hands, only to throw her out again and then guide her into a spin. Before long, they'd attracted a crowd. Bulbs flashed. Indi glanced around. People clapped along.

Smile, Todd mouthed.

She didn't *want* to smile. She was feeling things that…well, that she hadn't felt in a long time. And yet as he whirled her along she found herself grinning. It had been so long since someone had danced with her, and danced with her *well,* that the music made her want to throw her head back and wiggle her hips, but she couldn't because it somehow seemed wrong to be enjoying herself with Todd, while Benjamin was back at the hotel, sick.

The music stopped—quickly, abruptly—like an engine cut off midstream. The electronic tinkle of a piano took the place of an electric guitar and Indi knew what was coming next.

"No," she said, right as Todd pulled her toward him.

"Come on," he said as slower music began to be played. "Our audience will be disappointed if we don't."

Indi glanced right and left. The crowd around them had begun to break up, but there were still a few people watching them avidly. The way people stared at celebrities always perplexed her. Didn't they realize Todd was a flesh-and-blood man just like all the other males in the room?

"You look like you're on your way to a triple root canal."

"Do I?"

"If I'm so hard for you to tolerate, Indi, I can take you home."

Was that what she wanted? She'd stood back after he'd walked her to the door earlier, watching him greet his fans when they'd first arrived. He'd shaken more hands and signed more autographs than someone schmoozing for electoral votes. And he'd done it with a smile. A *genuine* smile. That'd surprised her, and made her think yet again that she could like him if given half a chance.

Still…

"It's just that this really isn't my scene," she said, realizing that somehow they'd begun to dance. Todd's arms held her loosely, but not so slackly that she didn't feel the warmth of his body. The intimacy of not only sensing his warmth but smelling his essence had her blushing.

"Then let's go." He started to let her go.

She surprised herself by placing a hand over the top of his arm. "Wait."

They stopped swaying for a moment, Indi realizing that his eyes weren't really brown. They were more hazel, with light green flecks near the center.

"Aren't you obligated to stay?" she asked.

"I'm not obligated to do anything beyond show up."

"Really?"

He shook his head. "It's an *appearance*, that's all. The other drivers will head out soon, too."

"Oh," she said. No wonder those fans who stood near the perimeter of the dance floor still hovered there, a few of them with pens and paper in hand. They knew their time was short.

"Honestly, Indi. I wasn't planning on staying here long. You can tell Benjamin and Linda that you didn't miss out, that none of the drivers hung out long."

"So you guys just smile to the crowd and then bail?"

"For the most part, yeah."

"That must suck for the fans."

"Not really. They know how the game's played."

That would explain the forward behavior of those women, too. They had to act fast to catch their idol's attention.

"So if we're ambushed on our way out, that's why," Todd added. "Although most fans are pretty well behaved, especially at a function like this."

"How do people get invited?"

Wait. Were they really having a conversation again? One without verbal sparing and disparaging remarks being flung back and forth?

"These are VIPs, or Snappy Lube employees, or friends of Snappy Lube employees. It's invitation only, which means you don't want to get whoever invited you into trouble by hunting down your favorite driver."

"Unless you stalk them on your own time."

"Excuse me?"

She told him about what she'd overheard, Todd's brows darting straight up. "You're kidding?" His head turned until he'd found the table full of women. Amber and Barbara waved. Diane rolled her eyes and shook her head, obviously as mortified by her friends' behavior as before. "I really do have an appointment with a physical trainer in the morning."

"I'd cancel it."

"Yeah. And maybe we should slip out the back. You ready to go now?"

Not really. For a moment or two she'd been able to forget about Benjamin and his illness. "Sure," she said.

But when his arms dropped away, the sudden loss of contact made her feel momentarily off balance— as if she'd been leaning on him for support.

"Do you know where the back entrance is?" she asked.

"When in doubt, follow the caterers." He guided her toward the buffet table set up at one end of the tent.

"Todd," a man called as they passed.

Todd ignored him. Indi glanced back in time to catch the disappointment on the man's face. And then someone else called his name. Todd quickened his pace at the same time he leaned forward and ducked, almost as if he tried to hide behind the silver-domed chaffing dishes.

"This is ridiculous," she muttered right as Todd found the exit. He bolted outside…and right into the path of an oncoming waiter.

"Hey," cried a young kid carrying a tray of food. And then his eyes widened. "You're Todd Peters," the guy said, taking a step back in order to get a better look. Unfortunately, the food on his tray didn't stay put. A gravy boat of oil-based dressing slid off the front.

Right onto Indi's dress.

"Oh!" Indi cried as the wet, gooey mess oozed down her.

"Oh, damn," the kid cried.

"Uh-oh," Todd said when he caught sight of her.

Uh-oh was right. Bits of parsley and minced garlic clung to the front of her dress, the oil turning the bright red fabric a deep maroon.

"Here," someone said, throwing a towel.

Indi wiped at the mess. But it quickly became obvious it was hopeless.

"We have bottled water in the truck," a woman said, her white catering coat bearing the name Anna. She pointed to a white truck with the words *Good Eats* on the side. "Maybe we can run some water over the front of it."

"I doubt that'll help," Indi said, still swiping.

"I have a T-shirt you can borrow," the woman said. "You could take the dress off—"

"You can clean up in my motor coach," Todd said, flipping open his phone and pressing a button. "Ron, are you around with the rental car?"

"Ron? Who's Ron?" she asked.

"He's my motor coach driver. I'll have him pick

us up in the SUV. Unless you want to ride back in the Snappy Lube car?"

"No, no—"

A man's voice cut her off. "I'm here," he said.

"Great," Todd said. "I need you to pick us up in the back of the Snappy Lube tent ASAP. Indi collided with a soup tureen."

"It's not soup. It's salad dressing," she said, surprisingly disappointed that her new dress was ruined.

"Don't worry," he said after snapping his phone closed. "We'll get it cleaned up."

"I hope so." But right as she said that, Indi noticed someone else had followed them outside. A young woman wearing a red dress rimmed with gold— Todd's colors—had her camera in hand.

"I'm sorry, Mr. Peters," the waiter said at exactly the same time the woman said, "Can I get a picture?"

"Sorry. Bad timing," Todd said, motioning toward Indi. "We need to go."

"You can send us the dry-cleaning bill," the woman named Anna called after them as Todd took Indi's hand and all but tugged her past food warmers and portable stoves, most of which seemed to be powered by a nearby generator that hummed and expelled noxious fumes.

"I feel like wet toilet paper," Indi muttered, realizing she'd walked away with the caterer's towel. Oh, well.

Todd looked over his shoulder again. Indi followed his gaze. The female fan had backed off, but she was following at a distance. Indi had forgotten how "difficult" it was to deal with fans.

"We'll get you cleaned up," Todd said, picking up the pace. "My motor coach is right over there." He pointed to the racetrack.

"Wait a second," Indi said, pausing. Night had fallen, but she could plainly see the giant grandstands that rimmed the track. A multitude of lights turned night into day, and now that Indi was outside, she could distinguish between the roar of the cars and the excited cheers of the crowd. "I'm not going in there dressed like this."

"You don't have to go in there," he said, trying to prod her forward again. "My motor coach is out behind the track," Todd said. "In a private lot. Nobody will see you."

Except him.

When she took off the dress, which she would have to if she wanted to try to salvage the fabric, she admitted. The realization dawned right as he pulled on her hand again; Indi put on the brakes a second later.

"What?" he asked in obvious exasperation, his attention sliding down and catching the galaxy of garlic before moving up and over her shoulders. The woman was still there, too.

"Just take me back to the hotel," she said.

"There's no point in you sitting in the back of a limo, miserable, when you can get cleaned up at my place."

That was just it. It was *his* place. His private quarters. For some reason Indi didn't like the thought of being alone with him. In a confined space. And then…stripping.

"I'd really rather go back."

"I'm not returning you to your hotel looking like that."

"It's not a big deal."

"It is to me," he said. "I don't want to have to explain to Benjamin that I ruined his favorite person's dress."

It was on the tip of Indi's tongue to argue further, but he had a point. She'd hate for Benjamin to think she'd had a less than perfect night.

So she waited. With any luck Benjamin would never know.

"Here's the car," Todd said a few moments later. "Get in before that woman snaps a picture of you in all your greasy glory."

Indi saw that it was true. They were about to have

their photo taken. Darn it. She got in, but not before her eyes were blinded by a flash.

Oh, great.

CHAPTER EIGHT

SHE HAD TO BE the most stubborn individual he'd ever met, Todd thought, sliding onto the seat next to her in the back of the SUV. And she smelled like an Italian restaurant.

"Don't you get tired of it?"

He shrugged, glancing out the window. "You take the good with the bad." But the truth was the only thing that kept him sane was escaping once in a while, out on the racetrack.

"Besides," he added, "I'm *not* really famous. Not like actors and actresses are. Half the time, when I'm away from the track, people don't recognize me. Or if they do, they think I'm a long-lost cousin. Or an old friend. I'm constantly asked what school I went to and where I grew up."

Her lashes lowered. Todd knew she studied him intently. "I used to get that, too. When I was a sportscaster."

"Wait a second. You did sports?"

She lifted that small chin of hers. "I was the first female sports broadcaster in our station's history."

"And that's where you formed your opinion of athletes?"

"Partly."

And he hadn't helped improve that opinion in the beginning, Todd admitted, although he was trying to make it up to her. "What made you quit broadcasting?"

He saw her tense. She looked away. "This and that."

He waited for her to expand on the comment. But she didn't. "That's overnight parking," he said, when he followed her gaze. "For race fans."

The track provided enough ambient light that one could perfectly see the revelry going on inside. RVs that were too numerous to count, each of them bearing the standard of their favorite driver, sponsor or car manufacturer, were parked tail to tail or nose to nose. Some fans had set up the accoutrements of home outside their vehicles—couches, televisions, even bars complete with bar stools.

"I've never seen anything like it."

"That's nothing," Todd said. "You should see Daytona."

She sat back again, Todd wondering if she'd even realized how close she'd come to him. So close that her eyes had looked as green as a race flag when she looked at him next.

"You must feel like a god sometimes."

"No," he immediately countered. "I feel more like a puppet." And it surprised him to admit as much, at least to her. But she was easy to talk to now that she wasn't slinging barbs.

"How so?"

"The demands on my time are too numerous. I'm always running from one engagement to another. And if I'm not making public appearances, I'm doing other things on behalf of my sponsor. Interviews, commercials, VIP dinners or lunches or breakfasts or whatever. Sometimes I go weeks before I get a free day."

"I had no idea," she said, her head resting against the back of the seat, static causing wispy strands of her upswept hair to stick to the leather.

"So while it might seem all I do is race and sign autographs, the reality is much different."

They were near the back of the track now, parking attendants slowing them down until they spotted the SUV's parking pass. The sound of the vehicles out on the track was louder now, as were the cheers of the crowd. Indi seemed lost in thought as she studied the massive grandstands.

"I feel bad about missing those appointments with Benjamin."

She turned to face him. "I know."

They turned right, the limo further slowing as a security guard checked to ensure Todd Peters was really inside the vehicle, and not a bunch of fans trying to infiltrate the driver/owner lot.

"Good luck tomorrow night," the man said as Todd rolled up the window.

"Thanks."

"I thought you raced during the day."

"Usually, we do. But tomorrow we race at night. Although there are other times when I race on Saturday night, when I race in a different league with a different kind of car—the kind that's racing tonight."

"And what's that?"

"The Busch cars are running now. I race them, too, from time to time."

"What's the difference between a Busch car and the car you'll race tomorrow?"

"Horsepower. Body weight. And a few million dollars."

"How much does it cost to run a NASCAR team?"

"About ten to fifteen million."

The hand she'd been using to wipe at her dress fell to her lap. "You're kidding?"

"At a minimum," Todd said. "NASCAR tries to

keep things affordable, but the teams keep getting more and more competitive and so it's costing more to stay ahead of the curve. That's one of the reasons why I bend over backward to please my sponsors, although I'm pretty lucky. My primary sponsor—Fly For Less—was previously owned by my team owner. It's pretty much a given that they'll keep on sponsoring me since he still owns a lot of stock in the company, unlike some of the other guys who don't know from year to year what name will be on the hood of their cars." He glanced outside. "This is it."

A second later his driver opened the door for them. "Do you need me to wait?" the man asked.

"Uh…sure," Indi answered.

The man nodded. Todd slid out first, offering Indi his hand. To his surprise, she took it.

"Does he hang around the track all day waiting for you to summon him?"

"Depends," Todd answered. "He works for the team during the day. At night he keeps an eye on the place, if I'm not around. He's more like an assistant—keeps the refrigerator stocked and the generator going—but at night he has his own hotel room."

"I see," she said, her eyes fixed upon the black-and-silver Prevost that sat at the end of a row of similar buses. Thick humidity clung to their faces, and even though cars thundered around the track, Todd could still hear crickets chirping in the grove of trees behind the lot.

"My home away from home," Todd said, her hand so tiny and delicate he was almost glad to let it go.

"And here I thought only rock stars owned things like these."

"Actually, drivers are a lot like musicians. We're always on the road. So our motor coaches become our homes away from home. Each bus is tailored to a specific driver's needs."

"All *I* need is some hot water."

"Right this way," he said, pushing on a numbered keypad. "Although I should warn you. I own a dog."

No sooner had he said the words than he heard an excited whine on the other side.

"That doesn't sound like a dog," she said as the door hissed open. "That sounds like a potbellied pig."

"He's an English Bulldog," Todd said, going inside first. "Hey, Lex. Come here, boy."

He heard Indi's footsteps behind him right as Lex reared up and jammed his nose in Todd's crotch. "Ouch, damn it. Why do you always do that?"

But the dog was through with him. Lex had spotted Indi, and it was love at first sight.

"He's baring his teeth at me," Indi cried out in alarm.

"No, he's not. He's smiling," Todd said, Lex's stub of a tail wagging so hard his whole rear end gyrated. "Lex has a movie-star grin."

"And an underbite you could hang things off of," she said, using her hands to keep the dog down.

"Yeah, but it doesn't detract from his smile."

By now Lex was doing his "I'm a happy dog" routine, tongue hanging down, stubby front legs half rearing as he tried to paw Indi's thighs.

"Uh, hi, Lex," Indi said when the dog balanced on his hind legs in front of her.

And then Lex froze, like a rearing horse, his nose lifting in the air as he caught a whiff of salad dressing. He grunted his approval before dropping back to the ground and licking Indi's ankles.

"Ooh," Indi cried as she tried to move out of the way.

"Lex, leave her alone," Todd said, going to her rescue. "Sorry about that," he said as he pulled the dog down.

"That's okay," she said. "He just took me by surprise. Dogs' noses are always so darn cold."

"Isn't that the truth," Todd muttered. "Bathroom's on the right," he said, holding on to Lex's collar.

"Thanks," she said, heading straight for it. Usually newcomers made some comment about the bus's plush interior. Or how spacious it was. Or the fiber-optic lights that encircled the ceiling. Indi appeared completely engrossed in making it to the bathroom ASAP. Not that he blamed her. It must suck smelling like a salad bowl.

"You want something to drink?" he asked, taking Lex to the front of the bus where his bed was located. "Down," he ordered.

Lex smiled.

"Don't try that with me," Todd said, wagging a finger at the dog.

"Nothing to drink for me," came Indi's muffled reply.

"Did she taste good?" Todd asked.

Lex wagged his tail.

"That's what I thought," he said with a smile, turning toward the kitchen. She might not be thirsty, but he was, and the Prevost's kitchen—it sat in one of four expandable compartments—was fully stocked thanks to Ron. He wished he could pull out a beer, but he never drank before a race and tomorrow was an important day. He might just make the Chase for the NASCAR NEXTEL Cup…

Don't think about that.

He pulled out a soda and popped the top, a bit of the liquid bubbling through the hole. The bus's water pump hummed with use. Todd figured it might take her a while to get the dress rinsed off and so he sat and called Lex over. The dog had been rescued by one of the local shelters Todd did some fund-raising for. His brown spots had caught Todd's attention, and, still stinging from Kristen's rejection, he'd impulsively brought him home. Life had never been the same since.

"Damn it," he heard Indi mutter.

"You need some help in there?" he called, pointing Lex back to his dog bed. Lex went the opposite direction, toward the bathroom, his stub of a tail wagging back and forth, nose sounding like a plugged up vacuum as he sniffed the ground.

"No," Indi yelled. "I don't need any help."

Lex found the crack in the door. He kneeled down on his knees and tried to suck the oxygen out of the bathroom.

"You sure?"

"No," she said again, her voice impatient. And then low, but still audible, even over Lex's snorting, she said, "I feel like an oil can."

"Lex, go," he ordered his dog, grabbing his collar and pointing him back toward his bed. "I have a shirt and sweatpants," he said. "You could change into those if you want to rinse the dress."

"That's all right."

"You sure? It might be easier."

The image of her naked rose in his mind. It didn't improve his mood.

"The dress is already off."

He drew back from the door as if it had reached out and slapped him. "Oh, well...you want a robe or something?"

"No."

He heard water splashing, looked down at Lex and shrugged. "Maybe we should both go to our beds," he said, then winced at the mental image *that* wrought. He chugged the whole can of soda just so it would scald his throat—which it did—but it didn't take his mind off things.

A few minutes later Indi emerged with a towel held over the front of her, the dress noticeably wet from top to bottom.

"It's ruined. Let's go," she said, still sopping up the moisture.

Lex looked from Todd to Indi, rear end gyrating, teeth bared. "Stay," Todd told the dog. Then he said to Indi, "You're not seriously going to ride all the way back to your hotel wearing a sopping wet dress, are you?"

"I'm fine. Let's go."

Her hand dropped, and it was then that he saw what the towel had concealed.

She wore no bra.

"You're right," he said. "You should go."

Her gaze became entangled in his own. She jerked the towel up. But it was too late. They might have been at each others' throats until recently, but Todd was a man, and Indi was a woman. And they were alone. In his motor coach. With only Lex for company.

"I told you this would be a wasted trip," she muttered as she zoomed by.

"Indi, no…wait," he said, catching her arms. "If the dress means that much to you we should stay and try to fix it."

"It's *not* the dress," she said.

"Then what is it? Why do you care so much about the darn thing?"

She jerked away. "Because Linda picked this dress out for me. Because it means something to *her.* Because when she slipped it over my head tonight I saw something in her eyes, something that made me want to cry because I knew, I just knew, she was wishing all her *own* troubles away. Only she can't do that and so I went along with her plans and I realized I really liked being dressed up. Only now the dress she picked out for me so carefully and, yes, lovingly, is ruined."

Her eyes hadn't filled with tears, but they may as well have. What Todd saw swimming in the depths of her eyes was akin to a bucket of tears.

"Indi, I'm sorry," he said, his hand reaching for her own. "I'll have Ron take it to the dry cleaners."

"It's okay," she said, shaking her head and looking away. "I just want to go back to the hotel."

He almost let her go, but something made him close the distance between them, made him clutch her shoulders. "The weight of the world is on your shoulders, too, isn't it?"

"No, it's not," she said. "My burden's nothing compared to Linda and her husband's."

"That's not true," he dared to contradict. "I see it when you think I'm not looking. I see the sorrow and the sadness and, yes, the fear. You love your clients like they're your own and when their illnesses get critical, it affects you like it does the family."

"What makes you say that?" she asked, her gaze wide and searching.

He picked up the towel she'd dropped, wrapped it around her shoulders, used it to pull her toward him a little. He was tempted to snuggle up against her.

Snuggle?

"I know because I know you're a good woman."

And he wanted to kiss her. Not because she was beautiful or because she had a hot body and a pretty face. He wanted to kiss her because he understood what it was like to have a job that created an unbearable amount of stress. Man, did he understand.

"Don't," she said softly.

"Don't what?" he asked, his head lowering a fraction.

"Don't start being nice to me now."

He kissed her before he could think better of it. He used the towel to hold her close. And the moment his lips connected with hers, Todd knew nothing would be the same. Kissing her was like sliding into a new race car—a pulse-pounding, hair-raising, adrenaline rush of an experience. He pulled her closer, let the towel drop as he palmed the back of her head, applied pressure in the hopes that she felt the same thing, too. And for a second, a split second, Todd tasted her, his body jolting at the soft texture of her tongue.

"Don't," she cried, wrenching away. "Don't kiss me."

"Indi," Todd said, unable to do much more than stare at her.

She bent, picked up the towel, jerked it around her, the water stain on her dress having spread lower. Without a backward glance she began to pass him. He lifted a hand to stop her, then thought better of it. In her current frame of mind she'd probably deck him. He glanced down at Lex. The dog had his head buried beneath his front paws, his eyes the only thing peeking out.

I know how you feel, buddy.

"How in the hell do you open this thing?" she said when she reached the door.

"Button there on the right," Todd said, coming up behind her. "But, Indi, I really think we should talk about this."

She pushed the button. The door hissed open. Thick, humidity-drenched air hit them. Indi took a step, then drew up short.

A woman stood at the bottom of the stairs. Lex must have caught sight of her because he was up in a flash, Todd catching the dog's collar at the last moment.

"You have company," Indi said, stating the obvious. She took the steps two at a time.

"Hey, Todd," the woman said, but only after eyeing Indi up and down. "I saw your light on and thought I'd drop by. You remember me, don't you?"

A brief image of naked flesh and tangled hair flitted through his mind.

Yeah, he remembered her, and he wondered which of the other drivers she'd befriended had gotten her a wristband to get into the lot.

"Don't bet on it," he heard Indi mutter.

"Indi, wait—" He let go of Lex's collar, but he had to turn to keep the dog from bounding outside.

"We met last year," the blonde was saying when he finally made it down the stairs. "And I was kind of thinking that maybe, you know, we could spend some time together again."

"I'm with someone," Todd said, reaching Indi right as she jerked open the SUV's door, Ron having tried to beat her to it. The man settled for holding the door for her.

"Well, then, maybe tomorrow," the woman said, having trailed behind.

"Yeah," Indi said. "Pencil her in for tomorrow. Right after the race would probably be good. Professional athletes enjoy a good romp after competing in an event."

"Indi, it's not like that. *I'm* not like that."

"Right," she said as she took a seat.

"And I wasn't trying to hit on you earlier. Really. I just—" He scratched at his hand, trying to think.

"Make sure you practice safe sex," Indi said just before the driver closed the door.

"For God's sake, Indi," Todd cried.

"*I* could stick around if you like," the woman said, her lashes flickering.

Todd stared between the woman and Indi, and as he did so, it hit him hard that he didn't want a one-night stand with her. Not with *any* woman. He was tired of the inevitable aftermath that always followed a fling—the woman's persistent phone calls, the notes left on his motor coach's door, the woman following him around in the garage. He wanted…he wanted.

Indi. Or someone like her.

"If you want, we could go out—"

Damn it. It was all too much. The stress of the upcoming race. Benjamin. Dealing with Indi.

He turned to the blonde. "Listen…" But damned if he could remember the woman's name.

"Lorraine," she said.

"Lorraine, I appreciate you dropping by, but I'm not interested."

The SUV's engine started. Todd resisted the urge to pound the window in frustration.

"No?"

He took a step, thought about yanking open the vehicle's door, but he stayed put, instead. The taillights lit up as Ron put the SUV in gear.

"No, I don't," he told Lorraine.

Because now that he'd kissed Indi, he knew there was something there, even if she didn't. The question was—would she let there be more?

CHAPTER NINE

SHE COULDN'T BELIEVE she'd fallen for his *I-know-how-you-feel-and-I-have-a-cute-dog* routine.

"Damn him," she muttered, the SUV making slow progress through the city streets. The race had ended right as Indi had left the track, meaning her and a few thousand fans tried to make their way back to their hotels. As a result their top speed had yet to exceed that of a tricycle, which meant the dress she wore had started to dry by the time they pulled into the hotel's parking lot. Unfortunately, it looked worse than before she'd tried to wash the oil away—if such a thing was possible.

"You sure you don't want to stop at a dry cleaner?" Ron asked again. He posed the same question when she'd first climbed inside. "Might be one open late."

"No, thanks."

"Well, here you are then," he said, rolling to a stop a few minutes later.

"Thank you," Indi said when he opened the door and offered his hand.

The lobby was full of race fans. She headed for the elevators, and noticed the full-size cardboard cutout of Todd that sat near the concierge's desk. She'd spotted it yesterday, but tonight the grin on his face seemed to mock her.

I kissed you.

And you liked *it.*

No, she hadn't, she mentally corrected herself. She hadn't liked it at all.

Liar.

She had a message from Linda when she made it back to her room.

"Call me when you get in," Linda's voice mail message said. "Can't wait to hear about your evening."

Indi shook her head and turned to stare out the window. The depression that consumed her from time to time overcame her, making it difficult to swallow. In the parking lot, people were still straggling in from the track, more than a few cars bearing antennae flags of their favorite drivers. The fans themselves carried bags filled with souvenirs, electronic equipment and seat cushions. They all looked so happy.

And Benjamin was two rooms away, fighting for his life. Damn it.

She shrugged off the dress and changed into sweats. Next she called the concierge to see if they offered dry cleaning. As she suspected, they did. Only after seeing the dress off did she dial Linda's number.

"How was it?" Linda said without preamble, but the words were whispered.

"Is Benj asleep?" Indi asked.

"He is."

"How's he feeling?"

"Better, if you ask him. But he's still stuffed up. Guess who we got a call from while you were out?"

"Who?"

"Dr. Ronald King."

"Who's that?" Indi asked, leaning against the pillows on her bed.

"Are you kidding? The King name is like racing royalty, or so my son tells me. He's the son of a famous race car driver, and an M.D. He's going to look in on Benjamin in the morning."

"Wow. How'd that come about?" Indi asked, but she could guess.

"Todd arranged it," Linda said. "This guy even called Benji's oncologist this evening. They're going to draw blood in the morning and check his counts. I told Benji that if the doctor approves it, and he's feeling better, he might—and I stressed the *might*— be able to go to the race tomorrow."

Indi sat up. "The race?"

"He does sound a bit better," Linda said. "I just worry that his immune system is weakened, but we should know if that's the case in the morning."

"You're thinking you might actually go *to the race.*"

"Yeah. Isn't that exciting?"

No. It wasn't exciting at all. It was a *disaster.* The whole way home she'd told herself not to be ashamed of herself for letting—yes, letting, because she could have drawn away—Todd kiss her. That even if she had let his lips connect with hers, it didn't mean anything. It had been a moment of weakness. Stupidity. Utter insanity. But ultimately, it was all behind her because she'd never see Todd again.

"Indi?" Linda said into the silence that had followed her words.

"Yeah. I'm here. And it *is* great news. Very, ah…exciting."

"So…tell me about your evening."

Indi quickly recapped her night with Todd, but she left out the part about the salad dressing and going back to Todd's motor coach.

"Sounds like you had fun," Linda said.

"Yeah. It was. He's a surprisingly nice man."

And he has soft lips.

Argh!

"Good. Well, Benji will expect a full report first thing in the morning. Call us when you get up."

"Will do."

But she knew it would be a sleepless night, and an even longer day tomorrow…if they went to the race.

"Please, God, don't let us go to the race."

BENJAMIN, HOWEVER, LOOKED tons better the next morning. So much so that Indi knew he was on the road to recovery—at least as far as his cold was concerned. Of course, he might have more color in his cheeks because he was excited to hear all about her evening. She told him everything (well, almost everything), glamorizing the event and putting extra emphasis on the two dances she and Todd had shared. Benjamin seemed more than satisfied, although Linda kept giving her pointed looks.

They got the results of Benjamin's labs while Indi was there, Dr. King having come by first thing in the morning to take the sample, just as he'd promised.

"They look good," Linda said, hanging up the phone.

Or as good as could be expected given Benjamin's illness. Those words were unspoken, but Indi could see them in Linda's eyes.

"Right on!" Benjamin cried, somehow mustering

the energy to spin his wheelchair around. It was a good-news/bad-news situation. She tried to be thrilled—and she was, for Benjamin's sake—but she wasn't happy about having to go to the race.

"What's the matter?" Linda asked while Benjamin went to the next room to call his father. Linda smiled at her son's excited squeal. Granted, he still sounded stuffed up, but his delight was obvious.

"It's just…" Indi shook her head. "I'm not feeling real well and so I was thinking I might pass on the racetrack."

"Something happened between you and Todd, didn't it?"

Indi straightened. "Linda. No. For goodness' sake. Of course not."

But Linda knew a lie when she heard one. "*What* happened?" she cried. "I know something must have because you wouldn't bail on Benji without good reason."

She wasn't bailing. Okay, maybe she was.

"Nothing happened," Indi repeated because the last thing she needed was Linda getting ideas in her head. "Absolutely nothing. We had a great time."

Lies, lies, lies.

"Oh, no," Linda said, wagging a finger. "You are *not* getting off the hook that easily. *What happened?*"

"Nothing. And you and Benj don't need me there

tonight," Indi said. "I've already seen the racetrack. You two go."

"Indi Wilcox," Linda said, sounding like the parent she was. "Don't think for a minute I believe you. And don't think you're not going with us. Benjamin expects you there. You know it and I know it. Besides, aren't you just the least bit curious what this NASCAR thing is all about?"

"No. I've had my fill."

"Something *did* happen," Linda murmured. "Well, well, well."

"Linda—"

They were interrupted by Benjamin, who came to tell them his dad wanted to speak to Linda.

But Linda hesitated a moment before she trotted off. There was even a hint of disappointment in her eyes before she went to get the phone.

Terrific. Now she'd alienated a woman who'd become a friend in recent months.

"What's wrong with Mom?" Benjamin asked.

"She wants me to go to the track with you guys this evening."

"You mean you're not?" Benjamin asked, a look of surprised distress on his face.

"Benjamin, this is *your* day. You should do this all on your own. You don't need me there."

"No, but my mom does. She counts on you. You cheer her up. Or did you think I was too young to notice how often she cries?"

Oh, Jeez.

"Indi," he said, his green eyes sad. "I know how sick I am. I hear the doctors talking. I don't want—" She watched him swallow, his frail hands clutching the arms of his wheelchair. "I don't want to make her cry now—"

"Oh, Benjamin," Indi said over the lump in her throat.

"And today, maybe if you go out to the track with us, she'll be able to forget—"

How sick he was.

Indi released a breath she'd been unknowingly holding in. "For a little boy, you're awfully bright."

"I skipped a grade when I was younger."

"You did?" She hadn't known that.

"I used to enjoy school…."

Before.

The deep breath she expelled was jagged with pent-up emotion. Everything was *before.* "All right, kiddo. I'll go."

"You will?" Benjamin said, his pale face filling with color, his eyebrows lifting almost to the brim of his ball cap.

"I will."

"Awesome."

Yeah. Awesome.

YELLOW FLAG

Is It Love or Is It Memorex?

By Rick Stevenson, Sports Editor

Recently, I wrote an article about drivers that are reviled, not revered, by NASCAR fans. In it I wondered whether drivers really care if they're despised by the racing public. Well, after today's press release, I have to wonder if Todd Peters took my words to heart. The announcement says that he intends to champion his "biggest little fan," one "*Miracles* child named Benjamin Koch," all in the hopes that "his association with the boy will help bolster his spirits as he engages in his battle with cancer."

Could this be a more obvious attempt at currying the public's favor?

I don't know if I'm being overly cynical, or if Mr. Peters truly has taken an interest in the child's welfare. All I know is my stomach turned when I read that all members of the media were welcome to speak to the child prior to the race at Richmond. Why? Why does Mr. Peters feel it's necessary for the press to meet little Benjamin unless it's to curry the public's favor? I suppose I should attend the event and find out.

But will I go?

More than likely not. I'll sit back. If Mr. Peters truly HAS turned over a new leaf, good for him. I'll be the first to shake his hand when next I see him. Until then, I remain jaded.

Call me a cynic, but there you have it.

CHAPTER TEN

"ARE THEY HERE YET?" Todd asked.

"Yes," Jen said. "The limo driving them in just cleared the front entrance. Benjamin should be here shortly."

Todd nodded. He'd just finished up a signing at a sponsor booth and so his driver, Ron again, piloted the golf cart. He was flying through the two-lane access road that circled the racetrack. Well, he went as fast as a golf cart could go without running over race fans, track officials and other unsuspecting individuals heading in various directions. But the speed was necessary. The last thing they needed was for a fan to spot him. That had happened in the past and it had never been pretty.

"Where are we meeting them?" Todd asked right as he braced his hands on the golf cart's dash.

"What the hell is this crap?" Ron muttered, jerking the wheel to the left and darting around the row of cars to their right. It was a line of vehicles waiting to get inside the infield.

"Motor home," Jen said. "It was too much of a hassle to get them an infield parking pass. What with space so limited inside the track. You know how it is."

Yeah, he did. Hell, there were times when even *he* had a hard time getting in.

"Hang on," Ron said as he steered the cart up an incline, one with a concrete wall on one side, the grandstands to their right casting a gray-brown shadow over them. The golf cart's engine strained as they made the climb.

Same track. Different day.

It was a thought he'd had more than once this past season. Nothing had perked him up. Nothing except dating Kristen. But that was over now. She and Mathew were a couple. And he was happy for them. It was just so damn monotonous. About the most exciting thing in his life right now was the prospect of making the Chase.

And kissing Indi.

"Here we are," Ron said, turning the wheel left. The driver/owner gate loomed ahead.

"What the hell is that?" Todd cried immediately, because even from outside the lot he could see the news vans and media personnel milling around the front of his bus.

"Those are the reporters I invited," Jen said, smiling proudly.

"Reporters." *Ah, hell.* "Jen, I don't want the media involved in this."

"Why not?" she asked, brows raised.

"Because this is private. It's between me and Benjamin, not the whole world."

Jen was shaking her head. "Todd, I don't think I need to tell you that you're not exactly loved by race fans. If you do happen to make the Chase, we could use a story like this. Something that makes people feel warm and fuzzy instead of wanting to throw beer bottles at you. Unless you like negative press?"

"I don't give a damn what the fans think of me," Todd all but growled, although he was more irritated at Jen for using the word *might* again. He *would* make the Chase for the NASCAR NEXTEL Cup. "Did you talk this over with Mrs. Koch?"

"Of course. She was fine with it—"

"Hold on," Ron said. Todd's butt slid forward as Ron hit the brakes.

"I'm not happy about this," Todd muttered. He might have a bad reputation thanks to previous run-ins with the press, but this was no way to repair the damage.

"I'm sorry," Jen muttered. "I just thought—"

Todd lifted a hand at the same time he jumped out

of the cart. "Hey, everybody," he called. "There's been a mistake—" But his words that were cut off by the arrival of a car.

"Is that them?" one of the cameramen asked, and it was obvious that it was. A limo pulled to a stop near the side of a news van, one of about five that lined the narrow road. That ought to make his neighbors happy.

"Todd, did you arrange for the limo?" someone from a local affiliate asked.

"When did you meet…Benjamin, is it?" one of the print reporters asked.

"What does Benjamin think of NASCAR?" someone else asked.

Todd resisted the urge to groan. Indi was the first to get out of the limo, and he could tell by the look on her face that she wasn't happy.

"Guys," Todd said, holding up his hands. "I really wasn't expecting y'all to be here. Is there any way you can maybe give Benjamin and me some time alone?"

"Is that him?" one of the national TV broadcasters asked. "Is that little Benjamin?"

Camera's swung toward the limo.

Ah, hell.

"Hi, everybody," Benjamin said right as his mom helped him into the wheelchair the limo driver had opened for them.

"Are you Mrs. Koch?" one of the reporters asked Indi after she made her way through the myriad of cables.

"No. I work for *Miracles*."

"Terrific," the guy said. "I'm Brad, from KRVR. We're one of Kentucky's largest radio stations and I'm sure our listeners would love your thoughts on Todd championing little Benjamin there."

"Oh, I'll give you my thoughts," Indi said. "But why don't we get Benjamin inside first. He hasn't been feeling well."

"Sure, sure," the guy said, retreating.

Indi headed right for Todd. "You know," she said in a low voice, "I really hoped I was wrong about you, but exploiting your relationship with Benjamin has to be one of the most hedonistic forms of self-promotion I've ever encountered."

"Indi. No. I didn't have a thing to do with—"

But she walked away, and Todd didn't have the chance to call the whole thing off because by now the reporters swarmed Benjamin. And bless the little kid's heart, he seemed to be enjoying himself. He had a grin on his face as wide as an ocean in a world atlas.

"She'll get over it," Mrs. Koch said, stopping by Todd's side.

Todd met the woman's gaze. "Something tells me it won't be in this lifetime," he said.

That feeling seemed to be reinforced when he opened his bus's front door and Lex all but bounded out, nearly tumbling ass over teakettle during his descent because he was so excited to have company. The dog headed straight for Benjamin's wheelchair, his stubby little body somehow managing to stretch to the boy's height. The media snapped photos, and Todd could see the derision in Indi's eyes.

"Benjamin, meet Lex." He grabbed his dog's collar, ordering him down, but the dog refused, his stub tail wagging so hard he literally rocked from foot to foot.

"Hey, Lex," Benjamin giggled.

"Watch out," Todd said. "He'll lick you silly if you're not careful."

"That's okay," Benjamin said, his grin so big his ears wiggled beneath his red ball cap. "I love dogs."

"Yeah," Todd said. "Me, too." And that had come as a surprise having never owned one before, but Lex was the closest thing to a friend he had right now.

He glanced over at Indi again. She'd turned away, and Todd could tell her arms were crossed.

"That is one ugly dog," one of the reporters muttered.

"Almost as ugly as his owner," Todd thought he heard Indi mutter.

"WHY ARE YOU SO MAD?" Linda said after scooting next to Indi on the seat. "I told you, his PR rep cleared everything with me."

They were in the very back of a stretch golf cart. At least that's what Indi called it. The canvas-topped vehicle had four rows of seats—Todd and Benjamin were in the second row and Todd's PR assistant sat next to the driver. Indi had made sure to put a row of empty seats between them.

"They should have never posed the question to you in the first place," Indi said as they headed out of the driver/owner parking lot. She'd refrained from maligning Todd to various reporters because she prided herself on her professionalism. "The man ought to be shot for siccing the press on you and Benjamin."

"Benjamin was excited about talking to the media."

"Benjamin doesn't understand he's being used."

"Why do you think that?"

"I recognize his ilk."

"You said last night he was nice."

"I was wrong."

Linda stared at her a long moment. "Did Todd make a pass at you?"

That was so close to the truth Indi's cheeks filled with color. She tried to hide it by turning her head and pretending interest in the tall grandstands to their left.

"He *did,* didn't he?" Linda cooed. "I'll be damned."

"Linda—"

"Did he kiss you?"

Indi refused to answer, but that turned out to be a mistake, because Linda pounced on her silence like a district attorney would a guilty defendant. "He did, didn't he? Indi, that's terrific."

"Are you *crazy?*" Indi asked, swiveling toward her, and grateful Todd was too far away to hear their conversation. "Todd Peters is the last person on earth I should let kiss me."

They were slowing down due to a security station up ahead stopping cars from entering the infield tunnel. A single post traffic light glowed red.

"Men like Todd can't be trusted," Indi mumbled, remembering the little blonde who'd shown up outside his motor coach.

"You only say that because of what happened between you and that quarterback," Linda said, placing a hand on Indi's knee. "But you can't judge every book by Sean's cover."

Just hearing Sean's name made Indi's stomach turn over. She was about to set Linda straight, but the driver stopped and Indi realized Todd would hear them without the whine of the rotary engine filling their ears.

They both grew silent. Indi glanced around. There were vehicles in front and behind them, a few of them passenger cars, their engines idling while they waited to be turned loose. It was cooler in the shadow of the racetrack that loomed up ahead of them. Racetracks looked like unfinished steel structures from the outside, Indi thought.

"Did you hear me, Indi?" Linda said once the stop light turned green and they lurched forward again.

"I heard you, but I'm still not going down that road again," Indi said.

Linda's blond hair caught the light. Indi noticed it was now streaked with gray. When had that happened?

"Indi, Sean was a fool," Linda whispered.

"Sean was a professional athlete, and like most pros, he couldn't keep his wee-little-winkie in his pants. I learned that the hard way."

"It'd be different with someone else."

The sun disappeared. They'd entered the infield tunnel, and for a moment the echo of multiple engines made it impossible to hear inside the passageway. "That's what I thought, too," Indi said. "I knew the risks. I'd been a sports broadcaster long enough to know what went on behind the scenes of most pro sports. The players with the girlfriends in every town. The multiple cell phones—one for the wife, one for the mistress. Heck, sometimes they even have more than one condo in one town. I knew all that. Thought I was smarter than those *other* women. Thought the wool couldn't be pulled over my eyes. Uh-uh."

They emerged from the tunnel like ants out of a hole and for a moment Indi was blinded. So was Linda, because she lifted a hand to shield her eyes, the wedding band on her finger scattering bright dots of light on the golf cart's roof. When Indi's eyes slowly regained focus she saw row upon row of empty seats—obviously, most people had yet to arrive—and the reflection of the sun against aluminum grandstands caused spots to dance before her eyes. Even though she told herself she could care less about racing, she still felt her interest pique as she glanced around her…until her gaze happened to fall on Todd sitting up ahead of her.

He turned to her. His eyes were hidden by a pair of dark sunglasses, but she could tell by the tilt of his head that the look he shot her was quizzical. She turned away.

"He might be different," Linda said, leaning toward her.

"Maybe, but I'm not about to find out."

Linda's lips compressed into a thin line. They'd made it to the center of the track, where big rigs in all the shades of the rainbow sat in symmetrical rows—like soldiers at attention—their back ends opened up to reveal sliding glass doors and shiny chrome door frames.

"Here we are," Todd said.

Indi braced herself for the abrupt stop that seemed inherent in golf carts.

"Hey, it's Todd Peters," a heavyset woman said the moment they stopped, the fan's camera bouncing against her white T-shirt that, oddly enough, bore the name and number of some other driver.

"No autographs right now, 'kay," Todd said. "Not until after I get little Benjamin here settled."

The woman immediately slowed. She smiled at Benjamin and said, "Lucky little boy," then faded back.

"You ready to go there, champ?" Todd asked. He headed toward the back of the cart where Benjamin's wheelchair hung.

"I've been ready for this my whole life."

Indi went cold. She caught Linda's eyes and she knew the woman thought the same thing she did.

How much longer would that life last?

And here was the reminder she needed—there

were more important matters at hand here today. This wasn't about her. This was about Benjamin. Nothing else mattered.

"Well, then, let's go," Todd said.

They crossed through security, the entrance they used between an outbuilding of some sort and a chain-link fence. The garage seemed eerily quiet considering a race was scheduled for that evening. None of the cars were in their stalls, almost like racehorses who'd already left the gate. A few crew members moved equipment to an unknown location, probably pit road. There were still fans milling about, too, more than a few of them led around in tour formation. They were lined up like visitors to an amusement park, their group leader holding up a sign with a major corporation's name on it. When he or she moved, so did the whole group. Indi thought they resembled a gaggle of ducks. The media was still around, as well. One or two reporters caught sight of Todd. They looked their way as if trying to determine whether they should pounce. Once they saw Benjamin, they didn't.

Other than Todd, however, it appeared as if most drivers were MIA. The NASCAR star moved along as if oblivious to the heads he turned. And perhaps he was.

Benjamin, however, was in seventh heaven. He

kept pointing to the big rigs, his rear end wiggling in his chair. From time to time Indi would catch a glimpse of his profile. His face was wreathed in smiles.

"I've never seen him so happy," Linda said, hanging back so Todd and Benjamin could walk alone.

"Yeah, I know."

"Oh, good," Jen said. "I found you."

"You did, indeed," Indi said, wondering where the PR rep had run off to the moment they'd arrived.

"I was afraid you might have separated from Todd and Benjamin, but you didn't, and so here you are and now I can schedule your meeting with Todd," she said, looking at Indi.

"Uh… What meeting with Todd?"

"He said he wanted some alone time with you."

"Uh-huh," Linda muttered. "He likes you."

Indi wanted to cover Linda's mouth with her hands. "Alone time?" she asked instead. "Why?"

"He didn't say," Jen said, her blond ponytail brushing her back as she consulted a clipboard. "He'll be touring the garage with Benjamin for the next half hour. After that he's off to a team meeting. Benjamin's invited to go with him, by the way. He's got another meeting after that, but you could have the slot between that and his visit to the media center."

"I don't want any slot at all," Indi said.

"But—"

"He never consulted me about a meeting."

"Really?" Jen asked. "Well, obviously it was important for Todd to meet with you today. He wouldn't have asked me to pencil you in otherwise."

"Tell Todd to call me," Indi said.

"Let me just go ask him what this is about then."

"Fine. You do that," Indi said. They'd stopped near the back of one of the haulers. Team members sat in director's chairs lined up off the back, most of them with a paper plates of food in hand, and all of them staring curiously. The smell of steak and pasta wafted over, reminding Indi she hadn't had a thing to eat today. "I'll just go get myself some food. There's a snack shack around here, right?"

"Oh, we have food inside the hauler."

Indi ignored the woman. "I think we passed one on our way in and so I'll just head that way."

"But—"

Again, she ignored her. "I'll be back in a flash."

Coward, Linda's eyes mocked.

Yeah, so maybe she was. Nothing wrong with that. Evasion was often an efficient way of avoiding conflict, and she'd been dodging men like Todd for years.

CHAPTER ELEVEN

"WHERE IS SHE?" Todd asked as he took his cell phone back from Benjamin. He'd had to shout to be heard because the grandstands across from the infield were filled to capacity and the roar of the crowd was similar to the rumble of an ocean.

"My mom says she's hiding out near the media center. Oh, hey, look. There's Lance Cooper," the kid said, pointing. His grin was so wide it tipped up the brim of his red ball cap.

"Hey, Lance," Todd called, the blond-headed driver giving him a wave just before he climbed into the back of a minitruck.

"Neat. He waved back."

"So he did," Todd said, navigating Benjamin's wheelchair between the front and back bumpers of maroon trucks. They were traveling through the garage, the vehicles lined up while they awaited the arrival of the drivers they'd ferry around the track for driver introductions. Todd had already done his bit, but there were still another twenty or so drivers left to go, which meant he had about ten minutes to find Indi because, so far, she'd done a good job of dodging him all afternoon.

"Mom also said Indi's been hiding there for over an hour and that she's standing behind a stack of tires so it's hard to see her unless you know she's there."

"You know, I really like your mom," Todd murmured, picking up the pace. The smell of food filled the air, many of the crews having set up barbecues so they could cook their evening meal. There were still more than a few fans in the garage, and a number of them tried to catch his attention, but he ignored them. No time to dawdle.

"She thinks you've got a crush on Indi," Benjamin added.

"Is that what she said?"

"She did." And then, "There she is," Benjamin said, pointing toward his mother. Linda waved, a wide smile on her face when she was once again reunited with her son.

"Did you see me inside the truck?" he asked excitedly.

"I did," she said. "And I saw you wave, too."

"It was *so cool*," Benjamin cried. "All those people in the grandstands staring at me, like they were wondering who I was. And it felt like the truck would tip over because the track was sloped so steep. I kept thinking the driver would duck down on the apron, but he didn't."

"Sounds like you're having a great time," Linda said, sending Todd a grateful smile.

"He is," Todd said.

"Well, good. Now," she said to her son. "Let me push you around a bit while Todd goes and finds Indi."

"You going to be okay?" Todd asked. Fortunately, the sun had already started to sink below the horizon and so it wasn't as hot as it had been earlier.

"Are you kidding?" Benjamin asked. "I plan on asking for autographs as drivers pass by."

"What?" Todd asked, dying to dash off but reluctant to leave Benjamin. The little boy had gotten under his skin. "You mean you want other drivers to sign your race cards?"

"Only so I can give them to the other kids at the hospital."

And it was comments like that which made Todd realize just how special Benjamin was. No wonder Indi was so committed.

"Well, if you don't get the ones you want, let me know. I'll make sure they sign whatever you want."

"Cool. Thanks."

"Good luck," Linda called as he turned away.

"Yeah, I think I'm going to need it," he muttered.

He didn't know why it was so important for to him to speak to Indi alone. If she thought him a jerk for using Benjamin to gain publicity, so be it. He knew the truth. But he still wanted to see her. *Before* the race, he admitted, scratching at his hand.

That was odd.

"Hey," a female voice asked. "Where you off to in such a hurry?"

Fortunately, it was a female Todd recognized and liked, at one point, *a lot:* Kristen McKenna. Funny, as he stared at her now all he felt was a tug of warmth that more resembled friendship.

"I have a quick errand to run."

"Well, you better hurry," she said, flicking a strand of blond hair away from her face. The ring on her finger caught the sunlight, but it didn't cause the momentary pang of regret that it usually did. "They're gonna want you in your car pretty soon."

"I know, I know," he said, then muttered, "Mom."

"Be nice. I could have you fired, you know."

Yeah, she could. But she wouldn't. She was their team engineer, and a consummate professional. "Hey, I'm not the one sleeping with the boss." Although he'd hoped for something more from her. Ultimately, their boss and team owner, Mathew Knight, had won out.

"You're the one responsible for the two of us getting together."

"Yeah, but only because I expected a raise out of the whole deal."

She reached up and kissed him on his cheek. A few months back he would have given anything to have her kiss him. But that was last year and now she was Matt's.

"Good luck today," she said. "Remember, if you don't make the Chase, there's always next year."

"I'd rather it be this year."

"Yeah, me, too," she said with an impish smile. "I told Matt I'd marry him during the off-season if we won."

"Then I guess I'll have to win," he said, and he meant it. He truly wished her and Matt nothing but happiness.

They parted company, Todd undoing the collar of his driver's suit. The familiar Fly For Less logo was a beacon for race fans and so he kept hearing his name as he dashed through the chain-link area that kept those without garage passes off pit road. But he kept his eyes lowered. The only time he looked up was when he passed the fueling area. The media center was just past it.

And there she was.

She did a good job of staying out of sight, too. If he hadn't known exactly where she was, he wouldn't have seen her cowering there behind a whole row of

stacked-up tires near the chain-link fence that surrounded the media center. Only her head was visible,
her focus seeming to be fixed upon the activity on
pit road. She didn't see him approach. That was
good. It meant she didn't have time to escape.

He took care to keep out of her line of sight before
whispering "Boo" in her right ear.

She jumped about a foot. Todd resisted the urge
to smile. And to chuckle in self-satisfaction.

He'd caught her.

"Thought you could avoid me, huh?" he asked,
giving her an eyebrow wiggle.

Her lips didn't so much as twitch.

"Nice hiding spot," he said, fingering a rubber
tire. The black surface was still hot, the car number
written on the firewall indicating they belonged to
one of the Roush teams.

"What are you doing here?" she asked. He saw
her glance behind her, but the tires blocked her in so
completely she had no place to go.

He shrugged and followed her former line of
sight. She'd been watching a camera crew film a pit
road report of some sort.

"Since you wouldn't come to me, I thought I'd
come to you."

"Really? Too bad. I was just about to go get
myself a soda."

"Don't do that," he said before she could dash past him. "There's really no need to hide from me."

She looked about to deny it, but he saw her lips press together, then her shoulders slumped. "What do you want?"

"To tell you I wasn't responsible for alerting the media about Benjamin. Jen did that."

"I know. Linda told me. So you're off the hook. Have a great race."

He stepped in front of her again. "Hey, an apology would be nice."

"Is that was this is all about?" she asked. "You tracked me down all the way out here just so I could apologize?"

No, he instantly realized. That wasn't it at all. He'd sought her out because he'd wanted to see her before he climbed into his race car. Because for some reason, it was important to him that she not think him a complete jerk while he drove around the track, although the scowl on her face indicated he'd missed the mark by about a mile.

"Actually, I tracked you down because I wanted to do this," he said, cupping the back of her head so she couldn't move away while he pressed his lips against her.

She stiffened.

Todd didn't care, because once their lips connected he admitted to himself that he liked Indi, and not in a way that felt like anything he'd experienced before. He actually felt something ache inside of him when she stiffened in outrage. He pulled away before she could haul off and hit him. He'd kiss her again after she calmed down.

"You're an amazing woman, Indi Wilcox," he said, looking deep into her outraged eyes. "I needed you to know that before I climbed into my car."

Her eyes softened, and just for a moment he thought he saw something flicker in her eyes. Whatever it was gave him courage.

"And I was just teasing about the whole apology thing. You don't owe me anything. In fact, I owe *you*. Let me buy you dinner."

She shook her head. "I don't think so."

He'd known she say that, but that wouldn't stop him from trying. "Maybe you'll feel differently after I win the race."

"Don't count on it."

He smiled. He couldn't stop himself.

"I'll see you after."

"Yeah. After." But there was a big old unspoken "maybe" after that.

Little did she know—there was nothing "maybe" about it.

CHAPTER TWELVE

"So, DID HE FIND YOU?" Linda asked when Indi walked up to the hauler where she and Benjamin were camped out until the start of the race. Night had yet to officially "fall" but overhead a myriad of bulbs shone down on them. The lights were everywhere, shining over the infield and around the perimeter of the track. Even so, there were certain parts of the garage that looked as dark as haunted houses.

"Yeah. And thanks a lot for telling him where I was."

Linda and Benjamin exchanged glances and Indi resisted the urge to groan. It was obvious they were trying to play matchmaker.

Pul-leez, Indi thought, resisting the urge to wipe at the spot where Todd's lips had rested against her cheek. It still buzzed where he'd touched her.

"Indi Wilcox?" a voice asked.

Indi turned, surprised to find a female crew

member standing behind her. From what she'd seen so far, the man-to-woman ratio was pretty lopsided.

"Hi," the woman said, her eyes friendly behind a pair of glasses. "I'm Kristen McKenna."

"Hi," Indi said back, wondering what the woman could want. She glanced at Benjamin, thinking it must be about him.

Sure enough, the woman said, "And you must be Benjamin."

"You're the team engineer," Benjamin said.

Leave it to Benjamin to recognize one of Todd's crew members.

"Actually, Dr. Ralph Helfrick is the head engineer. I just work for him."

"But you're engaged to Mathew Knight," Benjamin added. "The team owner."

"Well, yeah," Kristen said. "Jen's going to be busy dealing with the media during the race so she asked me to keep you guys company. Benjamin, Todd insisted you be up on the pit box tonight."

"Are you kidding?" Benjamin all but shouted. "Right *on*."

When she caught Linda's eye, they exchanged smiles. Seeing Benjamin so happy, watching the color fill his cheeks and his little body straighten up with renewed energy brought a lump to her throat.

"Okay, then," Kristen said. "You guys can follow

me. The crew's lining up for the National Anthem, but they're going to help you up on top of the box while the pace car's out on the track. Come on."

That was the start of a night that Indi would never forget. She'd never been much of a NASCAR fan— all she'd ever done when she'd been a broadcaster was read the stats—but hearing the crowd cheer after the National Anthem, and then having to plug her ears a split second later when jets flew overhead, and then just about jumping out of her skin when forty-three cars started their engines…well, she'd have to have been born without blood not to feel the electricity in the air.

"Isn't this neat?" Linda asked.

The two of them were sitting on a short stack of tires, Linda peering up at her son from time to time. A pit box, she'd learned, was actually a mobile toolbox complete with giant wheels and inlaid television screens. She could watch the race on TV if she stood in the right spot.

"He's having the time of his life," Indi said.

"Yes, he is."

And they had Todd to thank for it. And so, while a part of her still fumed over his audacious behavior earlier, a part of her felt flushed with gratitude for his kindness toward her little charge. If he'd been trying to make amends, he'd succeeded in spades.

That feeling only increased throughout the night. Benjamin got to wear a team shirt, which he pulled on so fast he darn near knocked his headset off. He cheered when Todd came in for a pit stop, which Todd did frequently because the night was fraught with caution flags. And through it all Indi learned the ins and outs of stock car racing. Even more so when Kristen offered her a headset, too, which enabled Indi to listen to Todd's conversations with his crew.

"How many spots did I lose, Dan?" she heard Todd ask after one particularly long pit stop.

"You lost four," Todd's crew chief replied. The man sat atop the pit box with Benjamin, Kristen and a man Indi learned was the team owner. Mathew Knight was recognizable from magazine covers and the bestselling book he'd written last year. She hadn't officially met the man, but he'd given her a warm smile before climbing up to sit next to Dan.

"Don't worry," Dan said. "You got four tires out of the deal. The other guys took two."

In one of the seats atop the toolbox, she saw Kristen squeeze the side of her headset. "You're sitting in tenth, Todd. That's good enough to get you into the Chase."

"Roger that," Todd said. He sounded different over the radio. More tense. Less boyish. She supposed that was to be expected given the gravity of the situation.

She'd been told by Kristen that tonight was an important race. And so even though Indi didn't know much about racing, she still wanted him to do well—for the whole team's sake. She knew enough about the NASCAR NEXTEL Cup Series to know that making the Chase for the NASCAR NEXTEL Cup was a big deal.

"Just keep out of trouble," Mathew said. "We don't need a win tonight. Just a clean race."

"Yes, we do," Todd said. "I want Benjamin to stand in Victory Lane."

"Ten-four," she heard Mathew say. "I couldn't agree more."

She saw Benjamin grin, and in the muted light of the racetrack he looked like any normal boy. He even wiggled in his seat from time to time, his legs dangling off the edge of the chair. He waved at a television crew who came into the pit stall to film Dan up on the box. On the LCD screen, she saw Benjamin's smiling face just before the network cut to a commercial.

Dan looked at Benjamin and the little boy smiled like a kid at Disneyland, and the grin reminded her so much of her nephew Kyle's, she had to look away.

"Hey, Todd," she heard Dan say. "We've got ourselves a television star. The network just showed a shot of Benjamin waving to the fans back home."

"Oh, yeah?" Todd asked.

"Yup."

"Well, it won't be the last time he's on TV tonight. They'll get another good shot of him when we're in Victory Lane."

For some reason, those words set Indi's heart pounding. Todd sounded so determined. She *believed* him.

She watched the television screen intently. Everyone around her appeared equally tense. Even Linda nibbled her bottom lip, her attention never leaving the screen.

On the track, cars picked up speed again. The thing that surprised Indi most about Richmond was that she could see into the faces of the fans across the track from them—they were that close. Thus their cheers sounded like the roar of rushing water. Before she'd been given a headset, she'd had to plug her ears every time the green flag had dropped.

"Clear outside," someone said. Indi wasn't sure who the guy on the radio was, or where he stood, but she knew his job was to keep Todd from colliding with other drivers. This appeared especially true on the restarts when the cars were lined up two by two, lapped cars on the inside, front runners on the outside. Someone had told her this was a dangerous time. Drivers who were lapped often played dirty pool. Their number-one goal was to get their lap back, and they didn't care how they did it.

"Take it easy on those tires," Dan said. On TV, Indi watched the front of the pack begin to stretch apart like taffy. She couldn't see Todd. He was too far back for cameras to follow, but she could see him when he passed by, which he did a few seconds later, the rush of cars causing her ears to ring even with the headset on.

"Do you think he'll win?" Linda asked after Indi pulled her earpiece away from her ear so she could hear.

"I think he's got a shot," Indi said because over the years she'd learned a little bit about the sport. By sitting in tenth, and on a fresh set of tires, Todd was poised to overtake more than a few cars. Would it be enough to win? That remained to be seen.

"How many more laps?" Linda asked.

Indi turned toward the leaderboard. It was behind pit road but it was tall enough and brightly lit so that she could clearly see the numbers. Next to number ten was Todd's number.

"We have about eighty to go."

"Is that a lot?" Linda asked.

"It's enough that nothing's for certain yet."

A few laps later Todd passed the car in front of him. Then the front-runners started fading back and before Indi knew it, he was in third place and Indi's heart pounded like shoes in a washing machine.

"Twenty-two-twelve," Dan said. "That's a good lap, Todd. A real good lap."

"What are the leaders running?"

"One-eighties. You're the fastest car on the track."

Todd didn't say anything. Indi scooted closer to the television screen, as did Todd's crew. Nobody looked away, not even when Todd zoomed by in front of them.

And then something happened.

The first and second place cars touched. She saw the whole thing on television. One car's rear end shot out. It touched the door of the second car. Both cars began to turn.

Boom!

She heard the sound of the collision over the roar of the crowd. Both cars bounced off the wall, the two sliding down low as if connected by tethers.

They were directly in Todd's path.

TODD SAW SMOKE.

"Caution, caution, caution!" rang through his ears, the words a split second too late. Oil splattered his windshield. Through the murk he saw the image of a car. It hung in front of him like it might dissolve like the specter it resembled. It didn't.

Todd jerked his wheel right.

He hit oil. Or water. Whatever. He lost it. His car spun as he burst through the debris cloud. He faced the grandstands. Trackside lights blinded him. Then…nothing. He faced the infield, and the eighty-nine car. It sat in front of him, stalled. His car slid down two degrees of banking, heading right for it.

"Low, low," rang out in his ears.

"I know," Todd muttered, bracing himself for impact.

But they never hit.

Another patch of oil shot him to the right. It also started him spinning again. He faced the grandstands once more. The fluorescents turned his windshield white. He faced backward next, then forward, backward again. His tires squealed in protest.

When he had a clear shot, he gunned it.

The motor responded with a crack of exhaust. His back end pitched left and right. Todd corrected. His body shot back. One, two, three thousand RPMs. He glanced at his gauges. All looked good. Had debris punctured a tire? Or worse? A radiator?

He'd know in a few seconds.

"You okay?" Dan asked.

"Fine."

Someone streaked by him on the outside. Then

another and another car. But Todd drew even with the fourth-place car, fading back to take fifth.

No lost lap.

"Good job there, driver," Dan said.

"Thanks," Todd said. The hand he used to push open the mic shook.

"How's it feel?"

He keyed the button on the steering wheel again. "Like someone's jackhammering the tires. Definitely a flat spot on all four. But the gauges look good and I've still got brake."

"Keep an eye on things," Dan said. "They'll open pit road in a sec."

He would, but he didn't need to tell Dan that. Throughout the caution lap Todd kept an eye on things. There was no increase in temperature. No loud boom of a blown engine. And when he jerked the wheel left and right, the steering felt okay. No broken sway bars or tweaked shocks.

"Okay, they're opening pit road next time around."

"Roger that," Todd said, taking note of where he was. Turn Three loomed ahead of him. Four more to go.

When he pulled in for his pit stop less than a minute later, Todd caught a glimpse of Benjamin's anxious face.

Relax, kid. I've got it handled.

The right side of the car tipped up. Then the left.

"Go, go, go," Dan yelled a few seconds later.

Todd braced himself for other drivers to pull out ahead of him.

Only three did.

"Way to go," Todd yelled. "That was a hell of a pit stop, guys."

"Why thank you very much," Dan said, amusement plainly evident in his voice.

Todd smiled. A year ago he and his crew chief had exchanged harsh words. Todd had been blown away to discover most of his crew hated him. Something that wasn't surprising given how he'd treated them. Actually, he'd treated everyone that way—his teammates, the media, other drivers...*especially* other drivers. He'd always been front-page news—and not in a good way. That had changed and Todd reaped the rewards of his crew's newfound loyalty by getting pit stops like the last one.

"Everything still look good?" Mathew asked tensely.

"It's fine, boss. We're okay. Tell Benjamin to practice his Victory Lane smile."

"He's *already* smiling," Kristen said.

"Well, that smile's about to get a whole lot bigger."

He set his sights on the car in front of him. Adam Drake was known for racing clean and so if Todd could get the jump on him, he felt certain Adam would let him go.

They rounded Turn Four. Ahead of him, up on the flag stand, Todd could see the starter lift his hand.

The green flag dropped.

"Go, go, go, go," echoed in Todd's ears. He sensed, rather than heard, the crowd cheer. The thirty-five cars left in the race surged toward the start/finish line.

"Take it easy on fuel," Dan warned before Todd had made it through Turn One, Adam's car dropping low so Todd couldn't pass. "Kristen tells me we've got enough to make it to the end, but I'd like to make sure."

"Roger that." But Todd would take it easy only *after* he took the lead.

A few laps later, the front-runners' cars drifted high and to the left. Lapped traffic blocked the bottom, but there was just enough room....

Todd pointed his front bumper between the two sets of cars.

"Outside, inside," his spotter said.

"Yeah, I know," Todd muttered, his hands clenching the wheel. His car wanted to slide up the track, a sure sign that he had a push. But Todd couldn't afford that, so he fought the wheel with everything he had, his arm muscles burning at the strain. If he could avoid hitting the brake just a moment or two longer…

Adam faded back.

Yes!

The field shot out of Turn Two. Well, at least the leaders did. The lapped cars faded back.

"Clear low."

"I'll just take that low spot, thank you very much," he muttered, his sights set on the second-place car. It was a black car or maybe dark blue. Hard to tell beneath the fluorescent lights. Frankly Todd didn't care. Whoever he was, he was going down.

Todd's jaw clenched. He threw his car into Turn Three. The driver in front of him didn't. Todd almost ran into the back of him before jerking the wheel to the left.

Not enough room!

He backed off the gas. Bits of rubber that signaled his proximity to the wall hit his undercarriage, *ping-ping-pinging* the heck out of it. He slid toward the wall. The pinging went away—never a good sign. Todd braced himself. His car shuddered. Contact. Uh-oh. He tried to duck left. He didn't expect his car to respond, only it *did*. His car *worked* next to the wall. It worked *good*.

He shot past the second-place car as if it stood still.

"Clear low."

"Good job, Todd," Dan said.

"Think I left some paint back there."

"Yeah. Thought for a moment you might leave more than that."

Todd almost laughed. That'd been awesome. He caught sight of the next car. Bright orange. White star in the middle of the bumper.

Lance Cooper.

"Tell Lance he's going down."

There was no response. Then Dan said, "Don't know that Blain Sanders will appreciate hearing that."

No, Lance's team owner probably wouldn't. But that was okay, because Todd intended to show the man exactly how good a car he had. He intended to show *everybody* that he didn't need to drive dirty to win a race.

Lance checked up before the next corner, which closed the distance between the two of them quickly. It was easier to pass on this kind of track than, say, Talladega in a few weeks. If he could just keep that high line a few times, he'd have him in maybe five laps.

It took *three*.

Todd's car was good when he hugged the wall. The bit of rubber that congregated there—the marbles—stood in his favor. It made his tight car loose in a way that gave him the best lap times he'd ever had at Richmond.

"Damn, Todd. You look like you're trying to qualify out there."

Todd didn't comment. He was too busy gunning Lance down. He was half a car length behind, but that distance closed quickly. Three feet. Two. A dive to the right and Todd was in his groove. Lance actually waved as Todd drove by. Todd waved back. Leave it to Cooper to know when he was licked.

It was his race to lose from that point forward. With every lap he pulled farther and farther away. A caution fell with twenty laps to go, thus negating Kristen's fears over gas mileage. On the restart Todd drove away from the field as if they were all in reverse.

"Two more laps to go," Dan said a few minutes later.

"Roger that," Todd said, and although he told himself not to smile, Todd couldn't help it. He hadn't won a race all year. Yet, he'd somehow made it into the Chase.

He'd made it to the Chase.

This whole time he'd been so focused on winning

the race for Benjamin that he hadn't given the Chase a moment's consideration.

He pressed the mic button on his steering wheel. "You guys ready to make a run for the championship?"

Todd could hear the excited cheers of the crowd when Dan spoke next. "Hell, yeah, we are."

The crowd was probably cheering for Lance, hoping he'd overtake him. But that wouldn't happen. Todd glanced right, out his main rearview mirror. He'd have to blow an engine in order for Lance to catch him.

And now you've probably gone and jinxed the deal.

Only he hadn't. A lap later he'd rounded Turn Four. Up ahead he could already see the checkered flag being waved.

"Whoo-hoo! Great job," Dan yelled.

"Benjamin, that win's for you," Todd said, knowing the boy was listening.

"Go ahead and talk to him," Todd heard Dan say, obviously speaking to the kid.

"Oh, my gosh, that was *so* cool," Benjamin said a split second later. "I can't *believe* you won. And that I'm talking to you right after."

Todd felt laughter build. "You're my good-luck charm, kid. Now you're going to have to go to *all* the races."

"You think I could?" the boy asked, his voice cracking at the end.

"We'll talk to your mom about it. Now get yourself over to Victory Lane."

He didn't bother with a burnout, but he did ask NASCAR for the checkered flag. He presented it to Benjamin the moment he exited his car.

"For me?" Benjamin asked over the excited cries of Todd's team members. The kid's skinny little arms wrapped around his neck when Todd scooped him up. Linda beamed and so did Indi.

"For you," he said.

"Gee, thanks," Benjamin said, green eyes shining.

"You can have my helmet, too."

Todd wouldn't have thought Benjamin's eyes could get any wider, but they did. "Right *on!* This is *so* cool," the boy said.

When Todd's eyes snagged on Linda, the woman had tears in her eyes. She came around to his other side and wrapped her arms around his middle.

"I just can't thank you enough," she said.

Todd would have squeezed her back, but he was afraid of dropping Benjamin. "Hey, whatever I can do to help."

"You've already done enough."

"Great job," Dan said, coming up to him next.

"Really top-notch job," his team owner said, Mathew's smile nearly as wide as Benjamin's.

"Congratulations, Todd," Kristen said, and then

she ducked out of the way at the same time she said, "Look out."

Todd tried to shield Benjamin, but they both ended up getting showered with some kind of soda. Benjamin laughed so hard he started coughing and for a moment Todd felt his breath catch. But Benjamin recovered quickly, squealing when someone tried to douse them again.

"Todd, Todd," the network's pit road commentator said. "How does it feel to not only win the race, but make the Chase, as well?"

Todd shifted Benjamin in his arms, whispering in his left ear, "Smile," before he turned toward the camera. "It feels great, Brad. Really great."

"Did you have any idea coming here that you had a shot at winning?"

"I really wasn't worried about winning. I just wanted to finish the race in one piece so Benjamin here wouldn't be disappointed."

"Who is this little guy?" Brad asked.

Todd filled the sportscaster in. Behind him, his crew continued to celebrate. He saw Lance Cooper walk by. The driver gave him a nod and a smile, which Todd returned.

"So you think Benjamin is your good-luck charm?" the commentator asked.

"He definitely is that, but he also helped me to see

how lucky I am to do what I do for a living, and made me realize that I want to help kids like him."

"Do you have any plans to bring Benjamin to other races?" the guy asked.

"Well, now, that's up to his mom and doctors, but I'm certain we'll chat about it."

"Oh, I'm going to more races," Benjamin said into the mic. And in his eyes was a certainty Todd only hoped proved true.

"Well," Brad said, "we hope to see you and Benjamin back in Victory Lane before year's end."

"Me, too," Todd said.

"Thanks," the commentator said to Todd off camera. "Good luck to Benjamin," he said before he walked away in pursuit of other top-five drivers.

And suddenly there was Indi standing right behind him.

"Come here," Linda said to her son. She held out her arms. "They need to present Todd with the trophy."

"He can stay here," Todd said.

"No, that's okay. Your arms must be killing you."

They were, but he didn't mind. Still, Linda looked insistent and so Todd set Benjamin gently back in his chair. "Stay close, 'kay?"

"'Kay," Benjamin said.

When he turned back, a man in a suit and tie had

a trophy in hand. Indi had faded back, but Todd met her eyes again.

She smiled.

The beauty of that grin took him by such surprise. He'd never seen her smile, *truly* smile. The grin seemed to come from deep within her soul, lighting her whole face up. He almost didn't clutch the trophy when it was presented to him.

"Congratulations," the man said.

"Ah, thanks," Todd answered, glancing back at her.

She seemed to be edging out of Victory Lane. She looked uncomfortable standing there amidst the revelry.

"Excuse me," Todd said, surprising Dan when he handed him the trophy.

"Where are you go—"

"Indi," Todd called. He darted away before anyone could stop him. She only looked up when he placed a hand on her shoulder.

"Hey, Todd," she said, the smile long since gone.

Too bad, he thought.

"Why are you leaving?"

She shrugged. "I don't really need to be here."

"*Benjamin* needs you."

"No," she said with a shake of her head. "He needs you more."

He knew the admission must have cost her. She stared up at him and Todd found himself thinking that the fluorescent lights made her eyes look greener, the lashes around them darker.

"Thank you," she said.

He touched her hand. "You're welcome."

"Todd, they're waiting for us," Kristen said, curiosity making her eyes look bigger behind the dark-rimmed glasses she favored.

"I'll be right there," he said. Kristen didn't look convinced, but she left them alone. "Are you going home after this?"

Indi nodded. "We leave in the morning."

"Then this is it."

"This is it," she echoed. And then, as if arriving at a decision, she tipped herself up and kissed him on the cheek. "I can't thank you enough for all you've done."

"It was the least I could do."

They both turned and looked at the boy. Someone had given him a new hat, one with the race's name on it and he was busy trying it on. Todd felt some of his joy fade when he saw how little hair Benjamin had left.

"This day truly was a miracle," Indi murmured.

"The next miracle will be to get him well."

The eyes that looked into his own were naked

with emotion. Sadness, sorrow, fatigue. Then her lashes dropped and she turned her face away. "Let's hope you're right."

He clutched the hand he'd touched earlier, forcing her to meet his gaze. "I *am* right."

He didn't want to let that hand go, but someone called his name.

"Congratulations, Todd," Indi said. And then she was gone.

CHAPTER THIRTEEN

"YOU, MY DEAR, are a miracle worker."

Indi shrugged out of her coat and hung it on a rack—another garage-sale find—before turning to face Maggie.

"Well, yeah, I know," Indi said, distracted. She'd been that way all weekend. Ever since Todd's little speech on national television, and their private conversation in Victory Lane....

"No, no," Maggie said. "I meant you've *worked* a miracle."

"Huh?"

Maggie's frizzy hair bounced with the same energy she seemed to exude. "You wouldn't believe the number of calls I've gotten from networks, newspapers and major corporations, all of whom want to talk to Benjamin."

"Really?"

Maggie's jaw thrust out excitedly as she bobbed her head. "But that's not the best news of all."

"It's not?" Indi asked, taking a seat. She had a feeling she'd need the chair's support.

"We got a call from headquarters."

"Oh, yeah?" Indi asked, knowing by the way Maggie dragged things out that she was purposely trying to build up to the moment. "What'd they want?"

Maggie leaned over her desk. "They asked if Todd Peters wanted to be our next celebrity spokesperson."

Spokesperson. Print ads. Media interviews. Commercials. She'd have to admit, Todd would be perfect for the job—if he accepted.

"But you want to know what's even more of a shock?" Maggie asked.

"What's that?"

"He *agreed.*"

"Great," she said, feigning enthusiasm because the truth of the matter was, she didn't want to think about Todd.

"He even said he'd donate his time."

"Did *you* talk to him?" Indi asked, curious.

"I did. This morning. He asked how Benjamin was. I told him I didn't know and that you'd call him back later."

Call him? No, no, no. She didn't want to call him. She just wanted to forget about the whole deal because when she recalled how rude she'd been to Todd at first, her whole body burned in embarrassment. She hadn't given the man a chance; she saw that now. She was just happy her unprofessional behavior hadn't soured him on working with *Miracles.*

"How is Benjamin, anyway?" Maggie asked.

"Good…well, as good as can be expected." She had stopped by the hospital on her way to work and she'd been relieved to see that his cold appeared much better. Now if they could just get that damn cancer to go away….

"Any word on his treatment plan?"

Indi shook her head. "No, but they're working on it. There has to be some new drug they can try."

"I'll keep my fingers crossed, but in the meantime, we'll need to get his doctor's permission to attend this camp Todd mentioned."

The Happy Campers Ranch. Indi had smiled when she'd heard the name. "I've already put some calls in."

She'd had plenty of time to do so during a two-hour layover on the trip home. Benjamin and Linda had gotten a ride on Todd's private jet. Indi had declined, preferring to fly commercial. Since she'd gotten in close to midnight last night, she'd had cause to regret her decision.

"Good," Maggie said. "And when you call Todd back, you'll need to set up a time for the two of you to meet privately."

"Excuse me?"

"That's the other bit of good news," Maggie said with a wide, oblivious smile. "You're getting a promotion. Todd Peters was so impressed with your work he requested you be his liaison. Congratulations."

"What?"

Maggie looked like a kid who'd been told summer vacation had been canceled. "What's the matter? I thought you'd always wanted a shot at doing national PR. That was one of your main goals when you joined *Miracles*."

"I know, but I just..." *Don't want to work with Todd.* "I'm not sure I'm ready."

But Maggie was like a hound dog with the scent of skunk in its nose. "What happened?"

"What do you mean 'what happened?'"

"Bull. Did you and Mr. Famous Race Car Driver hit it off?"

"No, we most certainly did *not* hit it off," Indi answered.

Maggie's grin faded. "Then this is a personality conflict?"

"Yes," Indi pounced. "That's it exactly. See if headquarters will give it to someone else."

"No can do. Todd made it clear he wants you. No Indi, he said, no deal."

"He did not."

"That's exactly what he said." Maggie's grin returned. "You must have made a big impression."

Oh, Maggie had no idea that was the truth, Indi thought.

"Look. Just talk to the guy. You may not get along with him, but obviously you hid it well. And he can't be all that bad if he's volunteering his time. Give it a shot."

GIVE IT A SHOT.

Yeah, sure, Indi thought. She hadn't known "giving it a shot" would mean meeting with Todd a week later. She'd expected it to be impossible to schedule some time with him. She'd watched the race this past weekend so she'd known he'd moved up a position in the Chase. She'd expected that to mean he'd be even more focused on racing. She'd been wrong. He'd agreed to fly out to California, although he could only spare a day, and to her surprise, he'd insisted on popping in to visit Benjamin.

But why *was* that a surprise?

She hadn't truly expected Todd to insist she come to him, had she?

No, she admitted, that wasn't it at all. What she'd expected was that Todd would forget about Benjamin the moment he was out of sight. To be honest, it wouldn't be the first time a celebrity had done as much. That hadn't happened and now she felt like a complete and utter idiot because yet again she'd completely misjudged the man.

So when she pulled into San Jose's Jet Center early one afternoon, she promised she'd treat Todd with the kindness he deserved. That was the least she could do. Still, she felt a fair amount of trepidation when she entered the Jet Center's plush lobby. Having greeted other celebrities before, she knew her way around, but the private terminal's marble floor and tall windows always made her feel a bit uncomfortable. She'd never achieve the kind of wealth it took to own a private jet, and that was a fact of life she usually shrugged off. Not so today.

"Well, well, well," she heard when she entered the main waiting area. "If it isn't Ms. Indi, *Miracles* worker extraordinaire."

She recognized the words, and the speaker, and the…

Dog?

Sure enough, when she turned, not only did she spot Todd standing by a potted palm, she saw his dog, Lex, too, the silly canine giving her that bulldog grin.

"You brought Lex?" she stated the obvious.

"Of course," Todd said, walking forward, an overnight bag held in one hand, Lex straining at the leash in the other. "I bring him everywhere."

"Hey, Lex," Indi said, bending down and being very nearly knocked over when the dog's paws landed squarely on her black slacks.

"Down, Lex," Todd ordered. His overnight bag slapped the floor when he released it to use both hands to hold Lex's leash.

"It's okay," Indi said, scratching under the dog's collar. Lex gave her another goofy dog smile. He had such an under bite that she could practically see all his tongue. Silly dog. "I don't mind."

"Obviously, he's glad to see you."

Yeah, but was Todd?

The question caught her by surprise. She stood up abruptly. "Did you have a good flight?"

"We did. Thanks."

And as he stood there, she had to admit that he looked good. More relaxed than she'd seen him before. And she hadn't realized how much taller than her he was until right then. Or maybe she hadn't *wanted* to notice. Just as she hadn't wanted to notice how blue-black his hair was. And how he always seemed to have a five-o'clock shadow that highlighted a very sexy, masculine jaw.

"You ready to go?" she croaked.

"Sure," he said.

"Good," she said, turning away before he noticed the color in her cheeks. "The drive over to the hospital shouldn't take longer than a half hour, especially during this time of day," she said, lifting the sleeve of her suit to check the time.

Her hand shook.

Nerves at facing Todd, she surmised. "Would you like to stop for some fast food or something before we head on over?"

"Nope. Lex and I ate on the plane."

Of course they had. They'd probably had a four-course meal, complete with dog biscuits. Didn't the über wealthy hire personal chefs? Any man who made close to half a million in a weekend could undoubtedly afford one of those.

"Well, then," she said, using her best tour director voice. "Follow me."

They garnered a few extra looks because of the dog, Lex's nails *clack-clack-clacking* against the floor. Thankfully the driver of the limo didn't bat an eye. Indi had worried he might balk at ferrying a dog around. Then again, he was probably used the whimsies of the rich.

She glanced up as a jet took off. Todd was stowing his bag in the back of the limo. It was one of those clear fall days where the sky looked so blue it seemed impossible to believe that just a couple weeks ago it had been raining cats and dogs.

"You didn't have to hire a limo," he said, coming around the back of the car.

"We didn't," she said, waiting for him and Lex to climb in. "The service is donated. Believe me, with traffic the way it is around here, you'll be grateful I'm not driving. People complain of neck aches after riding with me."

"Ouch."

"Yeah." Then Indi said thank-you to their driver, who tipped his hat at her, a gesture that seemed old-fashioned to the point that it made Indi smile.

She caught Todd staring at her when she slid in next to him.

"I'm sure it must be hard to let other people take the wheel," she said, suddenly uncomfortable all over again. She patted Lex's head—dog smell mixing with pine-scented air freshener—until Todd ordered him down. The canine must have been used to riding in cars because he settled onto the floor with a pleased grunt, the loose skin of his jowls spreading out around him as he dropped his head on his paws.

"You have no idea."

Inside the limo was her briefcase, but when she reached for it, Todd said, "Whoa, whoa, whoa. Let's wait until after I visit Benjamin to conduct business."

"Are you sure? There's a lot to go over." And Indi needed something to keep her mind off Todd's wide smile. And the memory of how those lips had felt when they'd touched hers.

Stop it.

That kiss had been…well, weird. He hadn't actually meant anything by it. Lord knows, he hadn't called her, and when they had spoken it had been to discuss his duties as a *Miracles* spokesperson, or to chat about Benjamin. Purely professional. And she'd been disappointed by that.

"After lunch," Todd reiterated. "Right now I want to hear about how you came to work for *Miracles.*"

"I'm not certain we should discuss our personal lives," she said, giving him a smile that must have looked chipped around the edges.

"Why not?"

A week ago she'd have made some snide remark, perhaps even ignored him. But that was before Richmond. Before he'd been so kind to her in Victory Lane and before she'd admitted to herself that she'd been terribly wrong about the type of man he was.

"Because, I don't know. I just think it's better if

we keep things professional." Because it just didn't make sense that she was having these types of thoughts about a man like Todd—a celebrity. Her last relationship with a man like him had ended in disaster.

"Would it help to know Maggie already mentioned your nephew?"

Her gut kicked so violently it took her breath away. She found herself staring at him in shock, and wondering which she wanted to do more—wring Maggie's neck, or stop the limo so she could dash out of the vehicle and avoid a conversation that seemed to be getting far too intimate.

"She shouldn't have," Indi said.

"She didn't tell me anything personal. Just mentioned it in passing. She explained it's why you give so much to the kids, because you've experienced loss firsthand."

Next to their limo, a kid had his car radio cranked up as loud as it would go. She pretended to use that as a distraction, only when she saw it was a teenager, she flinched.

Kyle would have been eighteen this year.

"I'm sorry."

She felt a hand on her knee, and looked away from the head-bobbing young man driving the beat-up Volvo.

"I don't think I realized until just this past week-end how hard this is on a child's family," he said.

"Are you certain you don't want to go over our publicity ideas right now?" Indi asked.

"I will if it'll make you feel better."

She had to look away again, because if she'd held his gaze for a split second longer he might have seen—

What?

That you're not as strong as you let people think?

So? Maybe, just maybe, it might be good to let her feelings all out.

"What do you want to see first?" she asked bright-ly. "The contract we drew up officially naming you as one of our spokespeople? Or the publicity ideas we're throwing around?"

"Neither."

"No?" She reached for her briefcase, anyway. "I've got some sample brochures for you to look at, too. And a mock-up of an ad we're thinking about running."

"Indi," he said gently. "I'm an uncle, too. I can't imagine what it must have been like to lose one of my nieces or nephews. I don't know how you do what you do now after dealing with something like that."

"Don't get too close."

"Excuse me?"

God. Had she actually said those words out loud? "Um. Don't get to close to me," she said. "I think I'm coming down with Benjamin's cold."

That wasn't what she had meant, and Todd knew it. She could see it in his eyes.

"It's too late," he said softly.

"What do you mean? If you wash your hands when we get to the hospital, you'll be fine."

"You're already close to Benjamin," he said.

"I wasn't talking about tha—"

"Yes, you were," he said, and this time, when he reached for her hands, he caught both of them. "And seeing him get sicker, knowing he might lose his battle. It kills you, doesn't it?"

She couldn't speak, couldn't talk over the sudden lump in her throat.

"I saw it in your eyes when we were in Victory Lane. It kills you every time, doesn't it?"

She looked away.

He squeezed her hands, tugged on them a bit, gently, yet sternly forcing her to look at him again.

"There *is* no keeping your distance, is there?" he asked, one of his hands tucking a stray wisp of hair behind her ear, and his touch… Well, his touch did things it shouldn't do.

"Todd, I—"

"Poor Indi," he said, his hand stroking the soft hairs behind her ear. "Poor, poor, Indi."

Okay, *that* wouldn't do. He would *not* pity her. She coped just fine—

But she realized just how weak she was, just how much she longed to connect with someone right then, someone who wasn't ill and who would leave her.

"Indi," he whispered just before his lips connected with hers.

CHAPTER FOURTEEN

HE EXPECTED HER to pull back. He was pleasantly surprised when she didn't. He lifted his hands to her chin, suddenly dying to know what she tasted like.

Vanilla. And mint, he added. She tasted clean and sweet and it was all he could do not to pull her into his lap.

"No," she said, moving her head to the right.

"Yes," he said, gently using a palm to turn her back toward him.

"Todd, I—"

He cut her words off with a second kiss, only this time he didn't hold anything back. When all she did was moan, he grew bolder. He cupped the back of her head, took another tentative taste, then another and another. He leaned her back, lifted a hand to her side. The blouse she wore, that damn clingy blouse that had been so sheer he could practically see right through it, afforded little more than a gauzy barrier between his fingers and her flesh.

"Todd," she gasped, turning her head when his fingers grazed the sensitive skin.

"I've been wanting to do that since the night you ruined your dress."

"My dress," she murmured, her head falling to the right when he lightly nibbled her neck. "The night you first kissed me."

"Yes," he whispered, moving up, nibbling her ears.

"That night the blonde showed up at your motor coach."

His mouth froze.

"The night I realized I was one of a bevy of girls you'd kissed."

He drew back. "Indi—"

"No, no," she said. "It's true."

"No, it's not."

"No?" she asked.

Okay, maybe it was. But that was all in the past. He'd been rebounding from Kristen when he'd met that woman.

And the others.

"Honestly, Indi, I had no idea that that woman would show up that night."

"I'm sure you didn't," she said, her hazel eyes full of disappointment. In him? Or herself? "And that makes it all the worse."

"Worse how?" he asked, his blood pounding.

"How many women has it been this past year?"

"I don't know," he said. "Does it matter?"

"Yes," she said.

"Why? That was before you."

"It just does," she said, straightening her hair when she realized he'd messed it up. Next she tugged down her shirt and smoothed her pants. She even reached for that damn briefcase again.

"Let's go over the contract."

He didn't want to go over a damn thing. "Indi—"

"No, Todd. Please. I don't want to talk about it. Where you and I are concerned, it's nothing but business from here on out." It *had* to be that way.

She released the catches on her briefcase. Inside was a laptop and several documents. "If you don't want to look at the contract, we can look at the mock-up ad that's on my laptop."

"Whatever," he said, sliding away from her and accidentally kicking Lex in the rear. The dog lifted his head, his eyes darting between the two humans as if he could sense the tension between them. Maybe he could.

What the heck was with her? "Here's your copy of the contract. You might want to read it on the way to the hospital," Indi said.

He took the sheaf of papers from her, but he didn't

look at it. He just set it on the black leather seat between them. He heard her release a sigh, knew she was upset that he wasn't doing as she requested. Well, tough. He'd never been so frustrated in his life. He should just do as she asked. Put his feelings toward her in reverse and back away as fast as he could.

Except he didn't want to.

He peeked at her. She was busy staring out the window, her profile backlit by sunlight. And though she didn't face him, he could still see the sadness in her eyes, a sorrow that always seemed to linger there. He couldn't even begin to imagine what it must be like to do what she did for a living. When he recalled how tenderly she always spoke to Benjamin, and how strong and supportive she was of Linda, Todd recognized the truth. Indi Wilcox was special. She might infuriate and inflame him. She might prod and provoke him, but beneath all that lay a heart of gold. Probably the biggest heart of anyone he'd ever met.

THEY ARRIVED at the hospital shortly after, the limo driver agreeing to take Lex on a walk since the dog couldn't come inside the hospital without special clearance. Indi hadn't spoken a word the rest of the way. That was fine with Todd. He needed to think about how best to pursue her because, yes, that's what he intended to do.

But the moment they walked into Children's Hospital, he put his concerns for Indi aside. He didn't know what he'd been expecting, maybe a hospital painted like a gingerbread house and filled with stuffed animals. But this was a hospital in every sense of the word. The main lobby had the requisite corridors that branched off from the reception area. The floors were linoleum, the carpet a serviceable gray. There were only a few brightly painted walls, but no cartoon characters running about. Actually, there was nothing to indicate that this was a hospital filled with children. *Sick* children.

"Can I help you?" said a tired-looking woman behind a bright blue counter. She didn't even look up when they stopped before her desk, just kept on typing on her keyboard. Todd wondered how often this type of place burned out the hospital staff.

"Hi, Sam," Indi said. "We're here to see Benjamin."

"Oh, hey, Indi," the woman said, looking up at last. "How was—"

She shot up from her chair.

Todd jumped back.

"Oh my God, you're Todd Peters."

"Uh, yeah," Todd said, always taken aback by reactions like hers.

"My boyfriend is your biggest fan," the woman said. "I mean, I'm a big fan, too. When Indi told me she was taking Benjamin to Richmond the other day, I told her she should take me along, too, only now look…you're here. I didn't have to go to Richmond—"

"Sam," Indi said. "I know you're excited, but, um, Linda wanted us to surprise Benjamin while he was getting chemo. You know how much he hates getting that, so we really need to move along. Todd will be around later." She glanced over at him. "I'm sure he'd be happy to sign autographs and whatnot."

"Oh, yeah, sure," Sam said, wilting into her chair. "Sorry. Mr. Peters—"

"Todd," he instantly corrected.

"Oh, yeah. Right. Todd," she said, her voice sounding almost giddy. "If you'd just sign in for me here."

Todd did as asked. Indi had already done her part, he noticed. She was halfway to the elevators by the time he'd finished. "Be back in a flash," Indi called out to Sam.

"Benjamin is getting chemo?" he asked as they entered the brightly lit elevator.

Indi nodded. "It's a new type. Experimental. They're hoping it'll work better than the last kind."

Because if it didn't…

They stopped on the second floor, and here again

it looked just like any other hospital—signs pointing patients the right way, doctors in blue smocks cruising the corridors, nurses, too. Indi checked in with another nurse's station, Todd suddenly aware that he was nervous.

"This way," she said a second later, her nondescript pumps making hardly any noise against the gray carpet.

By the time they made it to Benjamin's private room, Todd's heart beat as hard as it did on race day.

"Knock-knock," Indi said, tapping lightly on the door. She motioned for Todd to come in.

He had to force his feet forward because this was evidence, proof positive, that little Benjamin was sick. Terminally ill. At the racetrack it had been easy to forget that.

Not here.

The sight of Benjamin in a sterile hospital room, his tiny body engulfed by a huge hospital bed. Well, it was almost more than he could take.

Linda sat in a chair next to her son's bed and, though her eyes lit up when she saw him, exhaustion clearly clung to her eyes.

"Benjamin," she whispered. "Someone's here to see you."

Todd looked around. It was easier to do that than to look at the bed. Colorful posters filled the walls, toys and stuffed animals throughout the room. A television sat in one corner of the room—it was tuned to the Cartoon Network.

"Huh?" Benjamin asked, his eyes unfocused for a moment as he scanned the room.

Todd forced himself to look back at the bed. At Benjamin lying there, an IV strapped to his arm, the head that had been covered by a ballcap in Richmond completely bald.

"Todd," he cried, and what nearly broke Todd's heart, what made his breath catch, was how weak that cry was.

"Hey, tiger," he said softly, not wanting to disturb the other children on the floor.

"What are *you* doing here?" Benjamin asked, his little hands digging at the covers as if he was trying to sit up but was too weak to do so. Linda soothed him back.

"I came to visit you," Todd said. "I promised I would."

"I know, but I didn't think—"

That he'd actually show up. Why did everyone think that? "Surprised you, didn't I?"

"Mark's going to flip," Benjamin croaked.

"Who's Mark?"

"Don't forget to wash your hands," Indi said in a gentle voice.

And it was then that Todd realized he hung back, that he was afraid to go into the room, that the feeling in his stomach was the same ache he got when cars spun out in front of him and he had nowhere to go.

"Okay," he said. He knew he was stalling.

"It's over there," Indi said, giving him a soft smile, one that made him wonder if she understood why he'd hung back. If his reaction was common. "To the right of the door."

Go, her eyes told him. *You'll be okay.*

"Thanks."

"Mark's a Lance Cooper fan," Benjamin explained. Out of the corner of his eye he saw Linda lean forward and help prop Benjamin up. "He's going to flip when he hears you're here."

"Well, maybe after I'm done visiting you—" Todd's eyes caught on the IV when he turned around "—we'll go down and see him."

The IV looked so ominous, the amount of fluid in it surely too much for such a small little boy....

"That'd be great."

But a glance at Linda's face and Todd could tell that a visit with his neighbor wasn't in the cards. She shook her head just a fraction, chapped lips trying to smile. Todd nodded that he understood.

"How you feeling?" Todd asked.

"Okay," Benjamin said. "Tired."

And now that Todd was close enough to sit down he could see he was exhausted. Pale, too, his skin a grayish-yellow that set alarm bells to ringing.

"Are you still fighting that cold?" he asked.

"Nah. I still have the sniffles a bit, but it's not a big deal."

Indi scooted a chair forward and sat down, too. "They wouldn't have given him the chemo if he wasn't healthy enough to take it."

"Oh," Todd said, trying to come up with something to say. When he glanced around he spotted the checkered flag that he'd presented to Benjamin in Richmond.

Richmond.

How could a kid decline so rapidly in a matter of days?

"Does the chemo hurt?" Todd asked, scared to touch Benjamin, but wanting to clasp his hand.

"No. It just makes my mouth feel weird," the kid admitted.

Todd swallowed over the sudden lump in his throat. "You going to be okay to come to camp? I mean, I know we talked about it, but that was before…"

He'd taken a turn for the worse. It was obvious to Todd and likely everyone in the room that Benjamin was dying.

Dying.

Todd had to look away again.

"I don't know," Benjamin said in a weak voice. "My mom doesn't think it's a good idea."

Linda shook her head again.

Dying.

The word was a silent specter that hung in the room.

"Well, ah, yeah. Whatever we, ah, do, it's got to be okay with your mom, you know. So, um, if you can't go, I'll just have to come to you more often."

"You'd do that?"

"Sure, I would," Todd said. "I'll even be out on the West Coast in a few weeks for a race. Well, Phoenix, but that's pretty close."

But Todd didn't think he'd have the stomach to visit Benjamin again.

"Sounds good," Benjamin murmured, but his eyes had drifted closed.

"You tired there, buddy?" Todd asked, grasping at the chance to leave.

"Yeah," he whispered. "I am."

"G…gosh. Why don't I come back later? When you're feeling better."

"Okay," the child mumbled.

Damn it, Todd thought, standing. He couldn't take this. He just couldn't take this. *How the hell did Indi do this?*

"Indi," Linda said. "Maybe you can take Todd to the roof. He looks like he could use some fresh air."

Todd clawed at his shirt collar. His hand shook so bad it took him a moment to loose the first button.

"Yeah. Air. Sounds good."

Indi stared at him, clearly understanding what was going on. She stared at him in sympathy before leaning over Benjamin. "See you in a bit," she whispered.

"Bit," Benjamin echoed back.

"Come on," she said to Todd.

Todd waited until they were in the elevator, doors mercifully closed, before all but yelling, "Why the hell does he look so bad?"

"Todd—"

"What the hell happened? Was it his trip to Richmond? The new chemo?"

Indi calmly pressed the up button. "Your reaction is normal. It makes people angry when they see a child look as bad as Benjamin does."

"Don't give me that psychobabble. I want to know why he looks like that. I thought the trip to Richmond was supposed to help him, not make him look…"

The doors slid open.

"Like he's dying?" she finished for him, the two of them standing there, oblivious to the stares of the couple waiting to climb into the car.

"Get me out of here," Todd said, just about running away.

"Todd!"

He didn't know where he was going, just blindly followed signs. Stairs. A heavy metal door. He pushed on it so hard it crashed open.

"Todd," he heard again.

And then daylight. Blessed sunlight. And air.

"Todd, slow down."

He walked along a garden path. Someone slipped around him and blocked his way.

"You knew he was sick," Indi said.

"I didn't know it was this bad."

"Well, what the hell did you think? That he was just temporarily disabled?" The sympathy had faded. Now she looked ferocious, like a mother cat staring into the eyes of a dog who'd threatened her kittens.

"No. I mean, yes. Damn it," he cried, looking skyward, his hands clutching his hair. "I don't know what I thought."

His hands still shook. His heart still beat 190 mph. He was…

Crying?

No tears, he told himself. She would *not* see him cry.

"Todd," she said gently, a soft hand on his arm.

And Todd knew it was too late.

CHAPTER FIFTEEN

HE WAS CRYING.

Indi didn't know what to do. She watched him turn away.

"Sorry," he said. "Just give me a sec, okay?"

She let him go, Indi so riddled with emotions she felt like crying herself. How did he keep doing this to her? How did he continue to turn her world upside down?

He was *crying.*

She turned away and sat down on one of the benches that lined a path. The rooftop garden was an oasis. A grassy, tree-studded park meant to soothe the patients and the family members who needed a momentary escape.

It didn't soothe her today.

"I thought bringing him to Richmond would help him," Todd said.

He stood over her, his large frame blocking the sun. He had his hands in his pockets, but she could tell that they were clenched. His whole body looked taut with tension.

"Chemo is hard on people, Todd. This particular type of chemo is even harder than normal. It's a last-ditch effort to save Benjamin's life, and if it doesn't work…"

He sat down next to her. Sunlight burned into the shoulders of her dark jacket like hot hands. Indi shrugged it off, laying the jacket across her lap.

"He's not going to make it to camp, is he?"

"I don't know," she said honestly. "I looked into it the other day. There are doctors on staff, and the Carolinas Medical Center is nearby, but I'm not certain dragging Benjamin across the United States is a good idea. He's so sick, and to be honest, I don't think the doctors will allow it."

"Indi," Todd said, placing a hand on her thigh. For the first time, the touch was completely impersonal. His hazel eyes were intense, as if he'd done battle with inner demons and come out on the other side.

That's exactly what he'd done, she realized.

"Indi," he said again, and she knew he struggled for words. "I know it's a long shot. I know his doctors might not allow it."

She watched him swallow and Indi wondered who was this man sitting next to her. Gone was the cocky race car driver of Richmond. In his place was a man deeply rocked by Benjamin's battle with cancer.

"If I could just see that look on his face again, the one he had in Victory Lane—"

"Todd," she said, her own eyes filling with tears. Damn him. Why couldn't he be like some of the other self-centered celebrities she'd dealt with in the past? It made it so much easier to stay detached, to not have to think about the fact that she was losing another child in her life.

No.

She wouldn't go there. "Todd," she started again. "I know you want to help. I appreciate that you want to help, but I just don't see it happening—"

"I'll make it happen," he said, standing up.

"How?" she cried. "You can't just wave a magic wand and make Benjamin well enough to go."

"No, but I can ensure he gets the best care. That he's being treated by the best—"

"This is Stanford. One of the best children's hospitals in the world."

"Then I'll talk to the second-best. And the third. And the fourth. Damn it, Indi. I'm not going to sit around and wait for that kid to die."

Indi felt herself blanch, looked around, hoping there were no other parents or children nearby. There wasn't. They were completely alone.

"All the money in the world won't help some kids," she said.

"Is that what you do? Is that what you tell yourself to keep yourself sane while doing this crazy job? Is that why you've cut yourself off from feeling emotion? From allowing yourself to enjoy a damn kiss?"

"Don't you dare," she warned. "Don't you dare turn this into a personal attack on me."

"Why not?" he asked. "It's true, isn't it? You're afraid, Indi. Afraid to care. And not just because of what happened between you and that jock, who, by the way, was a total jerk if he screwed you around. You're afraid to open yourself up. And who can blame you?" he asked. "This is what you deal with on a day-to-day basis. Death. Death and the broken hearts of parents and family members."

"That's not true," she said, standing, too. "Not all the kids I work with end up dying. Many of them go on to live long, productive lives. They might be battling hemophilia or sickle-cell anemia, but they do it in such a way that they *inspire* me. I devote one hundred percent of my time and effort to this job for that very reason."

"Is that what you tell yourself?" he asked softly. "Is that why you refuse date after date?"

"What?" she huffed. "Who told you that?"

"Linda," he said softly. "She told me one of the doctors here asked you out on a date, but that you refused. She said you told her all doctors were 'players,' and I thought to myself, now why does that sound familiar?"

"Because it is true. You wouldn't believe some of the stuff that goes on in hospitals."

"And in law firms and marketing firms and private schools. Everywhere, Indi. No-good, lying scum are everywhere." He leaned toward her. "But how're you ever going to weed out the bad from the good if you don't give it a try?"

"This isn't about me," she said, the fight draining out of her. "This is about Benjamin, and I won't allow you to turn your frustration over his situation into a personal attack on me."

"You're right," he said. "That's exactly what I'm doing. This *is* about Benjamin. It's about *all* the Benjamins in the world. But unlike you, I'm not going to allow my sorrow to be the emotional death of me. I'm not going to give up—"

"I *haven't* given up."

"Haven't you?" he asked, his eyes never leaving her own. "Isn't that *exactly* what you've done?"

She refused to answer.

"I'm leaving," he said, turning away.

She let him leave.

"Stupid, ignorant man," she muttered. "Nobody wants to help Benjamin more than I do. I haven't given up."

But inside something whispered, *Haven't you?*

"Jen, cancel all my appointments," Todd said into his cell phone.

He pushed on the exit door, glancing over his shoulder to see if Indi had followed him. She hadn't.

Whatever.

"For tomorrow? That might be kind of hard—" Jen replied.

"For the rest of the week."

"What? Todd, I can't do that. You know how tightly booked you are. There's no way I can re-schedule your whole wee—"

"Do it," he said firmly, still looking for Indi even as the door closed. "I don't care what you say, just get it done."

"But, Todd—"

He hung up on her. Yeah, he'd probably pay the price for that later on, but what did it matter if one more woman was pissed off at him?

Damn, Indi.

You were pretty harsh on her.

Yeah, well, he'd needed to be.

The door to the elevator he'd called for slid open,

cool air from the lobby brushing his face. He headed straight for the reception counter.

"Sam," he said sweetly, leaning over the bright blue counter and giving the pink-smocked staff member his most dazzling smile. "I need a favor," he asked.

"What's that?" she asked with a flirtatious grin right back.

"I need to know Benjamin's doctors' names."

The smile faded. "Oh, well, I'd really like to—"

"Please," he said softly, leaning farther forward at the same time he revved up his smile. "Pretty please?"

"Todd, um. Yeah. I'm really *very* sorry, but I can't release patient information. It's confidential."

"I know that," he said softly. "But what would it hurt if you just wrote the name down on that pad of paper there, and I happened to see it. No one need ever know—"

"I would know," she said with a shake of her head, her frizzy ponytail falling over one shoulder. "I can't. Really, I just can't."

"There are two garage passes in it for you. I'll even make it hot passes. You and your boyfriend can pick the race."

She opened her mouth, closed it, seemed to consider his offer, but only for a millisecond. In the end she just couldn't do it. "Can't you just ask Indi to get that information to you? Or Benjamin's mom?"

He bit back an oath of frustration. Yes, he could. Of course he could, but he wanted to poke around first. Find out why Benjamin was regressing, see what they were doing to treat him, ask his doctors if there was any other medication they could give him. "I guess if that's what I need to do—"

"Yes," she said, pouncing on his acquiescence. "It is. I'm really sorry, but I just can't take a chance." She tried to ease the blow with a smile.

"You can still have the tickets," Todd said, straightening and tapping the counter impatiently.

"I can? Oh, gee, thank you so much."

"There's one last thing you can help me with," he said.

"Anything," she said.

"I'd like to bring an old friend of Benjamin's in for a visit."

"Certainly."

"It's a dog," he said.

Poor Sam looked stricken again. "Oh, Todd, animals aren't allowed."

"Sure they are," he said. "I saw a special on therapy dogs just the other day."

"Yeah, but they have to have special training."

"Who do I talk to about that?"

"Well, I mean…I don't know if you'd have time. Don't you have to, you know, race this weekend?"

"You leave the racing to me," he said, leaning against the counter again. There had to be somebody he could charm into helping him.

"I'll give you the number of the gal who brings animals in to visit, but I can't guarantee she'll help, or that she can get you approved."

Then he'd find someone else who would. Todd didn't back down from challenges easily.

His cell phone rang.

"Todd," Jen said. "I really can't—"

"I need the name of the best pediatric oncologist at the Carolinas Medical Center."

"But, Todd—"

"When you've got the number, call me back. Oh, and find out if he's a race fan."

"Todd. No. I can't—"

He flipped his phone shut. Okay, so now Jen would *really* be pissed. Oh, well. Next stop, Benjamin's room. After that, he'd call the dog lady. Maybe talk to someone in oncology that might be able to help him.

There was one thing Todd wasn't good at, and that was waiting. Benjamin's health couldn't wait.

He was running out of time.

GREEN FLAG

O Happy Days
By Rick Stevenson, Sports Editor

I'll have to admit, I was a little steamed last week when Todd Peters's PR rep called and canceled an interview. I took it as a sign that the old Todd Peters was back. You know the one: the guy that used to cuss pit reporters out, or hit cameramen on the way back to his hauler, or ignore reporters all together. I was all set to write a scathing article about my old pal Todd. Actually, about athletes in general, and how so many of them fail to use the resources their celebrity status provides to do good for others.

And then Dover's Happy Hour came around.

I happened to run into Todd's PR rep while Todd was out on the track. She was so über noncommunicative about where Todd had been that it got me curious. Being a journalist whose roots are investigative reporting, it didn't take me long to find out.

It seems Todd's been AWOL while he tries to

find the best medical care for *Miracles* child Benjamin Koch. You know the kid—the one with the million-dollar smile in Victory Lane. Seems little Benjamin took a turn for the worse and Todd's determined to do all that he can to help the boy.

Say *what?*

I'll confess, at first I didn't believe it. But several discreetly placed phone calls later, I verified the truth. Todd Peters has, indeed, taken a terminally ill child under his wing. Linda Koch, Benjamin's mother, said he's moved heaven and earth to fly Benjamin to the best specialists around the nation, all on his dime.

This isn't a media stunt anymore.

Linda Koch was clearly in tears as she told me the tale. Her son has rallied in recent weeks, something she feels certain has to do with Todd's constant phone calls and visits. She even mentioned that Todd arranged for Benjamin to attend a camp here in North Carolina where, surprise, surprise, Todd agreed to be one of the camp counselors.

So stop the press, ladies and gentlemen. If Todd Peters can be reformed, maybe there's hope for the other athletes. Word is Todd's team owner, Mathew Knight, is bringing in bad-boy open-wheel star Brandon Burke as wheelman for a second NASCAR NEXTEL Cup team. Maybe Brandon needs to attend the Todd Peters School of Philanthropic Endeavors. Perhaps *all* athletes should attend the school.

If only life were that simple.

But…*wouldn't it be nice?*

CHAPTER SIXTEEN

THE AIR WAS HOT and humid.

Again.

Indi rolled her suitcase through the jetway corridor at the Charlotte Douglas International Airport, wondering for the thousandth time why she'd agreed to come. It wasn't as if Linda and Benjamin needed her, she thought, waiting for her luggage to appear on the carousel, something she'd begun to suspect would never happen. With her luck, her baggage was on its way to the Bahamas while she was stuck here in North Carolina.

She released a sigh of frustration, although she was mostly frustrated for herself. Maggie had offered to tell headquarters she was too busy to travel. For goodness' sake, they had an office on the East Coast that could have handled the PR side of things. All they were doing was filming Todd and Benjamin together for use in a commercial and other media releases. And the corporate honchos that were flying in to shake Todd's hand could have done that without her. Most important of all, *Benjamin* didn't need her. He'd have both his parents here this weekend since they were taking a minivacation, their first in a long time. Even Benjamin would have someone with him to keep him company when Todd wasn't around. Mark, his neighbor from down the hall, was with him, too. Another patient adopted by Todd.

And yet here she was.

"I'll go in your place," Maggie had said.

But Indi had declined.

"I'm an idiot."

And there was her suitcase. Thank the Lord above. Now if she could find the rental car place.

"Indi," someone called as she exited the airport. The rental agency, it appeared, was off site.

Indi glanced around, spying, much to her surprise, Jennifer Scott standing near the driver's side of a dark blue Ford Tempo.

"Whew," Jen said, the willowy blonde looking far too calm, cool and collected considering the humidity that hung in the air and the rush of cars all jockeying to find a place to pull up to the curb. "I'm so glad I caught you. I've been calling your cell phone for an hour."

"I forgot to turn it back on."

"That's what I thought, so now you're going to have a million messages from me. Just ignore them."

"What's up?"

Jen smiled. "I thought you'd like a ride to Happy Campers," she said. "It can get a little confusing out in the back woods."

"But I've got a rental reserved."

"No need to do that. You can use one of the comp cars. It's all arranged."

"Oh, ah… Thanks," Indi said.

"No problem," Jen said, popping the car's trunk.

"I'll just call the rental agency and cancel," Indi said as she slid into the car.

"Go ahead."

It took her a moment to locate the number, but all was settled in a matter of minutes.

"So," Jen asked after she hung up, "Did you have a nice flight?"

"Fine. A little crowded. But no turbulence."

Jen nodded, her blinkers clicking while she switched lanes. "It used to be that you could stretch out on the empty seat next to you. Not so anymore."

Indi nodded, staring out at the Charlotte skyline. The airport sat a few miles away from downtown and off in the distance high-rises sprouted up like one of those airport trinkets, the kind with a miniature city in a glass globe. There were so many trees dotting the landscape you couldn't see the homes and businesses hidden behind the foliage. Some of those trees had leaves that were gold and red, the color of sherbet ice cream. Indi marveled at how pretty they were. In California, all you saw was an endless sea of concrete. Not so in Charlotte.

Very pretty. And…green.

"You know, Todd really likes you."

It took Indi a moment for the words to register, her startled *"What?"* all but shot out of her.

Jen smiled.

"I've never seen a scowl on his face like the one I saw when I mentioned you."

"That scowl isn't because he likes me."

"I beg to differ," Jen said with an emphatic shake of her head. "Trust me. I've never seen him react that way to a woman's name. Not even when Kristen threw him over for Mathew Knight."

"Huh?" Indi said.

"Yeah. Todd fell hard for her. Or at least he thought he did. He told me later it was more of a crush. Probably was, too, because now they are great friends. He even helped Kristen and Mr. Knight hook up."

"You're kidding?"

"Nope. 'Course he went a little crazy there for a while, dating this woman and that. But that ended a few months ago. I think he got tired of it all. That is, until he met you."

"Did Linda tell you to tell me this?"

"No," Jen said, her blue eyes quickly darting to Indi's before returning to the road. "Why?"

"Never mind," Indi said. "I just…" She shook her head because, honestly, she didn't know what to say.

"Anyway, I'm certain he likes you."

"What makes you say that?" Indi asked, even though she knew she shouldn't care. Her cheeks still stung when she remembered their last conversation.

And that kiss in the limo.

"I know he's really wrapped up in helping Benjamin. Honestly, that in itself is a surprise. The old Todd would have been so focused on winning the championship, he'd have said to heck with anything else. But that isn't what I was going to say. What makes me think he really likes you is that the other day when I told him you didn't want to catch a ride with Benjamin and Mark and their families, he looked crushed. But only for a second. And, see, that's just it. Todd never wears his emotions on his sleeve. He's not that way. But after he looked crushed, he got mad. Called you all kinds of names. Not *bad* names. Just things like stubborn and hardheaded and obstinate. I've never seen him so, so…volatile."

"It's stress," Indi surmised. "Not only is he worried about Benjamin, but he's got this whole Chase thing to contend with."

"But that's just it," Jen said, stopping at a light. She turned to face Indi. "He's never driven better in his life. Indi, he's poised to win the whole thing. He's got six more races to go. All he has to do is continue to race like he's been doing and maybe, hopefully, win one or two, and he's set. I think he's got a real shot, and so do all the experts. My phone's been ringing off the hook with interview requests. Of course, he's turned them all down."

Because of Benjamin. There had been a time when Indi wouldn't have believed such a thing was possible, but she'd come to the realization that she'd been so, so wrong.

"Unbelievable," Indi muttered.

"What?" Jen asked, misinterpreting why she'd said the word. "You don't think you're Todd's type?"

"Just what *is* Todd's type?"

"I used to think anyone with big breasts and pretty hair was Todd's type," Jen said, glancing over at Indi. "Not anymore."

"Gee, um…thanks. I think."

"No, no," Jen quickly corrected. "I'm sorry. I didn't mean it that way."

Indi smiled because she'd known that. She'd just

been giving the woman a hard time. The thing is, she liked Jen and that was strange considering she hadn't known her that long.

"Indi, you *have* to know you're gorgeous," Jen said, the car she drove accelerating as they merged onto an expressway.

"I don't know that at all," Indi admitted. "I worked in broadcasting, in Los Angeles, where everyone is drop-dead gorgeous. I don't think I'm anything special at all."

"You are," Jen said. "Trust me. You're tall and elegant and chic. Most women couldn't carry off those tan slacks and that silk shirt you're wearing. It would look blah on them. But you're so pretty the outfit looks stunning even though it's casual. Todd usually likes women in tight T-shirts, preferably with his car number on it." Jen smiled. "And yet here you are. And he likes you. Lucky girl."

Lucky girl?

Jen glanced over at Indi right then. She stiffened suddenly. "Oh, Jeez," she said with a horrified widening of her eyes. "You think I like Todd."

"Well, I—" Indi didn't quite not how to proceed, because that's exactly what she'd been thinking and it amazed her that Jen had read her so easily.

"Indi," Jen said sternly. "Todd and I are like brother and sister. Sometimes I want to kill him, like when he called me and asked me to cancel all his appointments that week he was out in California. You have no idea what I went through to do that, but that's beside the point. I'm just saying a lot of girls would love to date Todd Peters, but I'm not one of them."

"Me, neither."

"No?"

"No," Indi said firmly.

"Well, that's a surprise. But maybe that's why Todd likes you. He's always turned on by a challenge. That's why he races cars for a living."

"Oh, great."

"Anyway," Jen said, "About my dating drivers. I don't. At least not any that I've worked for."

"Does that mean you've dated drivers you *didn't* work for?"

"I've dated one or two. Not Cup drivers, though. I got into this whole business thanks to my dad. He raced open wheels. Sprint cars. Still does, but only on a local track."

"Why don't you want to date drivers?"

"Because the majority of them are jerks."

"Except Todd."

"Oh, Todd can be a jerk sometimes. He's the kind of guy who will tell you exactly how it is. That can be hard to take. But you know, nine times out of ten he's right. When I mess up, he usually points it out to me, but not in a really bad way. Just tells it like it is."

"And that's a good trait," Indi wondered.

"Some drivers will rip into you even when you've done everything right."

"I see."

"I'd take Todd over the majority of other drivers any day. And there's one other thing you should know. Ever since he met you, Todd hasn't looked at another woman. I know you might not believe that, but it's true. And I know he's been busy with Benjamin so you might think that's why. But, Indi, this is a man who's always, *always* with a woman."

They lapsed into silence again, and from that point forward Jen kept things impersonal. But rather than relax, the closer they got to camp, the more tense Indi became. She hoped she wouldn't run into Todd. At least not the first day. Sure, he'd undoubtedly come by to visit Benjamin, but she doubted he'd stay for long. The closer they got to the end of the Chase for the NASCAR NEXTEL Cup, the busier he would probably be.

"Here we are," Jen said a half hour later. Indi sat up. For a while now they'd been traveling through North Carolina's back roads so the fence-lined woodlands wasn't a surprise. A sign that said Happy

Campers Ranch hung over the entrance, the words done in a colorful script. There were horses grazing in bright green pastures on their left and right.

"It looks beautiful."

"It is," Jen said.

Of course, Indi had known that. She'd done research on the "ranch" prior to arriving. She knew it was situated on one hundred acres, and that the land had been donated by the power company that had originally owned the land Lake Norman was situated upon. From time to time Indi had caught sight of that lake off in the distance, Indi instantly recalling the first time she'd met Todd. She really *had* given him a hard time. And if she were perfectly honest, he'd taken it pretty well.

They crested a small hill, Indi leaning forward when she saw what sat on the other side.

"Oh, my," she breathed. "This is really something."

"Isn't it?" Jen said.

The Web site she'd surfed couldn't possibly convey the breathtaking vista that spread out before her. Situated at the tip of a small peninsula, the camp featured a beautiful lodge-type building that covered at least an acre of land. A porch jutted out from the front, wooden ramps leading up to double doors and spreading out beneath tall, paned windows. Off to the left and right were outbuildings. And a park. And a dock in the distance.

A dock with a very familiar Scarab moored to its side.

"Is Todd here?" Indi asked.

"He is," Jen said with what Indi swore was a sly smile. "He volunteered to be a camp counselor this week. The kids are *so* excited."

"But I thought he'd be busy during the day. Racing. Or maybe signing autographs or something?"

"Nope. He's made Benjamin his first priority. He drives over to the track, but that's not until Thursday morning and so he'll be here until then."

"Does he have any sponsor obligations this week?" Indi asked.

"Nope. Everyone's been really great about what's going on. Even the media. I know Todd's not doing this for publicity, but it's generated a lot of great exposure."

Jen pulled to a stop in front of the lodge. "Okay, so orientation is at one. Inside they'll tell you your room number. You're in the main lodge, by the way. That much I know. Consider yourself lucky. Todd has to share a room with six boys."

"Where are you going?" Indi asked when Jen stayed in the car.

"Back to the office in Concord. Todd might have

the week off, but I don't. See you later, Indi. Have a good time."

"Thanks," Indi said, trying hide her dismay. She went around to the back of the car and pulled her suitcase from the trunk. Then she told her feet to walk forward even though they didn't want to.

"Need some help?" someone asked.

And Indi didn't need to turn around to know who that voice belonged to.

Todd.

CHAPTER SEVENTEEN

INDI LOOKED GOOD.

Of course, she always looked good, Todd thought. But when she'd turned toward him Todd had been unprepared for the tentative smile she gave him, not after their last conversation.

"Hi, Todd."

He couldn't help but smile back. "You want me to take that?" he asked, holding out his hand.

"That's okay," she said. "It rolls."

"Not on this gravel," he said, closing the distance between them. "Here."

She kept her hand on the suitcase. Todd didn't move. This was it. This was where she'd tell him to get lost. After their last conversation, he wouldn't blame her.

"Thanks," she said instead.

She didn't hate him.

A million times since they'd last spoken he'd wondered if she did. The easing of his shoulders spoke volumes as to how much he'd dreaded their first meeting. She had, too, by the looks of it.

"How was your trip out?"

"Good," she said, following behind.

"You know, you really could have caught a ride out with everyone else."

"I know, but I didn't want to impose."

He stopped. She did, too. He wondered what to say, didn't really know where to begin. A hundred times in the past couple weeks he had thought about calling her. He hadn't, and that only seemed to compound how rotten he felt.

"About the last time we spoke," he said.

"No," she said with a shake of her head, her hair falling over one shoulder. "We don't need to bring all that up again."

"Yes, we do," he said. "I feel bad."

"Why?" she asked. "I needed to hear what you had to say, even if it *did* sting at the time."

"Yeah, but there was no excuse for blasting you like I did. Jen says I can be an ass sometimes and it's true. That day I was worse than usual. I felt so powerless. Impotent. It made me mad and I took it out on you." He set her suitcase down and touched her hand. "I'm sorry."

"Don't be," she said. "Your words had the ring of truth."

"Indi, no. Your devotion to kids like Benjamin is what makes you so remarkable. These kids—the ones here and the other ones just like them—need people like you. Who else is going to make their dreams come true?"

He saw her look away and wondered if she had tears in her eyes. For a moment he contemplated turning her head toward him, but he was afraid to touch her. Damn it, he *wanted* to touch her.

"Thank you," she said, meeting his gaze again.

"Come on," he said, needing to get away from her, because if he didn't move, he'd do something impulsive. "I'll introduce you to the people who run this place. They're all as remarkable as you."

He moved away, but he flexed his free hand over and over again, scratched at the top of it. What was this feeling he got every time she was around? He felt dehydrated, like he did after he'd been in a hot car for too long. Out of breath. Very nearly dizzy. Damn. Maybe he should pop in on one of the staff physicians.

"It's really beautiful here," she said.

"Yes, it is," he answered, stopping one of the camp counselors who crossed the main lobby—a spacious foyer with high-beamed ceilings and tall windows that overlooked Lake Norman.

"Have you seen Rob and Annie?" he asked the kid.

"I think they're outside."

Before they could take two steps, they heard someone cry, "Indi."

Todd watched Indi's face light up. His shortness of breath turned into full-blown cardiac arrest, at least that's what it felt like.

And Todd knew. He just knew that he'd started to fall for her. He wasn't sure when or how, but he couldn't deny the way he felt, and it made what he'd felt toward Kristen feel like puppy love.

"Benjamin," she said, the love she felt for the boy softening her features. "Look at you wheeling yourself around. That's *great.*"

"I'm having so much fun," Benjamin said, breathless. "Guess who's here?" he asked, wiggling in his chair. "You'll never guess who's here."

"Who?"

"Lance Cooper," Benjamin said like a kid announcing the big game's final score.

"Whoa," Indi said. "That's amazing."

"I know. Mark just about flipped," Benjamin said, referring to his friend from the hospital. The child had been thrilled to be invited and Todd hadn't minded giving an extra kid a ride out.

"Where *is* Mark?" Indi asked, tucking one side of her loose hair behind her ear.

He'd *kissed* that ear.

Nope. Best not to go there. Not right now.

"He went to get something to eat. I'm going to go find him. Want to come?"

"I can't," she said, grabbing the brim of his hat and wiggling it a bit. "I just got here."

"I know. I was waiting for you on the back porch."

"Aw, you didn't have to do that."

"I know, but I was feeling kind of tired anyway."

Indi's eyes dimmed. Todd saw it, even though he doubted Benjamin noticed. The kid was too busy rolling past them.

"See ya," Benjamin said.

"Hey, wait. Hold up there, buddy. I'll push you over there if you want to hang on a moment," Indi said.

"That's okay," Benjamin said.

"Go," Todd ordered. "I can have someone put your bag in your room."

"Are you sure?"

He nodded. "Go. I'll take care of it."

"Thanks," she said, dashing off because Benjamin was already out the door.

"She's devoted to the children," Linda Koch said.

Todd realized he'd been caught staring. "Yes, I know," he said, turning to Benjamin's mom.

"It won't be easy convincing her there's room in her life for a man."

Todd was surprised by her words. "No, it won't."

"You'd have to do it when other caregivers were around."

"Do what?" he asked.

There was a new serenity to Linda, one that caught Todd by surprise. Maybe she looked forward to spending some quiet time with her husband. Todd had been told *Miracles* had paid for a hotel room for the two of them in Charlotte. They wanted Benjamin to feel as if he were on his own here at camp.

"Convince her to go out with you," Linda said.

"Oh."

Linda stepped up alongside of him. "She came here for a reason, Todd, and I think Benjamin and Mark are just a small part of it."

"Really?"

"Really," Linda said. "And if ever someone deserved a chance at happiness, it's Indi."

"And you think I can give her that."

"I do."

Linda's words touched him in a way Todd didn't think possible. "Thanks," he said.

"Just don't break her heart."

"I won't," he said.

Linda smiled, her tired eyes brightening for a moment. "I'm holding you to your word on that, Todd Peters."

"I hope you do," Todd said, leaning in and impulsively kissing her cheek.

INDI EXPECTED Todd to follow behind her for some reason, but to her surprise, he left her alone. And so she found herself in the mess hall, a rowdy place where Indi learned the names of at least half-a-dozen children, or tried to. They were a wild bunch of boys and girls, most of whom acted like normal, healthy children complete with food-tossing tendencies and loud cries of delight, especially when the peanut butter side of a sandwich adhered itself to a window.

"Cool," more than one child exclaimed.

And that was the start of her time at Happy Campers Ranch where it was, indeed, a happy place to be. Not so much for Indi, though. She'd come to the camp to work, and that's exactly what she did. Once the camp directors realized she'd have very little to do except oversee the next day's filming of Todd and Benjamin, they decided to put her to work. She spent the rest of the first day overseeing the art room, and then dinner. Todd kept his distance, much to her surprise. Then again, Indi had made it abundantly clear she wasn't interested in him. Obviously he respected her wishes.

But as she walked one of the many riding trails that surrounded the camp the next day, she realized that a part of her was actually *disappointed* that things had cooled between the two of them. During their film shoot today, he'd hardly even looked at her.

Unbelievable, she thought.

She turned on her heel. On either side of the path, oak and pine trees kept the sun from reaching the ground, the shade they provided allowing ferns and reed-thin saplings to sprout up. It was early evening and a chill had settled in the air. The cold seemed to knock the wind out of the trees as leaves began to fall. They crunched beneath her feet, and Indi thought the North Carolina foliage was some of the prettiest she'd ever seen. Everything was so green.

The trees began to thin. Up ahead she heard high-pitched voices that could only belong to kids from the camp. Kyle would have loved it here, she admitted. Her nephew had always loved the outdoors. When Indi had been in her twenties, her mom and dad had insisted on a family vacation of sorts. They'd hiked trails and played in the water for days during that time.

It had been on vacation that they noticed Kyle seemed to sleep a lot.

He's just been fighting a flu for weeks, her sister Katie had reassured her.

Such a familiar story. Indi knew that all too well now. Many parents had no inkling of the illness that lurked in the depths of their children until it reared its ugly head.

"Don't," someone cried, a boyish giggle for all that it sounded breathless. "That tickles."

The pine trees that had grown so thick deeper in the forest grew scraggly in appearance, their needles lush at the top, but nothing more than twigs at the bottom. It allowed her to see through the trees and to the shore beyond. Not far ahead she saw the lake, its surface twinkling as if someone had sprinkled it with glitter. It blinded her for a second.

She saw Lex had his front paws on Benjamin's lap, the dog's tongue doing its best to lick the boy's hand.

"Hey," Benjamin cried, lifting his arms.

Indi smiled.

Benjamin loved that dog. After Todd had gotten clearance to bring Lex into the hospital the two had been nearly inseparable.

Todd.

He stood on a pebbled beach, tossing rocks into the dark blue water. His back was to her, but something about his shoulders spoke volumes. Was it the race this coming weekend that was troubling him? Or was it something more? Perhaps Benjamin.

They'd both noticed that he'd grown markedly weaker in the past few weeks. Of course, that might have something to do with the specialists who'd been poring over his medical charts and taking blood samples practically night and day, but Indi doubted it.

He was dying. She shook her head and inhaled against the injustice of it all. Oh, sure, they'd tried this drug and that. This new wonder treatment and that new enzyme inhibitor. But it always ended the same. In a matter of days, sometimes hours, Benjamin's body either reacted aversely to the medication, or it just plain rejected it. Through it all, they kept up with the chemo, but that did absolutely nothing these days and so Linda and Art Koch had decided to stop. That had bolstered Benjamin's spirits for a few days because he hated the way the chemo made him feel. But the end of chemo meant the end of something else. Benjamin knew that as well as his parents.

This camp would be his last vacation.

Indi wiped tears from her eyes. But, hey, this was part of her job, she reminded herself. She could deal with it. She started to turn away, but then changed her mind. Lex spotted her the moment she stepped out of the trees, his excited bark a signal to all that he'd found a long-lost friend.

"Lex, no," Indi cried as he barreled toward her, a pint-size bowling ball with four legs. Indi almost went down. "Lex," she scolded, but she couldn't stay mad for long. "Bad dog," she added with a smile.

"Indi. Come here," Benjamin called. "Todd's found a shell."

"A shell, huh?" she said, patting her thigh so Lex would follow. The dog gave her his patented smile, his tongue flipping out and hitting his nose. That caused him to snort and then sneeze, and Indi would have laughed if she'd been in a better mood. No wonder the kids loved him.

"What kind of shell?" she asked Benjamin when she stood by his chair. He wore his red ball cap. Usually the red fabric leached color into his pale face. Not so today. With the sun just above the horizon, Indi could plainly see the veins beneath Benjamin's skin, the smudges below his lower lashes and the sunken skin beneath his cheekbones.

He'd lost weight.

"We think it belongs to a crawdad. Look," he said, holding the shell out in the palm of his hand.

Lex apparently thought Benjamin held a doggy treat. He'd snapped the shell up in a flash, although how he got that low-to-the-ground body up high enough, Indi would never know.

"Hey," they both cried.

Indi saw Lex's jaw stop abruptly, a surprised look

crossing his face. He spit the thing out so fast she and Benjamin laughed out loud.

"Serves him right," she heard Todd say.

"Yeah, it does," Indi agreed, smiling in welcome.

"Hey, Indi," he said.

"Hi, Todd," she said, brushing the sand from her hands. She glanced at Benjamin. "You, ah…you need me to push you back to camp?"

"Nah. I like it here. The lake. It's so pretty."

Yes, it was. And he should enjoy it while—

Indi. Don't think like that.

"You stay here then," she said softly. "Enjoy yourself."

"I will," Benjamin said with a small smile. But then he brightened. "You and Todd can go for walk though."

"No, no," Indi said, waving her hands. "I'm tired. Think I need a nap."

"Come on," Benjamin said. "I'm the one who's sick, not you. What do you need a nap for?"

"Well, I—"

"It's a nice walk," Todd added.

"Grown-ups are supposed to walk on the beach together," Benjamin said, staring between the two. "You know, hand and hand, looking into each other's eyes, making faces at each other."

"Oh, please," Indi said.

But one of Todd's eyebrows had lifted. "Sounds like fun. You game?"

Indi was about to say no again, but there was a look in Todd's eyes, one that asked her to participate…for Benjamin's sake.

"Well, I—"

"Good," Benjamin said. "I'm just going to sit here. And watch." He folded his hands in his lap, Lex looking at all the humans as if deciding who to go with. He settled down next to Benjamin's chair. "You'll keep me company, won't you?" he asked. Benjamin's neck looked so thin and long, his shoulders gaunt beneath his bright red shirt.

"Come on," Todd said, holding out his hand to Indi. "Benjamin's orders."

Indi slipped her fingers inside his palm. She very nearly took a step away, increasing the distance between them, although that seemed like a silly thing to do given that they held hands.

They held hands.

And it felt…nice, Indi admitted, matching her steps to his. But she couldn't help glancing back at Benjamin. His eyes were closed, his head resting against the back of his chair.

"He's not feeling well."

"No," Indi said, clenching Todd's hands involuntarily.

He squeezed back.

Their eyes met, but Indi had to look away. She couldn't stand to see the concern in his eyes, not when it echoed everything she felt inside. This was the part where she needed to be strong. Where she had to show strength. For the Koches' sake. And for Todd, she realized.

"He's not going to last much longer, is he?" Todd asked, and she could hear a tremor in his voice.

She wouldn't look at him. "No, Todd, he won't."

"What's going to happen?"

She looked out over the water. She could see boats dotting the surface, their white hulls standing out against the blue backdrop. What she wouldn't give to be one of the lucky ones, a person who could spend the day relaxing in the sun, oblivious to the sadness in the world, to the tragedies that could unfold such as a ten-year-old boy losing his life.

"He'll have less and less energy. His appetite will fail. He'll fade in and out of sleep, become less and less cognizant of the world around him. In a few weeks his body will start to shut down. His liver will likely go first, then his kidneys—"

"Damn," Todd snapped, stepping in front of her and forcing her to look into his eyes. "You sound like you're giving a lecture."

Indi forced herself to look him in the eye. "You asked."

"Yes, but I didn't expect you to sound so…so…" She watched his Adam's apple bob. "So clinical."

"That's part of my job, Todd. I tell it like it is. I'm not going to sugarcoat it with pretty flowers on the side. Death isn't pretty."

He jerked her forward again and muttered, "He's looking this way." Indi looked back. The boy's head was turned in their direction.

"He's probably just keeping the sun out of his eyes."

"No, Indi. He's not. He's probably listening to every word you say."

"He's too far away. He can't hear a thing."

"What if he could? What if he just heard you catalogue everything that's going to happen to him? What if he's sitting over there wondering when it'll all start, when the process will begin that will ultimately end his life?"

"Todd," she said, placing a hand on his upper arm. "He already *knows* he's dying."

"He doesn't know that. All the testing we've done, all the doctors he's seen, something might still come up."

"Don't you think we'd have heard by now if something could be done?"

"Is that what you said to your sister about your dying nephew?"

Indi gasped.

"Did you?"

She shook her head, reminding herself that people dealt with grief differently. Todd's anger had nothing to do with her. He was just lashing out at the injustice of it all.

She knew exactly how he felt.

"I'm just trying to prepare you," she said softly.

"Well, congratulations. You're doing a hell of a job."

"Todd—"

He started to walk away. Indi told herself to let him go. He needed to come to terms with the truth, and no amount of arguing would help him to do that.

But she couldn't let him go.

"Todd," she called out.

He ignored her. She darted after him because she suddenly realized that *this time,* she didn't want to go through losing a child all on her own.

CHAPTER EIGHTEEN

"TODD," she called again.

He kept on walking.

"Don't ignore me," she ordered, catching up to him.

"What?" he snapped, knowing he was being an ass, unable to stop himself.

"We need to talk."

"No, we don't." Because he wanted to go back to Benjamin, pick the kid up and hug him to him and tell him everything would be all right.

"Damn it," he cursed, a part of him wishing he'd just stuck to driving cars. Life had been so much simpler then. The only person he had cared about keeping alive was himself. Nothing else mattered.

"It's okay," Indi said, seeming to read his mind. And this time, it was she who took his hand, she who gave him a conciliatory squeeze, she who looked imploringly into his eyes. "It's okay to be angry. I understand."

His hand went slack. He hadn't even realized he'd clenched her back.

"I don't think I can do this," he muttered.

"I never think I can, either."

And then she did something he would have never expected. She slipped into his arms. He stood there, his arms slack. And then he jerked her to him. He wrapped his limbs around her so tight he expected her to complain. She didn't. He felt some of the tension ebb out of him.

"Thank you," he said, although he had no idea what he was thanking her for.

"No problem," she said.

Maybe he was just grateful that she was there. Comforting him. Because that's what she did. She tried to prop up his spirits with her soul. He needed that. Needed other things, too. But that could wait. If it was meant to be at all, he admitted, because right then and there all he really wanted was to hold her. He rested his head against the top of her head. The silky strands felt smooth against his cheek. Her hair smelled like a warm summer day, her body felt as hot as one.

She leaned back and all at once her eyes grew serious. "This won't be easy, Todd," she said, glancing at Benjamin. "It'll be the toughest thing you've ever had to go through. Are you ready?"

He nodded. "I think so." *With your help,* he thought.

She started to move away, but he stopped her. "Stay with me."

He saw her search his eyes. He realized she thought he meant something else. "I mean, go out on my boat with me," he clarified. "It's primed and ready after taking the kids out today. All we'd have to do is grab some cold cuts from the cafeteria. We could eat out on the lake. Watch the sun go down."

Emotions played over her face. Her head turned for a moment. She stared out at the lake.

"We could be back before lights-out," he added.

"I don't think so."

"I'll tell Benjamin if you say no. You know how disappointed he'll be."

He heard her huff in exasperation, but a tiny smile crossed her face. "Benjamin might want to go with us."

"Then let's ask."

That brightened her spirits. Todd's insides did something funny at the pleasure that filled her eyes.

Too bad Benjamin turned them down.

Although in hindsight, Todd wasn't really surprised. It was obvious the kid hoped the two of them would get together. He might be ten, but he knew what a third wheel was.

"You guys go on without me," he said. "Lex and I will stay here."

The dog stood up when he heard his name, his snorts getting louder when he tried to lick Benjamin's hand. And when he couldn't reach the object of his adoration, he settled on the sides of Benjamin's chair.

"Hey, stop that," Benjamin said. "It'll rust."

They wheeled Benjamin back to his cabin where he quickly collapsed into bed, Lex trying to jump into bed with him. Todd and Indi helped the dog up. The cabin had four beds, but they were all empty. Most of the kids were at dinner, so Indi knew he'd be able to rest at least for an hour or so.

"So," he asked when they were alone again, "Do you want to go?"

The sun hadn't set yet, but it was fading fast—this time of year it always did—and so while Todd knew his way around the lake, he wanted to get going.

"I don't know," she said reluctantly.

"Indi," he said softly. "He'll be all right. It's only for a few hours."

"I know. It's just that...I'm not so certain we should do this."

"Do what? We're just going for a boat ride."

But was that really all? Indi could feel tension building within her, a tension that had nothing to do with Benjamin, she was startled to realize.

"Todd," she said softly.

"Come on," he said. "We both need this."

"Need what?" Because she thought he meant… But no.

"Time away," he said. "Time to ourselves."

Yes, they did, she admitted.

"Just for an hour or so," he added. And against her better judgment, she agreed.

Todd rushed her along. They went to the cafeteria where they selected cold cuts and some bread, then dashed over to the dock. The jetty stood at the end of a peninsula. It wasn't a big dock, nothing more than a collection of two-by-fours nailed together with pieces of foam nailed to the bottom to keep it afloat, but it worked. His boat sat on the right, lines at both the bow and stern keeping it close. No tarp covered the interior, not like the last time he'd taken her out and so it was a simple matter of untying the lines, which Indi helped him do.

"You ready?" Todd asked after climbing aboard. The wheel was to the right, a recessed hatchway in the middle that led to a tiny living area down below. He quickly sat down.

"I suppose," she said with an attempt at a smile.

"Relax. Believe me, you'll feel better once we're out on the lake."

She wouldn't look at him, and Todd would have

to have been born blind not to notice how uncomfortable she looked. Did she feel the tension, too? The slow burn that seemed to coil between them?

He forced his gaze away. The boat's engine roared to life. Water gurgled off the stern. Indi began pulling the rubber bumpers inside.

So she remembered from last time. Good for her, Todd thought. How many weeks ago was that? Four? Five. He hadn't even qualified for the championship yet.

"Better hold on."

She knew him well enough by now to instantly take a seat. Todd almost laughed, the first time he'd felt like doing so in ages. He gunned the engine.

"Todd," she cried, because, even prepared, she tipped back.

"I told you to hang on," he cried.

Speed was good. Speed made him forget. Plus, a couple of the kids playing near the shoreline cried out their approval. Todd could hear them hoot and holler over the rush of water against his bow.

Wind tore at his eyes. Flecks of moisture stung his face. He didn't care. When he glanced back, he saw that Indi didn't, either. She had her eyes closed, her face tilted toward the sun's remaining rays.

He turned the boat. The horizon tipped. He leaned sideways, enjoying the way the boat responded to his touch. The fiberglass hull slapped the water, jarring his body. The shore slid by, faster and faster, then faster still. The trees that dotted Lake Norman's pebbled beaches slipped farther away. He didn't know where they were going, didn't think Indi cared, either. All he knew was that the cool autumn air soothed his troubled soul. It also helped ease the tightening in his groin.

He'd have kept going for miles if the setting sun hadn't stopped him. This, he wanted Indi to see.

"Look," he said after cutting the engine. He pointed.

Indi followed the direction of his finger. She gasped.

Water and sky seemed to blend into each other—as if the sun had melted them and they all oozed together. Lake Norman reflected the colors. Or maybe the sky reflected the color of the water. It almost appeared that way. Over everything—their boat, the water, the shoreline not too far away—a neon orange set everything aglow.

"It's my favorite time of day."

"I can see why," she said.

"It's especially pretty when viewed from here," he added.

The boat gently swayed. Their wake caught up to them and caused it to rock even more. Indi and Todd simply stared at the horizon, the two of them watching as orange turned to red, red to gold, the three colors fading until all that remained was a cool gray sky that was already dotted with stars.

"And here I thought you had to go to the beach to see a sunset like this."

"You could see it every day if you lived here."

She glanced over at him.

Was that what he wanted, he wondered, staring into her eyes. For her to be with him?

Yes, he admitted. He wasn't a fool, and he knew Indi was special. A heart as big as hers would be a precious gift to hold.

"Where is your house from here?" she asked, deftly changing the subject.

"Way over there," he said, pointing to the east. "We're in Iredell County. My home is in Mecklenburg County—in Huntersville."

"It looks the same," she said, staring at the shoreline.

He nodded. "If you don't know the lake, you could get lost out here, that's for sure. But the lake is shaped like a leaf with the tip pointing north. So as long as you head either north or south, it's hard to get lost. Fortunately, this boat is equipped with GPS."

"Really?"

"And a refrigerator. And a stereo system." And a

few other things down below. Such as a bed. But he didn't mention that.

"All the comforts of home," she mused.

"Do you want some wine?"

"No, thanks," she said. "It'll make me sleepy."

Relaxed was good. Relaxed meant she might not mind if he kissed her.

Todd. For God's sake, get your mind out of the gutter. This isn't the time or place to make a move on Indi.

"How about a soda?"

That she took, along with the cold cuts they'd packed, although Todd noticed she didn't appear very hungry. He could understand why. He didn't have much of appetite himself.

"It's getting cold," he said after he saw her shiver.

"I should have brought a jacket."

"I think there's one down below. Let me go get it for you."

"No, that's okay. I can find it. It's down here, right?" she said, sliding past him and opening the door to the tiny cabin below.

"Yeah, but the closet's kind of hard to find if you don't know where it is," he said, starting to follow her and then stopping himself. He shouldn't go down with her.

"Where's the light switch?" she asked.

"On the right," he answered, swiveling in his chair and scrubbing a hand over his face. Cripes. What was with him? All of a sudden he couldn't get the image of Indi in his bed off his mind.

"Oh, look," she said. "How cute. Your bedspread looks like your race car."

"I didn't buy that," he said. "The boat was a gift from one of my sponsors."

"Some sponsor," she muttered. And then louder, "Where's the closet?"

"It's on the right."

"I can't find it.

"Just come on out. I'll get it for you."

"You even have a bathroom in here," she mumbled next. "What does a race boat need with a bathroom?"

"It's not a race boat," Todd said.

Indi jumped.

Todd stood behind her.

"Some Scarabs are built to race, but this one isn't. It's the luxury version. Sort of like a Ferrari compared to an F1 car. The closet's over here," he said, leaning toward her and reaching behind her.

She couldn't look at him.

"Here," he said a second later, handing her a sweat jacket.

"You didn't have to get it for me," she said,

taking a deep breath. The interior was teak, the lighting low, but she could still see into his eyes, still spot the intensity.

He must look like that when he races.

"I, ah…" Her suddenly sluggish mind struggled for words. "I could have gotten it myself."

"I wanted to get it for you."

"Thanks," she said, ducking her head at the same time she grabbed the jacket.

She caught his hand instead.

She glanced up in surprise. She told herself to move, but the strength of his gaze held her down. She couldn't breathe, the thump of her heart against her chest so hard she wondered if he could hear it.

"Todd, I—"

"Don't," he said softly. "Don't say anything." His head began to drop. "We always seem to ruin moments like this."

Yes, but that was intentional, she wanted to say. He'd been right. It was how she kept men at bay. She didn't want any emotional entanglements. She didn't have enough of herself to go around.

He kissed her.

The boat must have rocked, or perhaps her world tilted. Her knees lost all their strength.

"Todd," she tried to say, but he pressed her to him, his lips hard yet surprisingly gentle. And his touch made her whole body tremble. All he did was place his lips against her own. But that was all it took. She weakened even more. He must have sensed that because he held her up, but only for a moment, because in the next instant she sank toward the bed.

Had he done that? Or her?

She didn't know, didn't care. For once in her life she wanted to be impulsive. She wanted to forget for a moment that the world was a scary place, and that back at camp—

Todd came into focus, Indi realizing she'd closed her eyes somewhere along the way.

"I'm going to kiss you, Indi, like you've never been kissed before."

His hand rested near her side lightly, but it felt like a ten-pound weight. Her abdomen felt tense, her whole body heavy. A sensation she didn't recognize at first pulsed through her body.

Desire.

"But I've got to warn you," he said, his focus darting between her eyes and her lips. "If you let me kiss you, I can't promise I'm going to stop."

She didn't want him to stop. She wanted…

She wanted…

"Kiss me," she said softly.

Because she just *wanted*.

CHAPTER NINETEEN

TODD WASTED no time. He feared she might pull away. He feared she might change her mind, so when she opened her mouth, he pounced.

And nearly groaned aloud.

He could taste her. Could feel her soft tongue against his own. But more than that.

She kissed him back.

For the first time she answered his thrusts with jabs of her own, the tip of her tongue entwining with his own and just about causing him to groan.

He brushed a rib with his thumb, felt her arch against him in response.

Yes.

He lifted his hand higher, gently stroked the spot beneath the swell of her right breast.

This time she moaned.

Their kiss grew more desperate. Todd knew if he didn't stop soon there'd be no turning back. He'd

warned her of that, but still a part of him hesitated.
He pulled his lips away.

"Indi," he warned.

She wiggled against him, pressed the center of
herself against him. There…right there, the sweet
spot that made it *his* turn to moan.

"Touch me," she ordered.

He needed no second invitation. She arched
against him again and turned her head sideways. He
kissed the side of her throat, sucked in the taste of
her sweet flesh. A mark would be left there, but he
didn't care. It would be proof positive that this was
no casual union. This would be an experience unlike
any he'd experienced before.

This would be his first time with Indi.

HE WOKE UP LATER, much later. Sometime after their
first time together he'd found a spot and dropped
anchor. He'd called the camp and told them they
were staying out longer than anticipated and not to
worry. Then he'd gone back to Indi's arms.

He'd known she'd be a zealous lover. No woman
could give herself to things like Indi did and not be
passionate in other areas of her life. But the fervor
of their union took even him by surprise.

He lay there, Indi sleeping in his arms, her naked
body pressed up against his own. Something had

woken him, although he didn't know what. He'd left the door to the tiny cabin open and a cool breeze washed over them both. Perhaps that's what had disturbed their sleep.

He smiled, pulled her closer to him. Her head rested beneath his chin, her hair tickling her nose. He'd never cuddled with a woman before. Usually sex was a means to an end. Not this time.

No.

Not this time.

Her shoulders shook. He tensed, realizing in an instant what it was that woke him. She cried.

"Indi," he said gently, tipping up on an elbow. "What is it?"

She gasped in a sob. He tenderly turned her toward him. Though the only light in the cabin came from the running lights near the buoy, he could still look into her eyes. Tears pooled near the rim of her bottom lashes.

"Is it us?" he asked softly. "Do you regret what just happened?"

She shook her head.

Todd felt relief wash through him. "Then what is it?"

He watched her swallow, heard her suck in a breath. "I…can't," she gasped. "I just *can't*…."

He waited, swiped a stray lock of hair from her mouth. "Can't what?" he prompted.

"I can't stand to lose another one."

His throat tightened because at last he understood what she meant. "I don't want to lose Benjamin, either."

She buried her head in his arms. He held her so tight he worried she couldn't breathe. But she didn't seem to mind, she just cried harder. His own eyes grew hot, his cheek nestled against her hair. He would do anything for this woman, he realized. Anything at all.

"Sorry," he heard her mumble.

"Don't be," he said, kissing her silky strands. "You're due a breakdown."

"I bet this is the first time you've moved a woman to tears."

And there she went trying to make a joke. He loved that about her. Loved her passion and her zeal for life. He loved that she'd never cared about who he was. He might have known her for just a few weeks, but she'd taught him something completely unexpected. She had taught him there was more to life than racing.

"You go ahead and cry," he said softly. "Cry all you want."

She did, Todd thinking she must have had years of tears stored inside.

"I'm such a wreck," she said a long time later.

"No. What you *are* is human."

She looked into his eyes. Todd's heart slipped further away from the matrimonial market when he caught sight of Indi's misery. Could any other woman on the planet care as much as she did?

"I've never broken down like that."

"Obviously, you needed to."

She smiled, and his heart tipped right off the edge. "I can't help but think this must be a first for you."

She had no idea.

"Let me hold you for a while."

She bit her lip and shook her head. "Not now," she said, reaching up and pulling him toward her.

Todd went willingly. When it came to Indi, he'd never been able to resist.

THIS TIME THEY BOTH WOKE to the sound of a cell phone ringing. Todd was the first to sit up, his hand reaching out and grabbing it.

"Hello," he said groggily, and glanced out the window, which revealed it was early morning.

"Todd, it's Linda."

He snapped instantly awake. "What is it? What's wrong?"

He heard her sniffle. His heart started to pound even more. "They took Benjamin to the hospital this morning."

"What happened?"

By now Indi was sitting up, too. He watched her swipe her hair out of her face, her eyes searching his face for hints as to the news.

It wasn't good.

"He started bleeding last night. That's happened before. He's on so much medication his blood doesn't clot like it's supposed to. But last night Lex scratched him. Nobody thought it a big deal. But it wouldn't stop bleeding. The doctors on staff tried to control it, but when nothing worked they began to suspect something more was wrong."

"What'd they find out?"

"They ran tests this morning. Todd, his blood counts are off the charts. Of course, we knew they weren't good, but he's deteriorated so quickly." He heard more sniffs, knew Linda fought for control.

"We'll be right there."

"I didn't want to interrupt you," she sniffed. "I really didn't. You and Indi deserve some time together, but Benjamin wants to see you. Todd, he's so scared…."

"We'll head straight for my house," Todd said, thinking out loud. "It'll be faster than driving all the way around the lake. We can be there in less than an hour. Tell Benjamin we're on our way."

"I'll tell him," was all Linda said, but the words were barely audible.

"What's wrong?" Indi asked when he snapped the phone closed.

"Benjamin's in the hospital," he said, bending down and trying to find his pants.

"I figured that much," Indi said, getting dressed, too. "What's wrong with him?"

"Linda said his blood work is off the charts. What does that mean?" *Damn it.* Where was his shirt?

"His counts must be down," she said, going into clinical mode. He could tell. The face that'd been so full of passion last night looked as blank as a whiteboard.

"But they just checked all that before he left," Todd said, finding his shirt under the tussled covers and pulling it on. "How can he deteriorate so quickly?"

"Easy," Indi said, reaching up and pulling her hair back. She twisted it into a knot somehow, one with a ponytail hanging out the middle. "Some of the inhibitors he's on could have stopped working. His body might have built up a resistance. Infection is a common side effect."

"Linda said last night Lex scratched him."

"Did he bleed?"

"Linda mentioned that he did, but now I'm worried about infection."

"Bleeding is another sign his chronic myelogenous leukemia has gone into the blast crisis phase."

"Blast crisis?"

She nodded, the look in her eyes grim. "It's the final and most serious phase of the disease."

Todd bolted through the doorway and out into the cool gray morning. Chill air hit him square in the face.

It didn't help.

He took deep breaths, told himself he needed to calm down if he were to get them safely to his home. His boat could do upward of a hundred miles per hour, far faster than he could ever drive on city streets. Plus, there were no traffic lights.

"Sit down and hold on," he ordered.

It took him precious minutes to pull up anchor, and then a few more to stow it properly. By the time he twisted the key, his hands shook. Twin V-8s roared to life. It was still early morning and so a gauzelike mist hung over the surface of the lake. But he could see the shore. That was all that mattered.

He glanced down at the gas gauge. Good to go there, too. He'd have just enough to reach his house.

He hoped.

With one last glance to ensure Indi was sitting— she was—he jammed the throttle forward, nearly pitching himself out of his seat.

The cold air felt like ice crystals the faster they flew. And they flew. He made sure of it, a rooster tail shooting out from the back of the boat that was easily thirty feet long.

"Are you sure we shouldn't go back to camp?" she called out.

"Not this time of morning. Traffic on 77 will be horrible. If we head straight for my house in Huntersville, we can avoid the freeway altogether."

His eyes narrowed. His peripheral vision tunneled. The smooth water and pewter sky made it easier to focus. All he had to do was make sure he kept the shoreline parallel with the boat. He'd spent hours out here over the years and that time stood him in good stead. He reached the southern portion of the lake in record time. No way they could have made it that fast in a car. No way.

He rounded a peninsula, blew past the nuclear plant powered by the Cowans Ford Dam and spotted his home on the eastern edge of the lake less than five minutes later.

"Isn't your car back at the camp?" she asked when he slowed down.

"I have other cars."

It took them far too long to tie the boat off—at least to Todd's mind—the two of them making a dash toward his garage at such a rate of speed he could hear the dock rocking in their wake. Fortunately, he had a house key on his key ring or else he didn't know what they'd have done. Smashed a window maybe. That would have worked, he thought, letting them in a second later. He was in the mood to break something.

They made it to the garage in record time, Indi hardly sparing a glance at the cherry-red Mustang Cobra parked in his garage.

"How far to the hospital?" she asked, sliding into the black leather seat next to him.

"Fifteen, maybe twenty minutes. Depends on traffic."

He made it in a little over ten. Todd had no doubt there was an APB out on him by the time he arrived. He didn't care. All he cared about was finding Benjamin in the multistory hospital.

That turned out to be harder than anticipated. They were told to go to the Emergency Room. Only when they arrived there, they were told Benjamin had been moved. A frustrated phone call later and Linda informed them that Benjamin was in the pediatric ward's ICU. She met them at the elevator.

"How is he?" Indi asked immediately.

Linda, her face as pale as bone china, shook her head. "Not good," she said softly, her eyes rimmed with unshed tears. "They've been giving him blood. Pumping him full of coagulants. Doing their best to get the bleeding to stop."

Todd turned away.

"Can we see him?"

"They're bandaging him up right now. The spot where they inserted the IV, it keeps bleeding and bleeding…"

He hadn't realized he'd shut his eyes until he heard Indi's gentle shushing sounds and the soft cries of Linda's sobs. When he opened his eyes, the roomed seemed to tilt. Todd, a man who'd wrecked in cars at over 180 miles per hour and walked away, suddenly felt like passing out. He had to use the wall next to the elevator bank for support.

"Is Art here?" Indi asked.

When he turned around it was to see Linda nod her head, Indi's hands on Linda's upper arms. "He's in with Benjamin."

"We'll just wait until it's a good time for us to go in," Indi said.

How did she do it? Todd wondered. How did she keep it so together?

"Indi," Linda said, wiping at her eyes. "When you go in to see him, don't let him see…" She took a deep, shuddery breath. "Don't let him see your concern. I thought he was…" She took another breath. "I thought he was ready for this. He's been so brave. But, Indi, suddenly he's very scared."

And Todd had to turn away again because the

pain in Linda's eyes, the agony he heard in that one word—*scared*—was too much for him to bear.

"I need some fresh air," he said, jabbing at the elevator button as if the more he pushed it, the faster it would come and take him away.

Indi was too busy soothing Linda to give him much of a response. *Go on,* she silently mouthed.

Yeah, he'd do that because if he didn't, he might just throw up. Unlike Indi. She looked as serene as a Madonna.

Todd realized in that instant that he'd never be half good at this. God help him, he didn't *want* to be good at this at all.

BLACK FLAG

CHAPTER TWENTY

THEY ENDED UP having to wait hours before they were allowed to see Benjamin. Indi spent the morning canceling their appointments. The team from *Miracles* offered to come to the hospital for moral support, but Indi could tell Todd was in no shape to shake hands. That only became more obvious when they learned that Benjamin had been taken in for a full-body scan. The resulting diagnosis looked grim. Tiny tumors were now in Benjamin's liver.

"So that's it then?" Todd asked. "This is the beginning of the end."

Indi had to swallow before answering. "Unless a miracle happens."

She'd known he wouldn't take the news well. Ever since they'd arrived he'd looked about ready to pass out. For a man with olive skin, he had next to no color.

"Have we done everything we can do?" he asked.

Indi bit her lip for a second, then said, "We can pray."

They did that, too. But no amount of begging could stave off Benjamin's worsening condition. Indi knew from experience that he had less than a month to live, more than likely less than that.

"You can go in and see him now," one of the pediatric nurses said.

They both looked up from their position on one of two plush couches. The waiting room was typical of hospitals, Indi thought. Low lighting, natural beige carpet, box of tissues on the corner table out of the way for those people who suffered emotional breakdowns.

"Indi."

She found herself having to crane her neck back because Todd had stood up while she'd been taking stock of their surroundings.

"Oh, sorry," she said, smoothing back her hair. It'd come loose from the knot she'd tied it in. Maybe she should go to the bathroom and fix it before...

"Indi."

She jerked up. What the heck was wrong with her? She felt odd. Almost anxious. But that wasn't possible. She always held it together when visiting patients and their families. It was one of the things she was good at—keeping her cool. Staving off emotions. Being the shoulder to cry on.

"Let's go," she said as if he'd been the one

holding things up, not her. She walked away before he could see that her hands shook.

It wasn't a long walk, but it felt like it. Square, fluorescent fixtures lit the way, but Indi's vision seemed to darken around the edges the closer they got to Benjamin's room. A turn to the left here, another corridor, and all too soon the nurse said, "Go on in," in a soft voice.

"Knock-knock," Indi said, her standard greeting when entering a room.

This time, her voice came out as nothing more than a scratch.

"Come in," Linda said softly.

Indi looked toward the bed, only to immediately look away. She couldn't. Oh, Lord…she thought for a moment she couldn't breathe.

"Todd," a little voice said over the sound of the automatic blood-pressure machine. "You came." The words barely audible.

"Been here all day, buddy," Todd said, using the hand sanitizer without being told. Trouble was, Benjamin didn't have a free hand to clasp. Both hands were bandaged. One had an IV in it and one was resting atop a light blue blanket, bandaged from Lex's scratch. The ball cap he always seemed to wear had been removed, too, the hairless scalp a brazen reminder of what the child had been through.

Indi could see the horror on Todd's face, as well as the question he wanted to ask, but he couldn't ask because Benjamin would hear.

How had he regressed so quickly?

"All day?" Benjamin said, looking around the room.

Art, Benjamin's dad, stood silently in a corner. Indi realized he and Todd had never met.

"Todd," she said, having to clear her throat before she spoke. "Have you met Benjamin's dad?"

"Ah, no," he said softly, his own voice sounding hoarse. "Nice to meet you, Mr. Koch."

"Heard a lot about you," the tall man said, his dark hair and eyes making him look like he could be Todd's brother.

"And I've heard a lot about you," Todd echoed, his eyes shifting back to the bed. She saw him glance at Benjamin's arm, the one with the bandage on it, then up at the IV. She couldn't be certain, but she thought he paled.

"Sorry…had…to leave," Benjamin said.

"Hey, don't worry about it," Todd said. "You'll be back."

"No," Benjamin said, his eyes shooting to his mother's. "I don't think so."

Todd seemed to sense that the time for half-truths was over. He looked away without saying a word.

Indi felt her stomach begin to burn. The shaking in her hands seemed to worsen. She crossed her arms to hide it from the room's occupants.

"Sleepy," Benjamin said.

"You look tired, buddy," Todd said. "Maybe we should come back tomorrow."

"'Morrow's Thursday."

"I know," Todd said. "And I can be here all day if you want."

"No, ya can't."

"Actually, I can," Todd said. "I had Jen cancel all my plans."

"Practice," Benjamin said.

"Someone else can do that for me."

Benjamin shook his head. Indi knew what the effort must have cost him. She saw the boy grit his teeth, saw him try to sit up a bit. "Can't do that," he said.

"Benj," Todd said. "It's no big deal if someone else practices my car. In fact, they're bringing some new guy in. An open-wheel star—Brandon something or other—to do it for me. It's totally cool."

"No," Benjamin said, sounding as firm as a desperately ill child could sound. "You have to."

"Benjamin—"

"Maybe we could discuss this later," Indi said. She'd caught Linda and Art exchanging concerned glances.

"Todd, please," a little voice said. "Don't let someone else…" He blinked a few times, seemed to have to struggle to stay awake.

"Morphine," Linda said. "His spleen is swollen and it's causing him some pain."

Indi should have known. From here on out the child would be injected with a mix of painkillers and nausea medicine that would knock him for a loop.

The pain in her stomach worsened. She wondered if she were coming down with something. That would explain the shaking hands, too.

"Don't let someone else," Benjamin tried again, his eyes opening wide for a moment in a vain attempt to stay alert. "*You* drive," he managed to get out.

"But, buddy. If I do that, I'll miss out on spending time with you."

Benjamin's glassy eyes hardened. "Don't care." His lids fluttered for a second. "Championship," he said. "Important…you…win."

"Not to me," Todd said, moving closer to Benjamin's bedside. He reached out and stroked Benjamin's forehead. "Not to me," he said softly.

Benjamin looked as if he dozed off for a moment. All at once his little body jerked. Indi saw Linda flinch then start to move toward him. But it was nothing more than the child forcing himself awake, his eyes immediately moving to Todd's.

"Is to me," Benjamin said softly. "It is to me."

And the words were so clear, they had such a ring of truth to them, Indi knew Todd couldn't help but be moved.

"Is it really?" he asked.

All Benjamin could manage was a nod before his eyes closed again.

"Then it is to me, too," Todd whispered.

"YOU DON'T HAVE TO practice your car tomorrow if you don't want to," Indi told him later on. They were in the patient waiting room again, Todd standing, Indi sitting. "He's so full of medication he'll never know the difference."

Todd turned toward her. Behind him the Charlotte skyline could be seen through tinted glass. Todd stood in a patch of sunlight that surrounded his feet and crept up his legs. It was still early afternoon, but it felt as if they'd been there for hours.

"Really, Todd," she said, getting up and placing a hand against his arm. She felt better now that they were out of Benjamin's room. Funny. She hadn't been that close to an anxiety attack in ages. She really *must* be coming down with something.

"How much longer does he have?" Todd asked, his mouth barely moving because he fought so hard to contain his emotions.

"I don't know," she said, although she suspected she knew the answer. "These things are hard to predict."

"Don't give me that crap," Todd said. "You've been through this hundreds of times before. Now give me the honest truth. How much time?"

Her own temper immediately flared to life at the harshness of his words. For a second there she felt as if she spoke to the Todd of old. But then she reminded herself that this was a first for him. He'd never lost anybody close to him. "Two weeks," she said softly. "Three weeks tops."

"Damn."

"He'll be so out of it in another week or two, you could drive a golf cart around the track and he probably wouldn't notice."

"Then I'll have to win this weekend so he can watch me do that."

"Todd, he really won't know what day it is. The morphine, it'll knock him for a loop, especially at the dosage he's on."

"*I'll* know," Todd said.

"Wouldn't you like to spend time with him? Quality time? Next week his condition will worsen. He'll more than likely slip in and out of consciousness."

"Damn," he said again, louder. "I don't know how you do this, how you can sound so…detached."

"I'm just trying to tell it like it is."

"And I'm telling you I'm racing this weekend because no matter what you *think* you know, that child will know if I'm not in my car this weekend. He's a race fan. As sick as he is, as doped up as he is, deep inside he's still my number-one fan."

She heard his voice crack and reached out to console him, but he turned away before she could touch him.

"Todd," she said softly, finding it hard to believe that just last night he'd been touching her tenderly, holding her, comforting *her.* "Please—"

"No," he said, spinning back around to face her. His eyes had a sheen of wetness to them, but she noticed he didn't let the tears fall. "I'm not going to listen to your clinical reasons as to why I should park my car for the weekend."

"I wasn't trying to be clinical. I'm just saying you might want to spend some time with Benjamin while he's still lucid. When he passes—"

"No," Todd yelled in horror, and Indi flinched at the near animalistic sound of that cry. "He's not going to die. Not yet. Not ever."

She debated what to say, but in the end truth won out. "Todd, be realistic."

He took a step toward her. "You want realistic," he said. "I'll show you realistic. I'll show you that the will to survive can sometimes hinge on something as stupid as a car race. And that the inner spirit can heal a soul just as effectively as medicine."

"Not in this case."

"Oh, yeah?" he asked. "Just watch what happens when I win this weekend. Hell, when I win all six of the next races—"

"Todd, please," she said, trying to calm him down. "That's impossible. We need to be realistic—"

"That *is* realistic, damn it. I'm going to kick ass over the next few weekends. Not because I care about the championship, but because of what it will do for Benjamin."

"It won't do anything."

His face flushed. It seemed impossible to believe this was the same man who'd held her so tenderly. "You watch."

"Todd, *please*," she tried again.

But he was already gone.

CHAPTER TWENTY-ONE

HE DROVE LIKE A MANIAC all the way home. He didn't care that he'd left Indi behind. He didn't care that he was more than likely ruining what precious little chance they had at a relationship by yelling the way he had. He didn't care about anything other than proving Indi wrong. Proving them all wrong.

Benjamin would *not* die.

And the first step toward proving that was to win Saturday's race.

He put a call into Jen, told her to get a hold of the camp and fill them in. He hated to bail out on them, but he was in no mood to play happy in front of a bunch of kids. Next he called Linda from his cell phone. The last thing he wanted was for Benjamin to think he'd abandoned him, but Todd refused to visit him while Indi was around. Negativity was a deal breaker. He refused to put up with it.

If Linda seemed surprised by Todd's wishes to

visit her son when Indi wasn't around, she didn't let him hear it.

The last thing he did was put a call into one of the specialists he'd flown out to visit Benjamin. The man thought Benjamin might be a perfect candidate for a clinical trial currently underway but that they wouldn't know for certain until his DNA was tested. Apparently, the medication was the next line of defense for cancer treatment wherein they didn't fight the actual disease, but they treated the genetic abnormality that caused the leukemia. Todd didn't pretend to understand how it all worked; he just knew Benjamin needed to be in on the doctor's study.

Pronto.

He called him first thing upon arriving home, the day having turned into one of those stunning fall days that made a person think nothing could be wrong with the world. How far from the truth *that* was.

"I'm sorry, he's in a meeting," a woman said when Todd explained who he was.

"Tell him Todd Peters called, and that I need to know if that little boy he tested will work for the clinical trial he's overseeing."

"Got it," the woman said, the two words sounding uppity even to Todd. She hung up in his ear.

"Damn," he muttered, staring at the phone.

He turned away, wrenched open the door to his back patio and flung himself against the rail that separated the concrete flagstones from his yard.

His boat stood where he and Indi had left it what seemed like a lifetime ago. He'd have to put the rubber bumpers out sooner or later. They had been in such a hurry this morning he'd skipped it.

"Todd."

He must have jumped a foot. "Kristen, you scared me."

And then Lex came at him, the dog rushing between Kristen's legs and nearly toppling her in the process.

"Hey there, Lex," Todd said, squatting down and scratching behind his mouth so that his jowls flapped around.

"He sure does love you," Kristen said.

Todd nodded. "I've gotten pretty fond of the little bugger, too."

"I can see that."

"Thanks for bringing him by. I'm sure Jen appreciated one less thing to worry about."

"Yeah, you've got her running pretty hard canceling engagements and what not."

Todd stood up, Lex dancing around his feet and still begging for attention.

"She understands."

"Yes, she does," Kristen said, stepping onto the patio, the hair that'd been mouse-blond when he'd first met her now streaked with gold. "I'm sorry," she said. "I know how much the boy means to you."

"Yeah," he said, turning toward the rail. "Sometimes I wonder why I got involved."

She came forward, placing a hand on his arm. "Because Todd Peters, one of NASCAR's least favorite drivers, thanks to his rather rough driving skills, is really a man with a huge heart."

"Yeah…maybe so."

"Todd," Kristen said, her thumb stroking his arm. "It's okay to be upset."

He clenched the rail, the metal bar digging into his palms. It was cold, as chill as the freeze settling around his heart. "I'm going to win the race this weekend, Kristen."

"I know you will."

How ironic that Kristen believed him and not Indi.

"And the next weekend, too," he added.

"And we'll do everything we can to help you," she said without missing a beat.

His vision grew white, he stared out at the lake so long. "And the week after that."

"If you believe it can happen, so will the rest of the team," she said.

"I believe."

"Of course you do. That's what heroes do, fulfill the dreams of others."

"I'm not a hero."

"Yes, you are," she said. "To that little boy you're like Superman."

He tried to turn away. She wouldn't let him.

"To *millions* of kids you're like Superman, but even Superman could only help one person at a time. You will, too."

"I won't let him die."

"No," she said. "Of course not."

And somehow he found himself in her arms. There was nothing sexual about their embrace. It was the hug of two friends trying to comfort each other. And as Todd wrapped his arms around Kristen's slight form, he wished with all his heart it was Indi he held instead.

"We're here for you, Todd," Kristen said softly. "The whole team is behind you."

His nose plugged with unshed tears. "Thanks."

"No, *thank you,*" she said softly. "You've done us all proud, Todd. We're all so terribly proud of you."

"Just do what you can to help me win, Kristen. That's all I ask of you."

"You got it," she said, squeezing his arms at the same time she leaned back. "You got it."

RACE DAY DAWNED as stunningly clear and warm as the day Benjamin was admitted to the hospital. Unseasonably warm, the weatherman called it.

Perfect weather for kicking ass.

The garage was full of its usual prerace visitors. Charlotte seemed to be more crowded than other tracks. Todd suspected that had more to do with the track being located in the heart of race country than anything else. But whatever the reason, it drove him nuts to have to walk through the garage. Every ten feet he was stopped by someone wanting to wish him well.

He didn't need luck. What he *needed* was to get behind the wheel.

"You're due at the driver's meeting in five minutes," Jen said from alongside him.

They were just coming back from an autograph session, one that Todd had almost bailed from, and probably would have if not for Benjamin. Yesterday, when he'd visited Benjamin in the hospital, he'd been reminded that there were other kids out there who wanted to meet him and that Todd shouldn't blow them all off because Benjamin was in the hospital.

And what do you say to that?

Nothing, Todd reminded himself grimly. You did the autograph session and you made sure you spoke kindly to every little kid who showed up, and that you looked their parents in the eye and you told them how lucky they were to have their children, and that they should treat each day—

"Todd!"

"What?" he snapped back, although he had to think hard to remember what he and Jen had been talking about. They were walking back to his hauler and Todd had to work to recall what she'd been saying. Something about a driver's meeting.

"Are you okay with that?"

"Yeah, sure," he said, not having a clue what Jen had just asked.

"Are you sure? Brandon is new to all this and so I'm certain he'd appreciate your showing him around, but I've never met the man before so I'm not certain what to expect."

Oh, crap. What had he just volunteered himself for?

"He's supposed to meet us in the lounge," Jen said, checking around them as if expecting to spot the driver behind a stack of tires.

"Any word from Indi?" The question popped out before Todd could stop it. *What the hell was he doing asking Jen about Indi?*

"No," Jen said, glancing up at him, the ponytail she always seemed to wear hanging over one shoulder. "Sorry, Todd."

"Don't be sorry," he said.

He hadn't called Indi. But in his defense she hadn't phoned him, either. Maybe that was just the way Indi worked. How she closed herself down. Maybe she allowed men to get just *so* close before pushing them away. Maybe he was just the latest in a long string of men who been shut out while she dealt with another child's death.

"Anyway," Jen said. "About Brandon. If you could just take him over to the driver's meeting for now. Show him where it is and all that. We're still trying to find him a PR rep, but until then we're kind of in a bind. None of us expected Mr. Knight to put him in a car so fast so he's certain to feel a bit lost. I'm sure he'd appreciate having an old pro like you take him under his wing."

Somehow Todd doubted it. Drivers had some of the biggest egos around. They didn't need anything or anyone. He ought to know. Once upon a time he used to think like that, too.

"Hey, Dan," Jen said, waving to his crew chief. Dan patted Todd on the back as they walked by.

"Good luck with that one," Dan said, pointing with his clipboard behind him toward the hauler. "I thought you were difficult once upon a time, that was nothing compared to that asshole."

Todd stopped beneath the overhead door that

doubled as a car lift and hung off the back of the big rig. "What do you mean?"

"Brandon Burke," Dan said, running a hand through his graying hair. The color just about matched the metallic silver of the headset that rested on his shoulders. "He's a total putz. And coming from me, you know he's got to be bad."

Dan was one of the most levelheaded crew chiefs around. For him to be so torqued off it must be pretty bad.

"Great," Jen said. "Just great. I'm supposed to help him out until we find someone to rep him."

Dan all but slapped the back of Jen's red polo shirt. "Yeah," he said. "Good luck with that, too."

He sauntered away, Todd watching him with narrowed eyes. Whatever. He had other things to deal with this weekend than an arrogant, egotistical ass, which is what Brandon must be if Dan so instantly despised him.

He turned out to be all that and more.

"So you're the man who's ass I'm going to kick," the guy said the moment Todd and Jen entered the lounge.

"Ah, actually, this is our veteran driver Todd Peters," Jen said, obviously trying to play interference. "And you must be Brandon."

Brandon sat on the couch that ran along the far

wall. But instead of scooting over to make more room, he swung his legs up off the ground, effectively giving them no place to sit.

"Yeah, I'm Brandon," he said, the uniform he wore still bearing the name of his old sponsor. He had sandy-blond hair and sideburns that looked like they belonged to a cast member of the television show *The OC*.

Gimme a break, Todd thought.

"How you doing, old man?" Brandon asked, cocking an eyebrow at Todd.

"I'm fine," Todd said, then promptly turned his back on him.

"Dan's right. This kid's a punk. You can get someone else to show him around," Todd whispered to Jen.

"Todd," Jen said, her eyes imploring. "I'm sure he's just joking."

Todd glanced back at Brandon. The jerk gave him a stare that could turn race fuel into flames.

"Don't bet on it."

"See you later, old man," the guy called as Todd walked from the room.

The whole thing left a bad taste in Todd's mouth, so much so that he was in a rank mood by the time he made it to the driver's meeting.

"Is it true you've got the bad boy of open wheel of racing in your hauler?" Lance Cooper asked, the blond driver giving him his golden-boy smile.

"Don't want to talk about it," Todd said, taking a seat next to him.

Lance's smile faded as other drivers, crew chiefs and team owners settled down around them.

"How's Benjamin?" Lance asked.

"Not good," Todd said.

Lance nodded, scanned the crowd, his red uniform and Todd's blue uniform all but clashing. Their uniforms usually just about matched, but Todd had a different sponsor for this race. *Miracles* was riding on his hood. The car and his uniform a dark blue, his car number painted orange and white. "Sarah and I are going over to visit him tomorrow," Lance said.

"I'm sure he'd like that," Todd said as the NASCAR Event Director called the meeting to order, but before he could start in on his speech, a commotion broke out near the doorway.

"Whoo-ey," Brandon drawled in a mocking Southern accent. "Look at all them roundy-round racers."

"Brandon," someone muttered, Todd recognizing his team owner coming up behind him. And even though Mathew Knight leaned forward everyone in the room heard the "Behave," he all but snarled.

Brandon just smirked, his blue eyes scanning the room. When his gaze fell on Todd, his upper lip actually curled. "Yeah," he said. "I'll do that."

"I see why you don't want to talk about it," Lance leaned over and muttered. "What a charmer."

Other drivers weren't as kind. In fact, the chill in the room when Brandon sat down would have rivaled that of a meat locker.

"Okay then," the president of the speedway said. "Where were we?"

Todd's mood didn't improve much from there. He tried to focus on Benjamin, reminded himself that in the scheme of things, jerks like Brandon mattered about as much as the dead bugs that dotted his Cobra's grill. Still, as he climbed into his car, he found himself surveying the line cars stacked nose to tail in front and behind him. He paused for a second on the doorsill, looking left and right. Out on pit road behind him, someone tested an air wrench, the *bzz-bzz-bzz* such a familiar sound he almost didn't hear it.

"What's the matter?" Dan said.

Todd looked at the grandstands across the track. They were filled to capacity—men, women and children already standing up in excitement.

"Just wishing Benjamin was here."

And wondering what Indi would say if she were here.

"Have a good race," Dan said as he handed him his HANS Device and then his helmet. He leaned into the car as Todd set his headgear aside.

"Thanks, Dan," Todd said, checking his belts. "But we don't need luck for this one. We're winning this race no matter what it takes."

"That's a good attitude to have," Dan said, reaching in and patting him on the shoulder.

"It's the *only* attitude to have," Todd said as Dan did the catches on the window net.

"Hey, where's Brandon starting?" Todd asked the moment he plugged in his radio. He'd been so focused on Benjamin this week he hadn't even paid attention to where everyone else had qualified.

"Believe it or not, he's starting tenth."

Two back from Todd. That was unexpected. A bit of beginner's luck for the rookie.

"Watch him, Todd," Dan said in a low voice, as if Brandon might be listening in. "I don't trust that guy."

"I've dealt with his type before," Todd reminded his crew chief.

"I know, I know. But this guy's got a reputation that would do a rattlesnake proud. Watch out."

"Will do," Todd said.

But he really didn't think he had much to worry about. Drivers like Brandon usually got punted by the tenth lap. After calling everyone a roundy-round racer, Todd expected he'd be out of the race in less than that.

He was wrong.

When the green flag dropped, Todd focused on keeping his nose out of trouble. When a race was as many laps as this one, there was no need to be aggressive right off the bat. That obviously wasn't a principle Brandon Burke subscribed to.

"Guess who's knocking on your door," Dan said on lap twenty-five.

It had been a clean race so far and Todd was in the zone so he had no idea. "Who?"

Cooper? Drake?

"The snake."

Great, Todd thought, checking his mirrors. He couldn't see Brandon, but that wasn't surprising. With the race having been green for so long, the field was pretty strung out.

"What position?"

"Eighth."

And Todd was sitting sixth. Time to put the pedal to the metal out and show Brandon how it was done.

"How many until we pit?"

"Provided there's no cautions, about eight."

"Good," Todd said.

He scanned the track ahead of him. For the last ten laps he'd been feeling his car out, and with green flag pit stops coming up, he had a pretty good idea what needed to be done.

"Okay," Todd said. "Here's what we're going to do. We'll take a turn out of the left rear. Give me a half-a-pound less in the front right and we'll see if we can get this baby to turn."

"You got it," Dan said. "Seven now. Seven laps to go."

The grandstands sped by, the catch fence nothing more than a gray blur on his right. Flashes of color hit his peripheral vision—sponsor banners that hung on the backstretch wall. Individual faces were impossible to pick out at these speeds, but Todd knew the crowd had their eyes upon him.

"All right," Dan said a few laps later. "Three more laps to go now. Brandon just passed the seventh-place car. Try not to let him rattle your cage."

"You really think I should worry?" Todd asked.

"He's got a good car," Dan said, but it was more what Dan *didn't* say that alerted Todd to trouble. Usually Dan would say something flip. The fact that he was all but warning him to keep his cool told Todd a great deal.

"Just let him try me," Todd said, glancing in his mirror. The sun had started to set so it made seeing difficult, what with the glare off the windshield. All he saw were blurs of color that were cars in the distance. But he didn't need to see the jerk. By the time Brandon caught up to him, *everyone* would be ready to pit. The jerk wouldn't have time to catch him.

Or so he thought.

Todd didn't know what setup they'd used in Brandon's car, but it was better than his. The jerk was at his bumper in less than two laps, the familiar Fly For Less logo that was usually on Todd's car glaringly bright.

"One more lap," Dan said. "Leaders will pit in one."

"Inside," Todd's spotter said a second later.

Inside? What?

Brandon had to pit, too. What the hell was he doing challenging him with less than a lap—

Bam.

Todd felt the impact all the way to his toes. His foot actually jammed the accelerator before he lifted. When he glanced in his primary mirror, it was full of bright red bumper.

"That son of a—"

"Still there," Phil, his spotter, said.

Yeah, and trying to push him into the wall.

"We're coming in this lap," Dan said, and Todd could hear the edge of panic in his voice. "Check up, Todd. Brandon's got to come in, too."

He didn't want to check up. Damn it. They could enter pit road two wide.

But in the next instant he knew what Brandon was going to do.

"He's trying to block me."

"What?" Dan said.

"The guy's trying to keep me out an extra lap."

They were headed into Turn Three and Todd knew something had to give…and it sure wouldn't be him.

You wanna play? Fine. We'll play, Todd thought.

They entered the turn. Todd jerked the wheel.

It sounded like two freight trains collided.

His car shuddered. The blue front end jerked right. He held it steady, knowing he risked taking both of them out, but he was too angry to care.

"Still inside," Phil said.

Well, duh. Todd could *hear* that. His left front wheel ground into Brandon's door panel. Then, as suddenly as it started, the noise went away. Brandon had backed off.

Or had he?

The back end of Todd's car lifted.

Son of a—

His car started to skid. It took every ounce of skill he possessed to keep from going into the wall, although how he didn't touch it, he had no idea. His tires hit the debris field near the bottom of the concrete barrier. He felt his back end begin to slide, corrected, then felt it slip the *other* way. Left. Right.

Left. Right. Around Turn Four he zoomed. Cars passed him. He glanced up, looked for the caution light.

No yellow.

Damn it.

"Where am I?" Todd asked, his heart pounding against his uniform.

"You're all right," Dan said in a soothing voice. "Just bring her in."

If he could get there in time. He still clipped along at a good rate. The entrance to pit road came up fast— right at the exit of Turn Four. He checked his mirrors, pointed his nose toward the bottom of the track.

"Inside," Phil said.

"I know I've got people on the inside." Damn it. There were cars all over the place, but he had to make the entrance to pit road or else...

There it is.

He headed straight for it, regardless of who he might bump into along the way.

"Outside *and* inside," his spotter said.

I know. I know, Todd silently answered.

And then there was the cone. He hit the brakes, checked his RPMs.

"Thirty-five hundred," his crew chief cautioned, seeming to read his mind.

I know. I know.

"Here we are," Dan said. "In three…two…one."

Todd spotted his pit, jerked his wheel left. When he skidded to a halt he beat his steering wheel in frustration. Up went the right side, then down. The left was next.

"How does it look?" he asked.

Someone beat on his car with a rubber mallet.

"All things considered, not bad," Dan said.

When Todd glanced left he saw that Dan stood atop the pit box, peering down.

The left side of the car went down.

"Go, go, go," Dan cried, waving his arms in encouragement.

Todd jerked the wheel right, almost taking out another driver. "Where am I?" he asked, dreading the answer.

"You're in eighteenth place."

"Damn." From sixth to eighteenth because of Brandon.

"Just stay calm," Dan said. "Remember, he's our new teammate."

"I'm gonna kill that guy."

"Todd," Dan interjected. "You just stay calm. You've got a good car. You can catch up."

Two laps later, they dropped the green flag. But it was no good. Todd could feel his car's performance had slipped.

"Feels like I've got no bottom end," he told Dan.

"Let the tires wear down," Dan replied. "It'll come to you in a bit."

That remained to be seen.

The laps ticked off. Night fell. The overhead lights turned on. Neon streaks of light skated across his windshield. Todd tried to be patient, but it was hard. He reminded himself that this race was important, not because a win would propel him to the top of the points standing, but because of Benjamin.

He glanced to the right. Opposite the in-car camera strapped to his roll cage, right where a passenger car's glove compartment would normally be, his team had taped a name. Benjamin's name. Todd stretched a hand toward it, would have stroked the black writing if he could have reached it.

To hell with Brandon Burke. Todd had bigger fish to fry.

He focused forward. Beneath his helmet, sweat began to sting his eyes. His shoulders began to ache. He ignored the pain, just concentrated on getting ahead.

"That's the way to do it, buddy," Dan said. "One at a time. Pick your way through the field."

Had he passed some cars? Todd didn't remember doing so, but his vehicle *was* handling better. Much better.

"Where is he?"

"Second," his crew chief said, obviously needing no clarification as to who "he" was. "But he's got some lap traffic coming up. Gonna slow him down."

Good. Because while he ran this race for Benjamin. Scratch that. While he would *win* this race for Benjamin, it would be nice if he could teach that little punk driver a thing or two about stock car racing.

"Caution," Phil said.

The wreck happened behind him, making it easy for Todd to avoid. A good pit stop a few laps later did the near impossible.

It put him in the top five.

"Good job, guys!" he cried as he exited pit road.

"Why, thank you very much," Dan said, and Todd could hear the smile in his voice.

"Where'd I come out?"

"Fourth and sitting pretty," Dan said. "But you're gonna have to work some to pass the cars ahead of you. They've all been posting better ETs than yours."

"Never been afraid of a little hard work," Todd said.

He just wanted to catch Brandon.

Sure, a part of Todd knew it was silly to make that his primary goal. Well, other than win the race. He needed to race clean, not take his fellow teammate out. But it sure would make his day if he could do both.

And so he drove. He drove like he'd never driven before. Usually, he liked his car on the tight side, meaning he liked a little front-end drift into the corner. Today he had to deal with a loose car, his backside sliding all over the place. But that was okay. He remembered his dirt track days, and as he climbed through the field, he wondered if he shouldn't try a loose setup more often.

Damn if he didn't have Brandon in his sight by the time the end of the race neared.

"Fifteen laps to go at the line, buddy," Phil said.

Todd clutched the wheel. They were running out of laps and Brandon was a good five car lengths in front of him. What they needed was a caution, something that would bunch the field up. That didn't happen.

"Ten laps," Phil said. "Brandon just took the lead."

Crap. That was unbelievable given this was his first NASCAR race.

"Time to get it on," Dan encouraged.

The second-place car entered his line of sight. He didn't even know who it was, just focused on the dark blue bumper. It only took one lap for Todd to know he had him. The guy's setup was toast. Two more laps and he'd have him. And right in front of the guy was Brandon.

You're going down.

He passed the blue car like it stood still.

"Keep going, buddy," Dan said, and Todd could tell by the timbre of his crew chief's voice that he thought they had a chance to win.

Todd would have leaned forward had his belts allowed him. One more driver to pick off. Fate worked in his favor because his car tightened up.

"Six laps," Phil said, and he could hear the tension in his spotter's voice.

Fans leaped to their feet. He couldn't see them, but he could *feel* them. The hair on his arms seemed to stand on end.

He caught Brandon with four laps to go.

Todd's wheels had left circular marks on Brandon's door. Night might have fallen, and he might not be right alongside him, but he could still see the perfect ring his rims had left. When he ducked down on the inside, he could see them better.

"Hello," Todd said. "So nice to see you again."

And this time the dude was going *down.*

"Three laps to go."

Todd's car edged ever closer. Just a few feet away now. He could smell Brandon's exhaust. Could hear and see the back end drift free.

Brandon was loose.

Todd knew just the way to make it looser.

His feet hovered over the gas and the brake, one foot near each pedal. He didn't want to touch Brandon, just take the air off his spoiler. At these speeds it wouldn't take much, and the beauty was he didn't have to touch the guy. All he needed to do was stick his car's nose as close as he could... A good driver could actually *hear* the difference. It grew quieter, not a lot, but enough that Todd knew he was in Brandon's draft and that if he shifted the wheel just a fraction...

Brandon's back end broke loose.

Beneath his helmet, Todd smiled.

He nudged the wheel left and right, disturbing the air even more. Brandon got downright squirrelly.

"Two laps," Phil said.

Shoot. He could pass this guy in less than half a lap.

And that's exactly what he did, Todd waiting until the white flag before edging up against Brandon's bumper.

He never touched him.

Todd could have been a complete jerk and sent him into the wall.

But he didn't.

Right at the moment when he could have done it, Todd didn't.

Hero.

Kristen's words came back to him. At home, kids were watching, Benjamin one of them. He couldn't let those kids down.

"Clear," Phil said a few seconds later.

It would have been nice to check up. To watch Brandon have to swerve to avoid missing him this time, maybe even send him into the wall.

He didn't.

But Todd couldn't resist lifting his hand and giving Brandon a piece of his mind. The finger he waved at him was not the one telling him he was number one.

"Welcome to NASCAR," Todd said before stepping on it and leaving Brandon Burke in the dust.

WHITE FLAG

When Drivers Eat Their Wheaties
By Rick Stevenson, Sports Editor

I never listen to drivers when they boast of their bright future. I'm a big proponent of put your money where your mouth is. So when Todd Peters told members of the media at Charlotte that he intends to win at least four of the remaining races left in the Chase, I scoffed. Todd might slowly be edging his way onto my drivers-to-root-for list, but such a prediction seemed rather arrogant.

Until he raced.

Like so many NASCAR fans, I watched as Todd overcame setback after setback—a bad setup, a near spin out, and the aggressive driving tactics of NASCAR's newest wheelman, Brandon Burke—a man who's now Todd's teammate—and all with the light touch and cool head of some of NASCAR's brightest legends.

I'm impressed.

Todd is showing newcomers like Burke what it means to have class, both on the track *and* off. All this has me thinking that maybe, just maybe, Mr. Peters isn't as full of hot air as previously thought. Especially when it's obvious he's taking each race one at a time—for Benjamin's sake. Benjamin, you might recall, is the terminally ill child Todd's taken under his wing. The child's name was taped to the inside of Todd's car this past weekend, something the network cameras caught on film as Todd was racing. His hand reaching toward the kid's name was something I will never forget.

So, while I never thought I'd say this: you go, Todd. If you think you can win at least three more races, so do I. So does the entire NASCAR nation.

So does Benjamin.

Good luck!

CHAPTER TWENTY-TWO

"There!"

The word echoed off the courtyard around Indi, causing several people to turn and look her way.

"Todd," Indi said, glancing toward whatever it was that he'd slammed down. A tall, gold statue of some sort.

"Is that your trophy?" she asked.

"Yes, it is," he said, ignoring the stares of curious onlookers, although they probably had no idea it was Todd Peters beneath the red baseball cap. He wore the brim so low that it shielded most of his face. Covering his wide shoulders was a T-shirt with—of all things— the face and name of another driver. Camouflage, she realized. He'd come here dressed like a race fan. Good thing, too. The courtyard she sat in was in the middle of downtown and many race fans had yet to leave. The trophy might have given away his identity if he hadn't slipped out of the brown leather jacket he was wearing and used it to cover the shiny gold medal.

"The first of many," he added. "Just like I told you."

She turned her face away. She sat outside her high-rise hotel, out in the middle of a lushly landscaped courtyard with multiple levels and a fountain gurgling in the distance. There was a chill in the air, but Indi hadn't minded. She was due to leave for the airport soon and she wanted as much fresh air as she could soak in before the long flight home.

"I never doubted you'd win," she said softly.

He plopped down on the bench next to her.

"Don't hand me that, Indi. You know you did."

Maybe she had. "Congratulations," she said softly.

"You'll be congratulating me next week, too. And the week after that, as well."

Would she? When he hadn't called, she figured it was over between them.

Over before it had started.

"I hope you do win, Todd. It'd make Benjamin happy."

"Yeah, but to hear you tell it, he won't last long enough to see me win the Championship."

"We need to be realistic—"

"No," he shouted, turning heads again. He leaned toward her. "No," he said again, more quietly. "Indi, I have a job. A high-pressure job. But do I have a defeatist attitude when Lrace? No. Because if I did, I wouldn't have a job. Nobody likes a quitter and that's what you're doing with Benjamin—quitting."

"I am not."

"Yes," he said. "You are. And I understand why, too. It's self-defense. You close yourself off. Forbid yourself from caring. And I have to ask myself, have you done the same thing with us? Did you sleep with me because you cared for me? Or because you needed to escape the pressures of your job?"

She gasped. "Of course I care for you. I wouldn't have let what happened happen if I didn't. I'm not that type."

"Then why haven't you called?"

"Because," she said, exasperated. "I knew you were mad at me...about Benjamin. I was going to give you some time to cool down. Call you when I got back to California."

"I *am* mad at you. I'm furious at the way you refuse to *believe*."

"Believe what?"

He shifted on the bench and leaned forward. "Believe in *things*. In the people who surround and care for you. In the doctors who care for your clients. In *me*."

"I believe in you."

"Then why you haven't called?"

"I told you, I was giving you time to cool off. And, really, maybe you could have called me."

"I was waiting to see if I was right. If you'd use our argument at the hospital as a way of backing off. And you did."

"I did not."

"You didn't even drop by to say good luck on Saturday."

"I wasn't invited to the race."

"Don't be ridiculous. After what we shared, what the hell makes you think you *wouldn't* be invited?"

"Past experience, maybe. I don't know. The fact that you walked out of Benjamin's hospital without even saying goodbye."

"I was mad. Furious at the way you look at life. Here you are, working for a foundation that creates miracles for children, and yet you refuse to believe in those miracles yourself."

"That's not true."

"Isn't it, Indi?"

"No, it's not."

"Think about it."

"I *have* thought about it. Sure, maybe I am a little jaded, but if you'd seen as much death as I have, you'd lose a little faith, too."

"I'm glad you admit at least that much," he said, touching her hand—not grabbing it—just clasping it for a second. "And I don't blame you." He faced forward again and glanced up at the blue sky above. "I just can't be that way myself."

"I don't expect you to."

"When I get behind the wheel of a car," he said, seeming lost in his thoughts, "it's always with the attitude I can win."

"I know."

"Sure, there's always the possibility that I could wreck…or blow a motor, but I don't let that mess with my mind. What happens, happens, and I'd rather go into situations with a positive attitude."

"And it bothers you that I can't?"

He met her gaze, his hazel eyes intense. "It does, Indi."

She watched as he stood up and stared out at the buildings around them.

"It's no way to live," he said, facing her again. "It'll suck the life out of you. Make you hard. Wear you down."

She stared up at him. "That hasn't happened to me."

"Hasn't it?"

"No," she said with a shake of her head. "Sure. I don't look at life through a pair of rose-tinted glasses, but I'm not jaded."

"Yes, you are. Tooth and nail, you fight caring for people."

"I care for Benjamin."

"To a point," he said.

"And I care for you."

"Do you?"

"Of course," she said, having to raise her voice so she could be heard over a pack of cars that drove by.

"I don't believe you. If you cared for me, you wouldn't retreat behind a wall. But that's exactly what you've done. I can see it," he added quickly when she began to shake her head. "It's part of the reason you haven't called me. You're building up your defenses against the coming storm."

"That's not true."

"So I wonder," he said, ignoring her protestations, "what would happen if Benjamin didn't make it? What would it do to *us,* Indi? I care for you. Probably more than you realize. I want to be there for you, but something tells me you won't let anybody be there for you. It hurts too much."

"I don't understand what you're saying," she said, standing herself. "I let people care for me all the time. Look at Linda—"

"That's different. Linda is the mother of a client. I'm talking about letting people close to you. People like me, Indi. People who will be around *after* the devastation of a loss. Or have you maintained close contact with all your deceased client's parents?"

"That's a horrible thing to ask. Of course I have."

"Have you?"

"Well, maybe not all of them. But sometimes people don't want to be reminded about what they lost."

"How about your own family?"

She shrugged. "Families often grow apart after a loss. It's difficult to face each other when a loved one is missing."

"There you go sounding all clinical again."

"Well, what do you want me to say? I come from a family that was never really close. After my nephew died, we grew even more apart."

He looked deep into her eyes, so deep that Indi felt vulnerable and naked and exposed. "Why do I have the feeling there's more to this story than meets the eye?"

She looked away.

"So what are you saying?" she asked, fumbling for a way to change the subject. "That you want to throw in the towel? That you don't want to see me again?" It shocked her how much the words hurt.

"I'm saying you're a puzzle, Indi. That there are layers to you that I don't know, even with all we've been through. Layers that you've kept hidden from me. I'm saying you need to throw it all out there if you want us to work."

"It is all out there, Todd."

"Is it?"

She looked away.

From the corner of her eye, she saw him check his watch. "You're leaving in a couple of hours. You should probably get going."

Indi felt everything freeze up inside her. She wanted to say things, personal things that she knew she should share with him.

Suddenly, she was petrified.

"Maybe I should," she said softly.

He stuffed his hands in his pocket. "Goodbye, Indi."

"I'll call you when I get back to California."

"Will you?"

She nodded, even as her stomach tightened further. "Sure."

He held her gaze a moment longer, turned away, only to spin back to face her again. "Before I go, you should know Benjamin's been accepted into a clinical trial for a new type of drug."

"What kind of drug?"

"It's a new generation that targets cancer on multiple molecular levels. Benjamin's already been treated with a similar type of medication, but he developed a resistance. That's what makes him so ideal for this new type of drug. It tries to fix the cancer in the same way, only most people won't develop a resistance to it. He'll begin taking it this week."

"Wha—" She didn't know what to say. "Why am I only hearing about this now?"

"Because I didn't want to tell you," he said. "I didn't want to hear how Benjamin would be a long shot for this trial, how the drug might not work. I didn't want to hear you try to be 'realistic.'"

"I see."

"We're flying him back to California on Tuesday, health permitting."

"I'll be sure to drop in on him."

"You do that," he said.

And Indi could tell he wanted to say more. She watched his fingers flex, watched the muscles on his biceps twitch.

"Take care, Indi."

"You, too, Todd."

And then he turned and walked away.

CHAPTER TWENTY-THREE

"SO YOU JUST let him go?"

Maggie stared across at Indi sympathetically, Indi pretending an interest in her computer monitor. "It was obvious he was trying to break up with me."

It was Monday morning, and the office was quiet. Outside, rain fell, the *swish-swish-swish* of traffic a steady rhythm that made Indi drowsy. Or maybe she felt tired because she hadn't slept all night.

She kept going over and over her conversation with Todd.

"So that's it then?" Maggie said. "You go your way and he goes his?"

"I guess so," Indi said, clicking on a window on her desktop even though she had no idea why she'd opened that particular file. "Although I told him I'd call."

"And will you?"

"Maggie," Indi said, risking a glance at her friend. "It's not like we were boyfriend and girlfriend. More like...two ships passing in the night." And that, perhaps, was not the best analogy given what they'd done on one particular ship, or rather boat.

"Weren't you?"

She'd opened about *ten* files, Indi suddenly realized. She pushed away from her desk. Maggie didn't know about what had happened out on the lake. Nobody knew that. "He's a friend, Mags. That's it."

"That's not what the Internet says."

"Excuse me?"

Maggie clasped her hands on her desk. "You know how I'm always looking for new things on my favorite driver, Mike Morgan? Anyway, I searched Todd's name on the Internet and a whole bunch of message boards came up. Drivers are practically like rock stars. They have millions of fans, most of whom appear to be on the Internet."

"I know," Indi said.

Damn it, Indi. Focus. It's not like you don't have other kids desperate for a miracle of their own.

"As I suspected, there are whole Web sites dedicated to Todd."

"And your point?" Indi asked, knowing she wouldn't like what was coming next.

"You've been tagged as Todd's girlfriend."

"No," Indi said, her hands falling into her lap.

Maggie nodded, a few kinky strands of bangs (she'd pulled her hair back) falling over her forehead. "Apparently, you were spotted hugging each other at the hospital. And this woman…" Maggie turned to her computer, clicking on some keys. "This woman said that the friend of a friend of a friend who saw you two said you were acting like way more than friends."

"No way. That was reported on the Internet?"

Maggie's eyes were wide and earnest. "I'm telling you, what Todd had for breakfast this morning is probably here somewhere." She shook her head in derision, muttering, "Darn it. I wish I could find that site."

"Well, if you do, tell them they're wrong. Todd and I were two people drawn together over a little boy."

A sick little boy, Indi reminded herself. No sense in pouting over her nonrelationship with Todd when Benjamin still fought for his life.

"How is Benjamin, by the way?"

Indi tried not to look too glum. "Linda said he's doing as well as can be expected. She thought he might perk up when he heard he'd been accepted to this new study, but apparently he's at a point where he just doesn't care."

"That's too bad. Are you going to continue visiting him?"

It was a valid question. Technically, Indi had done her job. She'd granted Benjamin his miracle, and she was happy to have done it, even if it had resulted in—

She shook her head. No. She would not think about her and Todd. Every time she did she felt the nauseating, suffocating feeling that made her want to close her eyes and maybe cup her head in her hands and fight back tears.

She sucked in a breath. "I'll be visiting him. Of course I will. You know how I feel about him."

"Yes, even though I've told you a hundred times not to get too close. You'll burn yourself out doing that."

From the way Todd had made it sound, she'd already done that. "I know. I plan on heading over to the hospital on Wednesday, when he's supposed to arrive."

"I'm surprised they're allowing him to be moved, given the shape he's in."

"It's a special air ambulance. Todd's arranged it all."

Indi returned to her computer. She went back to clicking on keys, only suddenly she realized she was searching for her name and Todd's on the Internet.

Argh.

She pushed her keyboard away and stood up abruptly.

"I'm going out to get a coffee," she said, bending beneath her desk to grab her purse. When she straightened, Maggie's eyes were full of concern.

"Indi. What happened? And don't hand me that 'it was nothing' routine. Something big occurred between you and that driver. I can see it in your face."

"What you see is concern for Benjamin," Indi said.

"Does he know you can't have kids?"

Indi froze.

"Is that what this is about?" Maggie asked, her face full of compassion.

"I'll be right back," Indi said, fishing in her purse for her keys.

Maggie didn't say another word.

Does he know you can't have kids?

No, Maggie, Indi silently answered. That little tidbit of news never came up in conversation. And as it turned out, it didn't *need* to come up. It was over between her and Todd. Over before it had ever really started.

SHE SAW BENJAMIN the day he returned to California, but only briefly, and only after calling Sam, the hospital receptionist and checking that Todd wasn't around.

Benjamin looked awful.

Of course, she tried not to let that show as she walked into his hospital room. "How're you feeling?" she asked as she rubbed her hands together, her hands chilled by the alcohol in the hand sanitizer.

"Tired," he said. Benjamin's eyes looked huge thanks to the bruising beneath them. He wore no ball cap today, his head so completely devoid of hair that Indi knew his scalp would be smooth to the touch.

How many children had she seen looking like this? How many lives had been lost…

Indi.

"Did you get some sleep on the plane?" Indi asked, although the words seemed to bottle up in her throat.

"It was a long flight," Linda said. And she still looked tired from it, Indi noted. Her blond hair had been pulled back, but it looked as if it hadn't been brushed in a while. The jeans and T-shirt she wore were wrinkled, as if she'd pulled them from a suitcase where they'd been sitting for some time. "And even though he didn't have to move much, it still took everything out of him."

Indi nodded. Her hand found Benjamin's beneath the cover. He was in the same room as before, the same childishly decorated, NASCAR motif, white-walled hospital room, with all the same equipment:

IV, blood-pressure clip on his finger, television spewing muted sound from overhead.

And yet it all felt so very, *very* different.

"Why is Todd mad at you?"

Indi's hands froze. Her gaze shot to Linda's. The woman just smiled, although it looked brittle around the edges.

"I'm…well, I wasn't aware we *weren't* talking."

But she forgot who she was dealing with. She was staring into the eyes of a child who saw far too much, who looked upon the world with a wisdom that took her breath away. Benjamin knew that the days on earth were limited so it was smart to make the best of them.

"He's…good guy," Benjamin croaked.

"I know he is," Indi said, leaning toward him and smiling softly. "Just look what he's done for *you*."

Benjamin might be ill, but he was buying *none* of it. "You stayed out. On the boat."

"I…well, I…for a few hours," Indi said, turning briefly to Linda and trying to gauge how much she'd guessed.

All of it.

"Saw you…together."

What? When? Where?

"The beach."

"That was nothing, Benjamin. We're just—" She

was about to say *friends,* but Linda shook her head, her eyes warning her not to lie.

She *had* been about to lie, hadn't she? Worse, she'd been lying to herself—pinning the blame on Todd when deep down inside she'd known everything he'd said about her was true.

"We're just working through some things," Indi said, smiling and clutching Benjamin's hands. "Although to be honest, I'm not certain he even likes me anymore."

"Does," Benjamin said, his eyes earnestly imploring.

Indi's heart seemed to lodge in her throat. She could tell Benjamin wanted them to be together, but that was one miracle Indi just couldn't provide. "You get some rest," Indi said. "I'll be by tomorrow."

"I'll walk out with you," Linda said, bending forward and kissing her son. "Be right back."

Benjamin's eyes were closed before they'd even stood.

"What happened?" Linda asked.

Nothing.

The word was on the tip of her tongue, but just as Indi couldn't lie to Benjamin, she couldn't lie to Linda, either. The woman saw far too much.

"We spent some time together," Indi said, pausing in front of the elevators. "It was…"

Wonderful. And he'd been so sweet. And so tender when they'd made love.

"Nice," Indi finished softly. "It was really nice."

"Then what happened?" Linda asked. "Benjamin said you spent the night out on Todd's boat. But when I asked Todd if he'd talked to you, he shrugged you off like the two of you were nothing more than friends."

Indi tried to muster a smile for a nurse who passed them by, but it was hard. It was damn hard.

"Maybe we *are* nothing more than friends," Indi said once the woman had passed. "Maybe we bonded because of your son. Maybe it wasn't real."

"And maybe nobody knows if a relationship is for real or not until they give it a shot," Linda said. "Maybe none of them are real unless you take a chance and spend time working on it."

"What are you saying?"

"That you shouldn't just give up," Linda said.

"We hardly know each other."

"Don't give me that crap," Linda said, shocking Indi. Linda never swore. In all her months of knowing her, she'd never heard a curse word cross her lips. "I'm tired of it," she said to Indi. "Tired of all the crap that goes on. The other day Art and I were in the car and on the radio I heard this woman actually complain about the fact that her kid got sent home from school because of a fever. I wanted to call in and give that woman a piece of my mind because at least *her* child would get better."

"Linda—"

"No," Linda said. "Let me finish. If I've learned nothing else while watching my son fight this horrible disease it's that life's too short to mess around. And what saddens me more than anything…" All at once Linda's face crumpled. "What saddens me is that my son realizes that, too."

"Oh, Linda," Indi said, opening her arms.

"So don't wait," Linda said with a sniff, staying her with a hand. "Todd is a good man. A *really* good man. The money he's put out…I can't believe someone who barely knows us would do what he's done." Her chest expanded as she took a deep breath. "Don't throw this away."

Indi nodded.

Linda dabbed at her eyes. "I don't want Benjamin to think I'm crying over him."

"I know."

From the pocket of her jeans, Linda pulled a tissue out. She took another deep breath. "Anyway," she said after she'd collected herself, though her nose was still stuffy sounding. "Todd's perfect for you, Indi. The two of you give from the heart— totally. You're made for each other."

Indi took a deep breath, too. "But being involved with Todd won't be easy, Linda. He's a race car driver. Women talk about him on the Internet—"

"So? These days everyone's life is on the Internet. And trust me…I've seen the way that man looks at you. You've got nothing to worry about."

"But he's volatile. Being near him sometimes is like being wood around a keg of gunpowder. He has no patience. Not like Art. You and your husband are so perfect together. Todd and I always seem to be at each other's throats."

Linda let loose a huff of laughter, one that surprised Indi for the genuine mirth she heard behind it. "Is that what you think? That we have a perfect marriage?"

"It sure looks like it. Believe me, I've seen relationships crumble from dealing with a sick child. But not you and Art."

"Don't delude yourself, Indi. I wish he was around more. We argue about that constantly. Frankly, I'm surprised he went to North Carolina with me. What you see here, at the hospital, is vastly different than what goes on behind the scenes. We just don't let Benjamin see the cracks in our relationship."

"I had no idea."

"Of course not. Nobody likes to air their dirty laundry."

No. She supposed not, Indi thought.

I can't have kids.

It wasn't something she ever really thought about. She'd never been serious enough with a man to bring up the subject. Did she now? Would Todd even talk to her again?

He said for you to call.

"Don't let Todd go," Linda repeated. "Sometimes you have to hang on to find your miracles."

And maybe, just maybe, it was Indi's turn for one.

CHAPTER TWENTY-FOUR

THE SOONEST TODD could slip away to visit Benjamin was the beginning of November, his win at Charlotte creating corporate obligations he couldn't ignore. Those demands only increased when—against all odds—he managed to pull off a second win three weeks later.

He almost brought the damn trophy with him. If he left it in Benjamin's room, Indi would see it. But that would be childish and petty. She hadn't called him or made any attempt to contact him, so he supposed he had her answer regarding their relationship. It was over.

He just wished he could get over his disappointment. He hadn't felt such a sense of letdown since he failed to win the championship a few years back.

He'd win it this year.

Mathematically, it'd be difficult for someone to catch up. The NASCAR NEXTEL Cup trophy would be his. Yet he still wanted to win at least two more races if for no other reason than to prove a point.

"Todd," Benjamin said when he saw him, the little boy covered in shadow thanks to one of the rooftop's shade trees. Not far away, standing discreetly aside, one of the hospital's many volunteers stood by, the older woman giving Benjamin his space.

"And *Lex*," Benjamin said, squealing in delight.

Lex, the official therapy dog, had flown to California with Todd. The bulldog even wore an official yellow vest, which attested to his status as a therapy dog and allowed him to walk the halls without fear of being arrested by the doggie police. But all Lex cared about right now was greeting his little friend, the dog's stub tail waving hello. Benjamin, as sick as he was, half rose, but no amount of smiles could erase the child's ashen color, sunken eyes and general air of exhaustion.

"Come here, boy," Benjamin cried, his hands reaching for the canine.

It wasn't fair, Todd thought.

It just wasn't fair that this bright child had to suffer through this terrible disease.

For now, Todd vowed. Unlike Indi, he believed in a cure, and cure Benjamin they would. The doctors had already started Benjamin on a new regimen of drugs geared toward targeting the specific gene responsible for his leukemia. The more Todd heard about the multiple kinase inhibitor being used in the clinical trial, the more optimistic he became.

"How are you feeling?" Todd asked, but he had to wait until Benjamin and Lex were done admiring each other before he received an answer.

"'Bout the same," Benjamin said, and with his energy spent, he sat back down, his head resting against the back of his chair. He had a blanket over his legs today. Todd recognized his team colors on the blanket that matched the little boy's ball cap.

"Well, that'll change soon," Todd said.

"Hope so," Benjamin said softly. His hand hung off to the side of his chair. Lex was busy licking it.

"Did you watch the race this weekend?" Todd asked.

Benjamin brightened again. "You won. Gonna win the championship, too."

"Looks like it. But I'm not done winning races just yet. Got two more to go."

"Think so?"

"I do," Todd said, explaining what they'd done to prepare. He would have spent all day talking to the child if he hadn't noticed how exhausted Benjamin became. It descended upon him suddenly and so very obviously that Todd wasn't surprised when the volunteer standing nearby said, "I should probably take him back."

"Yeah. I think so, too," Todd said.

"No. Wait," Benjamin said in a surprisingly strong voice. "I don't want to go just yet. I was just waiting—"

"Todd!" a woman said, her cry one of surprise.

"For Indi," Benjamin finished with a wide smile, the child turning and looking toward the glass doors. "Now we can go. Todd, you stay here with Indi. Lex can go with me inside."

Todd realized they'd been set up.

Indi must have realized it, too. She hung back, staring at him with uncertainty in her eyes. "Benjamin," she scolded as he passed by.

"I'll just be inside," the child said, shooting them both a grin.

"You don't have to stay," Todd said as the hospital worker pushed Benjamin toward the exit, Lex in tow.

"No, I—" She squared her shoulders. "I've actually been wanting to talk to you."

"Oh?"

She nodded, swallowed. "Um, congratulations on your win."

"Thanks," he said, watching as Benjamin glanced back, the smile on his face one of supreme satisfaction. It was good to see that look on his face, even if he was a devious little devil, so Todd smiled back, shook his head and started walking the concrete pathway that circled the roof.

"Where do you race this next weekend?" Indi asked, Todd wondering if this was really what she'd wanted to talk to him about, or if she was just stalling. Stalling, judging by the tension around her mouth.

"Actually, we're close by. Phoenix," he said. "Made it easy to visit Benjamin."

"I bet they're keeping you busy now that you're poised to win the championship."

"Busy doesn't begin to describe it," he said, thinking of the media requests that poured in on a daily basis—sometimes as many as ten in an hour. "But I'm lucky because the media knows what's going on," he said, glancing where Benjamin had sat in a pointed way.

"The footage we shot of you in North Carolina looks good. *Miracles* is planning on running a spot during your last race. A thank-you and congratulations kind of thing."

"Indi," he said softly. "You didn't really want to talk to me about business, did you?"

She stood near the edge of a flower bed, pansies in a hue of colors turning their cat-shaped faces toward the sun. "No," she said. "I didn't."

He waited. She'd pulled her hair up off her head

in a sleekly styled bun. Instead of making her look like an uptight professional, it softened her face. Then again, she was so stunningly pretty, she'd look gorgeous in a Halloween mask.

"Todd, look…" She shook her head, and Todd could tell she searched for a way to begin. "A thousand times I wanted to pick up the phone and call you. To let you know that I heard what you said in North Carolina. And that you're right. There are things about me that you don't know."

He waited, not wanting to push her but feeling his whole body tense just the same.

"My family and I, you're right, we're not close." She looked him in the eye, the green in them more pronounced. "I have a sister that I barely talk to."

"Why not?" he asked because he sensed there was more to the story than he'd previously surmised.

She looked out over the top of the roof. In the distance the mountains that surrounded the Bay Area rose up around them, brown on one side of the valley, green on the other. She studied them for a moment, then said, "We've never been close because, well…" She swallowed. "To be honest, I've always been jealous."

He nodded, knowing that sibling rivalry often caused rifts in families. He was lucky. Not so with his family.

"But not because she was smarter or prettier than me." She seemed to take a deep breath, then looked him square in the eye. "I was jealous because I can't have kids of my own."

The words took a second to penetrate, and even then he wasn't certain he had heard her correctly. "What?"

"I can't have kids," she said.

"Why not?" Todd asked.

She shrugged. "A birth defect we discovered when I was thirteen. I have an ovary, barely. But my uterus is defective. A genetic anomaly, the doctors called it. One in a million women are born with it. I'm that lucky one."

"Indi—" He didn't know what to say, and yet it explained so much.

"I didn't think much of it when I was younger," she said, crossing her arms in front of her. "I told myself I didn't want kids. My sister could have all the grandchildren in the family. I focused on my broadcasting career. And then Kyle was born."

"Your nephew?"

She nodded. "I fell in love with him at first sight. Became the doting aunt. Much to my sister's surprise, I volunteered to babysit, watch Kyle during the weekends, whatever she needed. Whatever Kyle wanted, he got. Toys, clothes, whatever. Kyle brought my sister and I closer than I would have thought possible. And then he died."

"And it ripped your family apart."

"It ripped my heart out," she said, uncrossing her arms, her expression stoic and yet marred by a sadness so deep it took Todd's breath away. "I realized after he was gone that Kyle had become like a son. When he died, it was like losing my own kid. My sister and I drifted further apart. My job suffered. I got involved with that stupid football player."

"What football player?"

"Just some linebacker who seemed to be Prince Charming, but was really a toad. It seems silly now, but at the time it really tore me up. And then I found *Miracles*."

"And that became your new child."

She nodded. "I suppose in a way it did. But my involvement with *Miracles* doesn't change the fact that I can't have kids."

She'd been afraid to tell him. He could see that now, found himself closing the distance between them before he could think better of it. "Not having kids doesn't make you less of a woman."

She released a huff of disdain. "Of course it doesn't. I know that. But it's the reason I do what I do for a living."

"And *that* something makes you the most remarkable individual I've ever met," he said, cupping her face with his hands. "It's one of the many things that makes me step back and say 'wow' when I think of you."

He saw her face crumple, saw her inhale to stifle the tears, saw her hands clench and unclench. "I can't give this up, Todd. I won't."

"No one's asking you to."

"But look what it does to us. You're right. When kids get as sick as Benjamin, I shut down. I can't deal with it like a normal person, and in the end, that'll be the death of us."

He tipped her head up again, leaned toward her and said, "Who says?"

"I know from experience," she said, tears glittering on her lashes. "That night we shared on the boat. That one, magical night. It was a taste of heaven, Todd. I knew that, remarkable as it seemed, I'd found someone I could love."

"I know. I felt it, too."

"And look what happened afterward. We got in that horrible fight."

"It wasn't horrible."

"It was bad enough." She blinked back more tears. "I can't deal with that kind of stress, not you and all the sick children who need me more."

His hands dropped away from her face. "So what

are you saying? That you don't want to see me again?"

She didn't answer.

Todd bit back an oath of frustration. "That is what you're saying, isn't it?"

"It's the way I feel."

But then he looked at her—really *looked* at her. And what he saw nearly brought him to his knees. He saw a woman, one so devoted to the children she served that she'd give up the one thing she loved in life.

Him.

His breath caught. He searched her face, wondered if he imagined it. But, no. She wore her heart on her sleeve, and the look in her eyes called out to him, told him that she didn't want to lose him. That it nearly killed her to stand in front of him and deliver her speech. That she wanted more than anything to collapse into his arms.

And that's exactly what she *would* do. Lean on him, damn it. Starting right now.

"Come here," he said.

"No," she said, her eyes imploring. "You're not going to make this harder on me."

"I *am* going to make it hard, damn it. Because if there's one thing I've learned, Indi, one thing *you* need to learn, too, it's that life is a team effort. Some days are miserable, but that's no reason to throw in the towel on the whole shebang. You shouldn't, either."

She didn't say anything.

Todd swiped a hand through his hair, swung away, then turned back. "You know, for someone who devotes her life to children, you sure don't know how to have a life of your own."

"I know," she said. "But what I'm trying to tell you is that's by choice."

He stared into her eyes, seeing a steely determination in them. It was the same iron will she used to get her through the tough times and Todd knew he'd have a tough time breaking through... If he'd ever be able to do so at all.

"So this is it then? You don't want to see me anymore?"

He saw her eyes begin to glisten, but she held her ground. "No."

He shook his head, looked away, ran a hand through his hair. "This is stupid."

She didn't say anything.

"You know, in all my years of racing, there's one thing I've learned. You can have the best cars, the best engines, the best sponsors in the world, but if you don't have the will to win, it won't make a damn of a difference." He took a step toward her. She stiffened, but he held his ground. "You, Indi, don't have the will to win because if you did, you wouldn't throw this all away."

"Todd—"

"Goodbye, Indi," he said. "Tell Benj I'll be back late tonight."

CHAPTER TWENTY-FIVE

BENJAMIN LOOKED disappointed when she entered his hospital room alone. Even Lex stood up, and Indi would swear the canine looked behind her as if expecting to see his master.

Sorry, Lex, she thought.

"Where's Todd?" Benjamin asked.

"I, ah…" Indi motioned for the dog to stay where he was. "I think he left, but he said he'd see you later tonight."

"But I thought the two of you…"

Would kiss and make up. She'd known he'd think that, especially after he'd worked so hard to set this whole thing up.

"I mean…aren't you, you know, seeing each other again?"

"No, Benjamin, we're not. Todd and I are…" She searched for a word to explain what they were. "Todd and I are just friends."

"But…the two of you—"

"Where's your mom?" Indi asked, turning behind her as if she might spy her right there.

"She's in the library, looking some stuff up on the Internet."

"Well, then, I'm probably going to miss her."

"But—"

Indi was glad she wouldn't see Benjamin's mother. The last thing she needed was Linda's knowing eyes scanning her up and down. "Tell her I said hello. And tell Todd good luck this weekend."

"*You* tell him."

What had happened to that tired-looking boy she'd caught a glimpse of up on the roof? Playacting, she realized. Pretending to be exhausted so she and Todd could be alone up on the roof. Clever child.

"I've got to get back to the office," Indi said.

"You broke up with him, didn't you?"

"Benjamin, I was *never* with him."

"Yes, you were. That night at camp. You stayed out with him."

Indi sighed, though she tried to keep it inaudible. "We were just talking."

Benjamin raised skeptical eyebrows, or he would have if he'd had any. That reminded her that he was sick so she should keep her visit short. "I'll see you tomorrow, kiddo."

She glanced down at Lex, and what broke Indi's

heart, what made her even more sad, was that she knew it was the last time she'd see Todd's dog.

"Bye, Lex," she said softly. The bulldog stayed down on his blanket but tried to crawl toward her on his belly, his droopy clown eyes bright. "Take care of Benjamin for me."

SHE SPENT the rest of the week trying not to think about Todd, but that was hard. Every time she dropped by the hospital she was forced to stare at constant reminders of him: the autographed team jersey Benjamin had been given. The checkered flag. A signed photo. It got so that Indi almost dreaded her visits.

And yet perversely enough, when Sunday rolled around she found herself glued to her television set. Todd was a hot topic. The television commentators couldn't speak highly enough of him and all that he'd done for Benjamin. Indi ended up turning the volume down so she wouldn't have to listen.

He won the race.

She shouldn't have been surprised. And she wasn't. What surprised her was how much she wanted to pick up the phone and congratulate him.

She went to see Benjamin the Monday after the race. Her second surprise of the week was how much better he looked. He reminded her of the Benjamin of old when she entered his hospital room. So much so that her eyes immediately went to Linda's.

Wow, Indi mouthed.

He's feeling better, Linda answered back, her smile one of the first Indi had seen in recent weeks.

"Did you see it? Did you see it?" Benjamin cried. "Todd won another race. And he dedicated it to me. Again." The word was almost a squeal.

A *squeal.*

Indi felt a burst of hope that was so great it made her eyes burn. "Yeah, I did watch it," she said gently.

"It was so great. He clinched the championship. No way anyone could beat him now. And this morning, when I talked to him, he told me I get to go to the awards ceremony next month."

"Really? How great."

"Mom said, if I keep feeling better, I can go."

"How are you feeling?" Indi asked.

"Great," Benjamin said, his face animated, the white sheet pulled up to his armpits, for once, not as pale as his face. "I can't wait to watch the race this weekend. Todd said he'd try to fly out here this week, but that he wasn't sure he could make it. He said he's going to be on *The Tonight Show* and that the producers mentioned they might want me to go on the show with him."

"Wow. Neat."

It was the longest speech Benjamin had given in recent weeks and it made Indi's attention dart to Linda yet again.

"Okay, we're all walked out," someone said behind her. "But don't ask me to do that again. Your dog is obviously concerned about his waistline, judging by how much jogging he did."

Benjamin's dad stood in the doorway, and he held Lex's leash.

"Lex," Benjamin called, distracting the dog who'd been about to make a run at Indi. "Come here, boy."

"Not up on the bed," Linda cried as the dog started to run, although that was hard to do. The linoleum floor made it impossible for him to get any traction. "You know the rules. When he visits, he has to stay on his bed."

"Aw, Mom."

"That's the rules," Art said, pulling back on the leash and bringing Lex to the corner of the room. "And you know what Todd said about obeying the rules."

"You break them, he's taking Lex back," Linda reminded her son.

"Todd loaned him Lex?" Indi asked, because she didn't quite understand what Lex was doing here.

"No," Linda said, her smile turning softly whimsical. "He *gave* him Lex."

"What?"

Art nodded after unclipping the dog's leash and telling the dog to stay. He stood behind Linda, placing a kiss on her head before leaning forward and poking at Benjamin's side. The child squeaked in mock fear.

"He said it was obvious Lex loved Benjamin more than him," Art said. "And so he gave the dog to Benj."

Lex didn't love Benjamin more than Todd. She'd seen the dog with Todd. Lex loved everybody, but most especially his owner. And his owner loved the dog.

"He's an amazing man," Linda said, glancing up at her husband. "If I wasn't already married…"

"Careful," Art said. "I can still have him banned from this room."

They all smiled. Actually, Benjamin giggled and Indi, who stood there watching it all, suddenly felt like a third wheel.

"Well, I just popped in to see how you're doing," she said, bending down and giving Benjamin a kiss.

His "ewww," made her straighten and give him a teasing smile. "Hey, these lips have kissed—" *your favorite driver* "—Lex," she said, her whole face suddenly so warm she was certain Linda spotted her blush.

"Lex is a dog," Benjamin cried.

"And you're lucky to have him," Indi said, her eyes stinging all of a sudden.

What a *nice* thing for Todd to do, she thought.

"I'll walk you out," Linda said.

"No, no. That's okay."

"Come on," Linda said, using her mommies-aren't-to-be-argued-with voice.

But Linda didn't say anything until they were out of the hospital, and even then it was only two words.

"Call him."

"I can't," Indi said, knowing instantly who she referred to.

"Call him," Linda said, using "the voice" again.

BUT WHEN SUNDAY ROLLED around, Indi still hadn't picked up the phone. She paced around her small apartment all morning. Only later did she realize it was anxiety. She was nervous about Todd's race, not nervous that he would win it, but nervous about his safety.

That tension only grew worse the closer it got to the green flag dropping. She found herself glued to the TV, watching the prerace shows in hopes of catching a glimpse of him.

Was he nervous? Did he feel ready to race?

Did he miss her?

The last thought was ridiculous, because, of course, he didn't miss her. He was probably glad to be rid of her, but as the green flag dropped, she wished—oh, how she wished—she'd called him.

Instead she watched him race.

She turned down the volume again. She couldn't take listening to the commentators downplaying his chances at winning another race. Such a feat was unheard-of, they said.

They didn't know Todd Peters.

By lap ten he led the race. By lap twenty he was ten car lengths ahead. He drove like a man possessed, only giving up the lead twice. He took that lead back in a matter of laps. As the race neared its end, Indi found herself turning up the volume.

"…going to make history with his four wins during the Chase," one of the announcers was saying.

"Who would have thought that Todd Peters could win a championship so decisively?" his partner responded.

"Obviously Todd did."

"And Benjamin Koch," the first guy said.

"Yeah, let's not forget who Todd's racing for. The little boy who's so sick with leukemia. But I bet you Benjamin is bouncing in his bed right now."

And Indi knew the announcer was right. She

knew her little friend was no doubt giddy about being mentioned on TV. She knew he watched Todd make every lap. She knew that when Todd took the checkered flag, which he did, that Benjamin was no doubt delirious with joy.

Indi cried.

It was silly—after all, it was just a race—but she knew how much this meant to Todd. And Benjamin. To the whole team, really. They all wanted to win. Not for winning's sake, but for Benjamin's.

She went to the phone, picked it up, set it down again. Who would she call?

There was no one.

You sure don't know how to have a life of your own.

And it was true. Sure, she had families she could call, friends she'd made through her job. But they weren't real friends, just acquaintances. She had nobody other than Maggie, not even her sister.

Damn it.

She paced her apartment, her heart thudding against her ribs so hard it felt like she'd just run a marathon.

Call him.

Call who? she asked herself. Todd didn't carry a cell phone in his uniform. She was pretty certain of that.

Call Jen.

Indi picked up the phone again. Todd was just pulling into Victory Lane. Indi's fingers dialed Jen's number by rote.

Jen answered on the second ring. Indi was so shocked she didn't know what to say.

"Jen, it's Indi."

On TV she could see Todd climb out of his car.

"What?" Jen said. "Indi, speak louder. I can't hear you."

Of course Jen couldn't hear her. There were thousands of screaming fans cheering Todd's name.

"Can you give Todd a message?" Indi yelled into the phone.

And then Jen did the unthinkable. Indi saw her do it right there on television. The moment about three seconds behind the actual action. She walked into the camera's view, tapped Todd on the shoulder and stepped in front of the trackside commentator so he couldn't shove a microphone in Todd's face. Then Jen handed Todd the phone.

"Who is it?" she heard him ask, and it was strange because on TV his lips hadn't moved...yet.

Indi almost hung up.

"Indi," she heard Jen yell.

Indi turned away from the TV.

"Hello?" came Todd's voice a second later.

She lost her voice, had to swallow back tears. *Oh, Todd. I'm so proud of you. So very, very proud of you. And so happy for you.*

But all she said was, "Congratulations."

I miss you.

"Thanks," he said.

You sure don't know how to have a life. "You ran a great race."

You don't know how to win.

"Thanks," he said again.

You're messing this up. Because she *did* want to win. As she stood there in her living room, all by herself, she realized she wanted to win Todd's heart.

"I'm proud of you, Todd," she said at last, her throat clogged with tears. "I really am."

She could hear his teammates cheer. On TV a bottle of champagne was uncorked.

"Gotta go," he said.

"Yeah,.I see that. Bye, Todd. Take care."

"You, too."

And that was that. A few seconds later she saw him turn back to Jen, saw him hand the phone back. When he faced the cameras on TV his eyes showed no emotion.

Indi's vision blurred. Her hands shook to the point that she had to wrap her arms around her middle to keep from sobbing.

As she listened to him give his postrace interview, Indi admitted something profound.

She'd fallen in love with Todd Peters.

Only she'd blown it on the last lap.

CHECKERED FLAG

CHAPTER TWENTY-SIX

BENJAMIN'S HEALTH improved. Whether it was Todd officially winning the championship, or the new drugs the doctors had him taking, Indi didn't know. She only knew that the fun-loving, wisecracking kid of old had returned.

Two weeks later, tests confirmed what they'd all begun to suspect: the kinase inhibitors had begun to work.

But it wasn't until a few days before the NASCAR NEXTEL Cup Series awards ceremony that they knew for a fact he was on his way to remission. The damaged genes causing his leukemia were being reprogrammed, and though it would be several years before they could officially label him "cured," the prognosis was good.

November passed, Indi spending the Thanksgiving holiday with the Koches. Benjamin had been allowed to go home so he was in high spirits and he wheeled himself around the Koches' spacious adobe-

style home nestled in San Jose's east foothills, Lex
following him wherever he went. The day had
dawned unseasonably warm, one of those fall days
where leaves floated to the ground on a soft breeze
and the sky was so clear you could see a sliver of
moon hanging in it.

"I'm so glad you could come over," Linda said.

Indi turned away from the window she'd been
looking out of. Art and Linda's home overlooked
the Bay Area, their dining-room window offering
an unobstructed view of the south end of the San
Francisco Bay.

"I'm glad I could make it," she said, glancing down
at the table Linda had lovingly decorated with gourds,
dried corn and a ceramic turkey just about the size of
a real one. Fine china plates dotted the surface of a
table covered by a beige cloth. It all looked so beautiful.

"Indi," Linda said, slipping a gold ring over an
off-white napkin. "I know this is a sore subject, but
have you talked to Todd lately?"

Indi, who'd been reaching for a napkin ring so she
could help, froze. "Ah, no," she said. "Not since he
won his last race."

Linda nodded, picked up another ring. "Have you
thought about calling him?"

"No," Indi said, the gold metal ring cold in her

hands. "I think it's pretty clear that he doesn't want to talk to me again."

"What makes you say that?"

Indi glanced down. She could see the reflection of the light fixture that hung over the table in the smooth, metal surface. "He barely said two words to me on the phone."

"Well, you didn't exactly call him at a good time."

"I didn't call him. I called Jen. She's the one who handed the phone to Todd."

"And you expected him to pour his heart out to you on national TV."

"No." Yes. Lord, she didn't know what she'd expected. Maybe nothing. Maybe everything.

"It doesn't matter," Indi said, sliding the ring on the napkin. "It's over." *Thanks to her own cowardness.*

"It doesn't have to be."

"What do you mean?"

Linda left the room. When she came back, she handed Indi an envelope.

"What's this?" Indi asked, peeking inside.

"Confirmation that we're on the list of confirmed attendees for the NASCAR NEXTEL Cup year-end awards ceremony."

"Neat."

"There are three names on that list. Benjamin, Art and me. Art's not going."

"He's not? That's too bad."

"You're going instead."

Indi almost dropped a napkin ring. "Oh, Linda. No. I can't."

"You can and you are," she said.

"No. Really—"

"Indi Wilcox. I haven't watched my son fight for his life just to stand around and watch life pass me by. Or pass you by, as the case may be. Our time on this earth is too short. If your job at *Miracles* has taught you one thing, surely it's that."

"Yeah, but—"

"You're going," Linda said, her words more strident than Indi had ever heard. "This is your last chance, Indi. Your last time to tell Todd exactly how you feel."

"I don't feel anything."

"Liar. You love him."

"Linda—"

"You love him and I'm not going to let you ruin it out of some stupid sense of obligation to your job." Linda moved to Indi's side, placed her hands on her shoulders. "I owe you so much," Linda said, as for the first time in weeks, Indi saw tears come to Linda's eyes. "If not for you, Benjamin would never have met Todd. And if he hadn't met Todd, we might never have heard about the clinical trial for that new drug. Because of you I have my son back, for how-ever long that might be. Come with me to New York. Please."

It was one of those moments where her life could go either way, Indi knew. If she stayed in the Bay Area, who knew what would happen? But if she went to New York…

She might end up a winner after all.

"ALL RIGHT," Jen said from behind Todd. "I've got you sitting next to Mr. Knight. Next to him will be Kristen, and beyond that Dan, Ralph…"

Jen's words faded away. Todd stared out at the Manhattan skyline visible outside the glass elevator. On the street below, NASCAR fans lined the side-walks, one of his cars clearly visible with its orange number eighty-two on the roof.

"You okay with that?" Jen said.

"Mmm?" Todd asked, turning back to his PR rep who stared at him impatiently. "Am I okay with what?"

"Have you been listening to a word I've said?" she asked, the elevator stopping at a floor. Todd smiled when a crew member from another team entered the car. He looked as uncomfortable as Todd felt in his tuxedo.

"Congratulations," the burly guy said.

"Thanks."

"Have you been listening?" Jen asked, her voice lowered.

Actually, he hadn't. He'd been thinking about Indi. About how she'd called him that day in Victory Lane. About how sincere she'd sounded when she'd congratulated him. And how hard he'd had to work to keep his voice carefully neutral.

"I was thinking about my speech," Todd improvised.

Jen nodded. "Do you have it with you?"

"Yup," Todd said. "It's up here." He tapped his head.

"Uh-oh," Jen said right as the elevator doors slid open. The lobby spread out before them. Christmas lights twinkled from the potted plants that lined the walls and support columns. The lobby was dimly lit and lushly decorated with huge poinsettias and multicolored glass bulbs hanging from every available surface. Christmas was in the air, at least in New York. Todd wondered why the thought depressed him when usually it was his favorite time of year. His mom and dad always made it into a big production, and this year he had more to celebrate than most years.

Speaking of his mom and dad, they would both be here tonight, along with one of his sisters. The other two couldn't make it because they had kids in school. But he knew they'd be watching at home.

"Congratulations," someone else called.

Todd lifted a hand. This year, the awards ceremony would be held in a ground-level ballroom
located near the back of the hotel. That meant he had
to cross the lobby to get to it. Race fans stood behind
a roped-off area, the entire crowd erupting into
cheers when they saw him.

"From bad boy to NASCAR angel," Jen whispered in his ear. "You and Benjamin have really
touched the fans' hearts, Todd."

"Where *is* Benjamin?"

"He's inside," Jen said as they rounded a corner
and walked down a long corridor after passing
through a makeshift security station. They hadn't
even asked for his ID.

"What table is he at?" Todd asked.

"He's near the front. Sitting with your parents
and sister."

Todd nodded. Good. He'd been so busy with pre-
ceremony interviews he hadn't had time to see the
boy, although he'd talked to him on the phone.

And he sounded so much better, Todd thought.
Thank God for that.

The names of meeting rooms were above the
doors, but one could plainly see that the room at the
end of the hall was where they needed to go. The
double doors were wide open, spectacularly dressed
people lounging around outside. He saw a few of his

fellow drivers, drinks in hand, more than one of them saluting him.

This was it. His night. His time to shine.

Enjoy it, Todd.

"Everyone should be taking their seats pretty soon," Jen said. "You can go on inside. Just be at the head table in no less than fifteen minutes."

Had they cut it that short? Apparently so. But no matter. He wasn't much in the mood for talking, although it was good to see his mom and dad sitting so proudly near the front of the stage, a beaming Benjamin by his father's side. Linda sat next to her son, the seat next to her empty.

"The man of the hour," his dad said. Was Todd mistaken or did he see tears in his old man's eyes? It was hard to tell. William Peters had never been the demonstrative type. When Todd had been growing up and racing go-karts, all he'd ever get in the winner's circle was a quick hug and a pat on the back. Tonight his father just about cut his breath off when he hugged him.

"Jeez, Dad."

When Todd leaned back, his father stared across at him through eyes gone misty with tears. "I'm so proud of you," he said.

"Thanks," Todd said, wondering why the words pricked at his insides.

I'm so proud of you.

Indi had said the same thing to him in Homestead.

"What about me?" his mom said. "Do I get a hug?"

"Mom," Todd said. "You look great."

And she did. One thing about his mom, she had class. Tonight she wore a sparkling black gown that hugged her trim figure, her gray hair shortly cropped, as it always was, her jewelry discreetly elegant.

Mom would probably approve of Indi.

His sister demanded his attention next, but not for long, because Benjamin was the star of the table.

"Where's Art?" Todd asked after playfully pinching Benjamin's cheek. The kid's hair had started to grow back. Look at that.

"He couldn't make it," Linda said, her eyes momentarily dimming.

"You going up?" Dan said, coming up behind him and clapping him on the back. He referred to the table set up on the left of the stage. "They're telling us to take our seats."

"I'll go on up if you will," Todd said,

"Let's go."

He waved goodbye. Todd glanced around the room as he climbed the stairs in front of the stage. The room was dimly lit, but the round tables sparkled. His fellow drivers were trickling in from outside. The light fixture overhead arched off the sequins on the ladies' gowns and caused them to twinkle. Cameras were discreetly placed around the edge of the room. Tonight's ceremony would be broadcast live. Todd paused on the top step. Behind the podium sat the championship trophy. It stood on a pedestal all on its own, the projection screen above it shedding light onto its surface so that it glowed.

He'd waited years for this championship.

Then why did he feel so empty?

"Here we go," Dan said, unbuttoning his tux as they took a seat.

"Yup. Here we go."

And so the night began. Todd sat through the endless speeches, dinner, and then the main presentation. He just about melted beneath the spotlights that were switched on once they started broadcasting. The other nine drivers who made the top ten were introduced one after the other. And then it was his turn.

The audience came to their feet, applauding when his name was announced as this year's champion. He hardly noticed. He headed straight for the podium and stared out at the audience.

And saw Indi.

She stood next to Linda, her palms seeming to come together in slow motion.

Indi.

The smile she gave him was tender, the look in her eyes causing him to stand up straighter, to swell with pride. How had he not noticed her arrival? Why hadn't she told him she was coming. Now he understood the empty seat next to Linda.

Linda beamed up at him, too. The whole table beamed, more than one pair of eyes filled with tears. Benjamin, however, just clapped. Energetically, enthusiastically clapped.

Todd felt his heart tip over. He clutched the edge of the podium and struggled for a moment with his breathing. What did he say? Suddenly his mind went blank.

He looked into Indi's eyes.

And he knew *exactly* what to say.

He lifted his hands. The audience quieted and took their seats. Todd breathed deeply, swallowed, then took another deep breath because suddenly he was all choked up.

"I used to think that winning the championship meant everything," he began. "A few years back, that's all I wanted." He glanced back at his teammates, at Mathew Knight and Kristen and Dan. "Last year, thanks to a new owner, I learned that winning takes a group effort. This year, thanks to one very special little boy, I learned that winning isn't everything."

He met Benjamin's gaze. "Thanks for that, kiddo."

Benjamin smiled. The audience applauded. Todd had to wait for things to quiet down before speaking again.

"I was going to stand up here and list everyone by name who helped me get here, but I realize now that that would be impossible. It took a team of dedicated individuals to get me here tonight, and it took another team of completely different individuals to get me to this level."

He smiled at his family. They knew who they were.

And then he looked at Indi. The breath left him again. She was still smiling at him, but it was one of those bunched-up grins that told him she was trying hard not to cry. He knew how she felt, could feel his upper lip quiver as he stared down at her. He knew why she was here. He could see the reason in her eyes. The love in her gaze was as bright as the spotlights that lit the stage.

"Many of you know that I've dedicated this year's championship to a little boy who's shown me the true meaning of courage. But what you don't know is that there's another person who's taught me the meaning of unselfish love."

The room went quiet. It was odd how he noticed that. Odder still that it seemed as if he and Indi were the only two people in the room.

"Indi Wilcox," he said, his voice suddenly raspy.

"You've taught me so much this past year. You've taught me how to love someone other than myself. You showed me the meaning of self-sacrifice. You're a champion of children, and you've taught me what it means to be a true winner."

Tears poured down her cheeks, the look in her eyes so profound, Todd found his chest expanding in pride. He glanced around the ballroom, raising an eyebrow at his fellow competitors. "She also got me so mad one day that I vowed to win at least four races of the Chase." The audience laughed. A few people applauded. "But nobody's perfect."

And then he sobered again. He stared into her eyes, pouring everything he felt into his gaze.

"I love you," he said softly.

Tears continued to stream down her cheeks. He could see them sparkle beneath the overhead lights.

I love you, too, she mouthed.

It felt as if he grew ten inches taller. And he knew for a fact that his grin probably blinded the viewers at home.

"I won those four races of the Chase, a feat that's unequaled in this sport. And so I'm going to do something else that's never been done before. I'm going to ask someone in the audience a question."

He held out his hand to Indi, stepped to the left of the podium.

She looked suddenly frozen.

Come on, he mouthed.

She shook her head.

He leaned toward the mic. "Get up here," he ordered.

She probably wouldn't have done it but for the fact that Linda just about pushed her up. Benjamin urged her on. His family clapped. The whole place erupted into cheers, especially when he went down to her and started to tug her to the stage.

"Todd," he heard her say.

He turned back to her. "You owe me this much, Ms. Indi Wilcox."

And she knew she did. She probably suspected what was coming, too. Or maybe she didn't, because when Todd got down on one knee, he heard her gasp.

"Indi Wilcox," he asked her, the audience going dead quiet in order to hear his words. "Will you marry me?"

Her eyes closed. He saw her shoulders begin to shake. It was only when she met his gaze again that he realized she was sobbing, the joy in her heart visible to all those who watched on TV.

"Yes," she said softly, her arms slipping around him. "Oh, Todd. *Yes.*"

The cheer that erupted was the loudest in NASCAR's awards banquet history. Never again would such a sound be repeated. But to the two people up on stage all they heard was the beating of their own hearts. That is until Todd said, "I love you," in her ear.

"I love you, too," she said just before he kissed her.

Feet stomped in approval. The network broadcasting the event went to commercials—much to viewer's disappointment—and at the table near the front of the stage Benjamin Koch looked up at his mother.

"I *told* you this would happen," he said.

"Yes," Linda said with a grin and a nod. "You certainly did."

"Just like I told you I'd beat this disease."

"I know."

"You're going to talk to them about being a surrogate for Indi, aren't you?"

"I am."

Benjamin glanced back at the stage, Linda leaning to the left so she could hear him better. "They're going to live happily ever after," he said softly.

And you know what?

They all *did*.

Dear Reader:

As many of you know, I lost my father to cancer this past year. Watching him fight for his life was one of the hardest things I've ever had to endure. When he finally lost the battle on June 20, 2006, I was beyond devastated.

The irony is that I'd long since planned to write a book centered on a terminally ill child. I just didn't know the child would have cancer, or that I would be pouring my heart out onto each page. Much to my surprise, the experience turned out to be cathartic because in *this* book, the story ends happily.

I'd like to thank my oldest friend on the planet— and I don't mean old-old, just that I've known her since before bras and panty hose. Jaime, your help on this one was invaluable. Although, come to think of it, you were a pretty big help with the last one, too. Hmm. This is getting to be a trend. But I still refuse to call you *doctor.*

Dr. Michael Figueroa at the Cancer Care Consultants in Redding, CA, spent a good half hour with me on the phone helping me to understand the ins and outs of CML (chronic myelogenous leukemia). Thanks for all your insights on how to fight this terrible disease.

I'd also like to thank the Lucile Packard Children's Hospital for spending time with me on the phone. One person in particular was extremely helpful. She didn't want to be named, but thank you *so* much. (Enjoy the books!)

Lastly, I'd like you to know that a portion of *TOTAL CONTROL's* royalties will be donated to the Victory Junction Gang, a camp for terminally ill children founded by NASCAR's Petty family. If you'd like to help, too, you can visit www.VictoryJunction.org where you'll find information on this very worthy cause.

All my Best,
Pamela

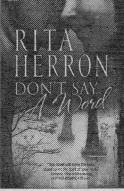

REQUEST YOUR FREE BOOKS!

2 FREE NOVELS
FROM THE ROMANCE/SUSPENSE
COLLECTION PLUS 2 FREE GIFTS!

YES! Please send me 2 FREE novels from the Romance/Suspense Collection and my 2 FREE gifts. After receiving them, if I don't wish to receive any more books, I can return the shipping statement marked "cancel." If I don't cancel, I will receive 4 brand-new novels every month and be billed just $5.49 per book in the U.S., or $5.99 per book in Canada, plus 25¢ shipping and handling per book plus applicable taxes, if any*. That's a savings of at least 20% off the cover price! I understand that accepting the 2 free books and gifts places me under no obligation to buy anything. I can always return a shipment and cancel at any time. Even if I never buy another book from the Reader Service, the two free books and gifts are mine to keep forever.

185 MDN EF5Y   385 MDN EF6C

Name	(PLEASE PRINT)	
Address		Apt. #
City	State/Prov.	Zip/Postal Code

Signature (if under 18, a parent or guardian must sign)

Mail to **The Reader Service:**
IN U.S.A.: P.O. Box 1867, Buffalo, NY 14240-1867
IN CANADA: P.O. Box 609, Fort Erie, Ontario L2A 5X3

Not valid to current subscribers to the Romance Collection,
the Suspense Collection or the Romance/Suspense Collection.

Want to try two free books from another line?
Call 1-800-873-8635 or visit www.morefreebooks.com.

* Terms and prices subject to change without notice. NY residents add applicable sales tax. Canadian residents will be charged applicable provincial taxes and GST. This offer is limited to one order per household. All orders subject to approval. Credit or debit balances in a customer's account(s) may be offset by any other outstanding balance owed by or to the customer. Please allow 4 to 6 weeks for delivery.

Your Privacy: Harlequin is committed to protecting your privacy. Our Privacy Policy is available online at www.eHarlequin.com or upon request from the Reader Service. From time to time we make our lists of customers available to reputable firms who may have a product or service of interest to you. If you would prefer we not share your name and address, please check here. ☐

BOB07

The latest novel in The Lakeshore Chronicles
by *New York Times* bestselling author

SUSAN
WIGGS

From the award-winning author of *Summer at Willow Lake*
comes an unforgettable story of a woman's emotional journey
from the heartache of the past to hope for the future.

With her daughter grown and flown, Nina Romano is ready to
embark on a new adventure. She's waited a long time for dating,
travel and chasing dreams. But just as she's beginning to enjoy
being on her own, she finds herself falling for Greg Bellamy,
owner of the charming Inn at Willow Lake and a single father
with two kids of his own.

DOCKSIDE

"The perfect summer read." —Debbie Macomber

Available the first week of August 2007
wherever paperbacks are sold!

MIRA®

pamela britton

77187	TO THE LIMIT	___ $6.99 U.S.	___	$8.50 CAN.
77103	ON THE EDGE	___ $6.99 U.S.	___	$8.50 CAN.
77098	IN THE GROOVE	___ $6.99 U.S.	___	$8.50 CAN.

(limited quantities available)

TOTAL AMOUNT	$ _____
POSTAGE & HANDLING	$ _____
($1.00 FOR 1 BOOK, 50¢ for each additional)	
APPLICABLE TAXES*	$ _____
TOTAL PAYABLE	$ _____

(check or money order—please do not send cash)

To order, complete this form and send it, along with a check or money order for the total above, payable to HQN Books, to: **In the U.S.:** 3010 Walden Avenue, P.O. Box 9077, Buffalo, NY 14269-9077; **In Canada:** P.O. Box 636, Fort Erie, Ontario, L2A 5X3.

Name: _____

Address: _____ City: _____

State/Prov.: _____ Zip/Postal Code: _____

Account Number (if applicable): _____

075 CSAS

*New York residents remit applicable sales taxes.
*Canadian residents remit applicable GST and provincial taxes.

HQN™

We *are* romance™

www.HQNBooks.com

PHPB0907BL